Raves for Selma Eichler
and the Desiree Shapiro mysteries . . .

Murder Can Spook Your Cat

"A very realistic character . . . the mystery is creatively drawn and well plotted."—*Painted Rock Reviews*

Murder Can Wreck Your Reunion

"A fast-paced, enjoyable read."—*The Mystery Review*

"Another wildly hilarious mystery."—*The Snooper*

Murder Can Stunt Your Growth

"A poignant and satisfying conclusion . . . the real pleasure of this book is spending time with Desiree Shapiro . . . just plain fun to read."—*I Love a Mystery*

Murder Can Ruin Your Looks

"Highly entertaining . . . witty insights and warm-hearted humor."—Joan Hess

Murder Can Kill Your Social Life

"P.I. Desiree Shapiro has a wonderful New York way with words and an original knack for solving homicides. Intriguing and   author of *Whose Dea*

D0956247

Also by Selma Eichler

Murder Can Spook Your Cat
Murder Can Wreck Your Reunion
Murder Can Stunt Your Growth
Murder Can Ruin Your Looks
Murder Can Kill Your Social Life

MURDER CAN SINGE YOUR OLD FLAME

A DESIREE SHAPIRO MYSTERY

Selma Eichler

A SIGNET BOOK

SIGNET
Published by the Penguin Group
Penguin Putnam Inc., 375 Hudson Street,
New York, New York 10014, U.S.A.
Penguin Books Ltd, 27 Wrights Lane,
London W8 5TZ, England
Penguin Books Australia Ltd, Ringwood,
Victoria, Australia
Penguin Books Canada Ltd, 10 Alcorn Avenue,
Toronto, Ontario, Canada M4V 3B2
Penguin Books (N.Z.) Ltd, 182–190 Wairau Road,
Auckland 10, New Zealand

Penguin Books Ltd, Registered Offices:
Harmondsworth, Middlesex, England

First published by Signet, an imprint of Dutton NAL, a member of
Penguin Putnam Inc.

First Printing, January 1999
10 9 8 7 6 5 4 3 2 1

Acknowledgments

My thanks to—

Major Alan G. Martin of the New York State Police, who, as always, came to the rescue on law enforcement matters; fortunately (for me) his expertise extends to the Drug Enforcement Administration;

Martin Turkish, MD, who once again supplied much-needed medical advice, in this instance enabling me to provide the proper treatment for my poison victim;

Kim Gruber, RN, for her input on broken bones;

My agent, Luna Carne-Ross, and my editor, Danielle Perez, for their valuable contributions;

And my husband, Lloyd, for his poison research—as well as for everything else.

And a special thanks to—

Penny Thomas and Joanne Calabrese for so patiently answering all of my many questions on airline procedures.

Chapter 1

It was a familiar voice—and one I'd hoped never to hear again. "Please, Dez, don't hang up," it pleaded.

I promptly slammed down the receiver, astonished at how quickly my mouth had gone bone-dry on me.

It took less than a minute for the phone to ring again. I let my answering machine handle things this time.

"I need to talk to you. Please. Just listen for a little while, okay?" For a moment I stood there mesmerized, staring at the machine. "I don't blame you for not wanting to speak to me— honestly, I don't. I behaved like a pig. Believe me, I'd never have gotten up the nerve to call you if the situation wasn't . . . well, critical. Pat says she told you what's happened. To my wife, I mean. It was really—" A half sob now, a second or two of silence, and then the voice went on.

"But what I'm calling about, Dez, is that I could be in trouble. Terrible trouble. I know I don't deserve it, but I was hoping that maybe I could convince you to help. It's . . ."

I reached over and, teeth clenched, turned off the machine. And then, my legs steadier than I'd have imagined possible, I shut off the lights and left the room.

Five minutes later I was soaking in the tub, up to my chin in fragrant, soothing bubbles.

"Well," I announced silently to myself, "you certainly showed *him*."

Chapter 2

As soon as I got to the office the following morning, I dialed my friend Pat Martucci.

"I heard from Bruce last night," I informed her tersely.

"Yes, I know. He said he was going to call you." And before I could respond: "He's pretty desperate, Dez. He thinks the police may suspect him of murdering Cheryl."

"That would be nice."

There was a long pause before Pat said softly, "I can't really blame you for taking that attitude. But Bruce isn't a murderer. A louse, maybe." And then she amended hastily, "No. A louse, definitely. But not a murderer."

"You can't be sure of that."

"He really cared for Cheryl. I'm sure of *that*. And so is Burton," she added, referring to her live-in love, who also happened to be both Bruce Simon's cousin and close buddy.

"And Burton wouldn't be at all prejudiced, would he?" I put to her snidely.

"Maybe he is. But I'm certainly not. I think Bruce deserved to be . . . well . . . *stoned* for that stuff he pulled on you."

Stoned? Why not castrated? But I refrained from posing the question aloud.

"You can't really think Bruce is capable of killing someone, though, can you?" Pat demanded.

Actually, who could say what that man was capable of! In the months I'd dated him, Bruce had lied to me, insulted me, and humiliated me. And that was his more benign behavior. What finally provided the jolt I seemed to require in order to get my brain in gear again was his neglecting to apprise me of the fact that he had a fiancée back in Chicago. Must have slipped his mind, huh? I know it's mean-spirited of me, but my one consolation in all of this was that he hadn't been playing fair with her, either—this same Cheryl Pat was insisting he'd been so crazy about.

Still, it was hard to picture Bruce pushing his new wife—or anyone else—in front of a train. But then, it's usually hard to imagine someone you know committing a horrendous act like that.

"Well, *do* you?" Pat was saying.

"Do I what?"

"Do you really think Bruce is capable of murder?"

"If being a P.I. has taught me anything, it's never to make that kind of a judgment."

"So I, uh, gather you've decided not to help him."

"Listen, Pat, I'm not the only private investigator in the world. I'm sure Bruce can get someone else to look into Cheryl's death. As a matter of fact, he never had a very high opinion of my investigative skills, anyway. In his mind, all I was capable of was dogging straying husbands." (Which, in truth, was at one time the high end of my business. But that was long before Bruce Simon made his unfortunate entrance into my life.) "He'd be much better off finding someone he can put his faith in."

"But he has faith in *you*," Pat protested. "Lots of it." And now she waited for a response that didn't come. "Maybe you're right, though," she said at last. "Maybe Bruce should get someone else." Then giving me absolution: "And no one can say you don't have every reason to feel the way you do, either."

I didn't get any work done at the office that day. (Not that I had all that much to do.) I was too busy trying to justify myself to myself.

What did he expect, really, after the way he'd treated me—that I'd drop everything just because he was in some kind of trouble?

The man had chutzpah; I'd give him that. But this was something I'd discovered a long time ago. Less than five minutes after I met him, actually.

It wasn't that I wanted to see him get hung with a crime he didn't commit, you understand. (Although being a true Scorpio, for a while there the idea wasn't exactly repellent to me.) But the thing is, wouldn't it make more sense for Bruce to hire someone who wasn't going to be bogged down by all these ill feelings toward him? Of course it would.

I spent almost an hour driving myself crazy and succeeded in working my way up to a five-star headache, which two Extra Strength Tylenols did little to alleviate. I absolutely refused to let Bruce affect my appetite, however. So at a little past noon, after rejecting the idea of venturing out into this August scorcher—a record breaker, the weatherman had warned that morning—I had a sandwich at my desk. A ham and brie with honey-mustard dressing. And I thoroughly enjoyed it, too.

Just as I was consuming the last mouthful, I received a visit from Elliot Gilbert, one of the principals of Gilbert and Sullivan, the law firm that rents me my office (or, more accurately, cubbyhole) space. He wanted to know if I'd finished my report on this insurance case I had been handling for him—a very simple task, by the way, and the sole demand on my time at present. I was forced to admit that I still hadn't completed it and, moreover, that I was thinking of cutting out early today. "I have a headache I can't seem to shake. Would it be okay if you got the report first thing in the morning?"

I was assured that the morning would be fine. But Elliot— one of the nicest, most obliging people you could ever meet— would have had a problem saying no even if we were dealing with something he needed for court in five minutes.

"Are you sure it's all right?"

This response, too, was predictable. "Absolutely. You just take care of yourself."

Anyway, at around two I grabbed my attaché case—inside of which Elliot's insurance file now lay in wait for me—and vacating my office, prepared myself to explain the reason for my early departure to Jackie. And let me tell you about Jackie. . . .

This woman—whose services I can only afford because of my arrangement with the Messrs. Gilbert and Sullivan—is probably the best secretary in New York. The trouble is, however, that she could also qualify as the most impossible secretary in New York—thanks to a very strict work ethic, a tough-love approach to bringing up her employers, and a genuine and often smothering concern for our well-being. (And I won't even mention that her oversensitive nature has, on occasion, driven me right up the wall.)

"What's the matter? Aren't you feeling well?" she demanded upon hearing of my intention.

"I'm okay. A headache, that's all." Actually, my head was much better by now. The truth is, wrestling with this Bruce thing had left me terribly antsy, and I was just anxious to get out of there.

"That's why you're going home early?" Jackie's tone bordered on the incredulous. "Take a couple of Tylenols."

"I did. But evidently this isn't that kind of headache."

"What kind of headache *is* it, then?"

At that point the telephone rang, and Jackie was forced to cut the interrogation short.

Ignoring the "Wait" she mouthed, I beat it out the door.

Not more than five minutes after walking into my apartment, I put up the coffee (which turned out to be so excruciatingly bitter it didn't live up to even my usual rock-bottom standards). Then, convincing myself that I might as well try to get it out of my hair, I sat down with Elliot's file. Somehow I managed to concentrate, wrapping up the remainder of the work fairly quickly.

And now I took some grapes from the refrigerator, switched on the TV, plopped down on the sofa, and prepared to watch a couple of deliciously lascivious talk shows.

After I was about three minutes into the first program, my jaw dropped almost to my chest, where it remained for most of the show.

Are those people for real, do you think? There they sit, revealing the most intimate details of their lives to millions of people—and for reasons that make no sense at all. One woman said she was appearing on TV like this because she was pregnant with her husband's brother's child and wanted the audience's advice on whether to tell her husband the baby wasn't his. I mean, didn't it occur to this ditz that her on-air confession had taken that decision out of her hands?

Anyway, I was all caught up in the histrionics of an angstridden eighteen-year-old girl who admitted to carrying on with her fifty-plus stepfather while her poor mother lay in a coma—when the phone rang. It wasn't easy to tear myself away from Cindy and her newborn conscience, but I answered it.

"It's me again," Bruce Simon said timidly. "Just hear me out for a couple of minutes. Please."

"Go ahead." It's possible that close to an hour's worth of talk show had weakened my brain.

"I tried to reach you at your office before," he explained. "But they told me you'd already left. You're not sick, are you?"

"No, I'm fine. And I'm listening. So say what you have to say."

"Yes. All right. Thanks," Bruce responded hurriedly. "You know that my wife was hit by a train last Thursday."

"Yes, I do know. And I'm truly sorry for your loss, but—"

"Thank you. What I wanted to tell you is that I think the police suspect Cheryl may have been murdered. And it's very likely she was. But they also think I might have been the one to push her off the platform. Why would I, though? I loved . . . that is, Cheryl and I were . . . the thing is, we—"

Apparently, he was attempting to soft-pedal his affection for his wife in the event I might find it upsetting—all this concern for my feelings a first for Bruce. I broke in to spare him any further discomfort. "It's okay. I'm not the least bit disturbed to hear that you loved your wife."

"Oh, I didn't mean— What I'm trying to make clear is that there was no reason for me to want Cheryl dead. I swear there wasn't. You do believe me, don't you?"

"I don't know if I do or not. But, for the moment, anyway, I'm willing to give you the benefit of the doubt."

"Will you investigate her death for me, then?"

"Why me, Bruce? I'm hardly your advocate. In fact, if you want the truth, I'm afraid that I have very little use for you. Why not bring in someone who's at least neutral, who doesn't already recognize you for the snake you are?"

Now, if you think that I was being unnecessarily harsh with this man in view of the tragedy he was coping with, I can only tell you that in deference to this tragedy, I actually swallowed most of what was on my tongue.

Bruce had to have had some reaction to my words, but he was apparently able to suppress it. "I'd like you to look into this because you're smart, Dez," he answered, his tone even. "And I know you to be a fair person. I'm certain that you won't let what went on between us—the crap I pulled—affect your doing your job."

Well, he'd never complimented either my intelligence or my ethics before. Another measure of his desperation.

"Look, let me give you the names of a couple of colleagues of mine. Also smart. And also fair. They'd—"

"No, please. I have a very strong feeling—a *sense,* you might call it—that you're the only one who can help me."

Naturally, I protested, maintaining that he was being foolish. After which Bruce protested my protest, insisting I was his sole hope. Well, the windup was that I finally agreed to look into Cheryl Simon's death. Sucker that I am.

But then I suppose I'd known that I would—on some level, at any rate—from the very beginning.

Chapter 3

The next morning—Tuesday—I did very little more than push papers around my desk.

Jackie coaxed me out into the stifling humidity at quarter to one, and we went around the corner for hamburgers. And then after I got back to the office, I occupied myself by talking on the phone, taking unnecessary trips to the ladies' room, and pushing the papers around my desk some more. Finally I hauled out my "To Do" file and paid a couple of overdue bills.

Well, one thing I had to concede. I might not be thrilled about working for Bruce, but if I wanted to continue making the rent, I sure as hell needed to be working for *someone*.

At any rate, I was almost glad when four o'clock rolled around and I had to leave for my every-six-months dental cleaning, which, this time, I'd managed to stretch out to a year and a half.

When I got home I heated up the remains of the eggplant parmigiana in my freezer, left over from when I had my across-the-hall neighbors Harriet and Steve Gould in for dinner. To accompany the eggplant, I fixed a copious salad that contained everything in the vegetable bin that couldn't get up and walk away. The meal's finale was to be my all-time favorite dessert: Häagen-Dazs macadamia brittle. As fortification for tonight's meeting with Bruce, I intended to allow myself two helpings with my coffee.

It was exactly nine p.m. when I stood in the lobby, pressing the buzzer to Bruce Simon's Chelsea apartment.

I can't say I wasn't nervous as I rode up in the elevator to the seventh floor. I hadn't seen Bruce since right before Christmas—almost eight months ago. And I'd never been happier to say good-bye to someone, either. Yet do you want to know what was troubling me the most right now? I was actually worried that, in spite of everything, I'd still be attracted to the man. Which gives you an idea of how trustworthy I consider myself. And I guess with pretty good reason, where Bruce was concerned.

I mean, how could I have ever been so dippy about him in the first place? Let's just take the physical considerations. He's almost the complete antithesis of the needy-looking little men I normally find so appealing (this preference being the result, I suspect, of an unfulfilled maternal instinct). While Bruce is short—which is kind of a prerequisite if you're into needy-looking little men—his five feet six or seven inches are much too muscular for my taste. What's more, he carries himself like a marine drill sergeant. And to add to this military mien, his dark hair—what little there is of it—is worn short, almost like a crew cut. And as long as we're on the subject of drill sergeants, you can throw in his tendency to be totally overbearing, too.

Anyway, he was out in the hall, in front of his door, waiting for me. The second I set eyes on him again I realized, with a wave of relief, that he did absolutely nothing for me anymore. Even though it was a far more sympathetic Bruce I was looking at tonight.

Tonight the shoulders inside his short-sleeved navy sport shirt seemed to droop. The hazel eyes were moist. And the smile that at times I had found so infuriatingly sardonic was forced now. And wistful.

"Come in," he said, stepping aside so I could enter the apartment that less than a week ago he had shared with his bride.

There was very little furniture in the living room—just a blue damask sofa, a blue-and-cream-striped club chair, and a large, square, glass-topped coffee table. The floors were bare, and the three large windows here were covered by old broken-down venetian blinds, apparently pressed into use for the sake of privacy. It was evident the couple had never finished decorating the place.

"Sit down, sit down," Bruce urged.

I took a seat on the sofa and instantly discovered that I'd made an unfortunate choice. The cushions were down-filled and deeper than I'd expected, presenting me with one of the big drawbacks of only growing as high as five two: My feet didn't reach the floor. Now, in addition to this not being terribly comfortable, it always shoots the hell out of my confidence. I mean, how can someone whose legs are dangling in midair like that possibly project a chic and sophisticated image? As Bruce settled himself in the club chair opposite me, I slid as far forward as possible, until the tips of my toes, at least, made contact with the parquet flooring underneath them.

"You're looking well," he said.

I'm afraid I simpered my "thank you." Then I self-consciously patted my glorious hennaed hair.

"You've lost a bit of weight, too, haven't you?"

How little the man actually knew me! Not only hadn't I taken off so much as a gram since we'd last seen each other, but I hadn't even attempted to. I don't find it necessary to either alter or apologize for the fact that I'm a full-figured woman.

I suppose my expression reflected what I thought of this obvious and misguided attempt of his to rack up a few points, because Bruce shot out of his chair now, no doubt anxious to absent himself for a couple of minutes. "Oh, I haven't offered you anything to drink. What would you like?"

"Nothing, thanks."

"Not even a Pepsi?"

"No, I'm fine."

He resumed his seat reluctantly. "I suppose we should get on with it then. I don't know how much Pat's already told you. . . ."

"She just provided some basic information. But let's pretend she didn't tell me a thing, okay?"

"Whatever you say. I'm not quite sure where to begin, though."

"Why don't you start with the day Cheryl died."

Bruce's eyebrows rose inquiringly, so I provided a little shove. "You had breakfast together?"

"Yes. Around seven-thirty. Cheryl wasn't flying that day. She was a flight attendant—in case Pat hasn't mentioned it."

She had, but I nodded noncommittally. "And then what did you do?"

"At eight o'clock or so I left for work. And incidentally, according to the doorman—and one of the tenants verified this—Cheryl left the building almost immediately after I did. Anyway, I got to the office, I don't know, it must have been about eight-fifteen, eight-twenty. And I—" He broke off abruptly. "Is this what you want to hear? My itinerary?"

"I think it would be a good idea if you filled me in. Particularly if the police actually do suspect that you might be involved in Cheryl's death."

"All right," he agreed, sighing resignedly. "Well, at a little past nine a client of mine stopped by the office to see me for maybe a half hour. Or maybe even less. He just wanted to go over one or two points in this new campaign I'd presented to him the week before." (Bruce is in public relations.) "Then at ten-thirty I had an appointment with another client over on East Twelfth Street. And after that I stopped in at Barnes & Noble—the one on Seventeenth, at Union Square. I figured it was a good chance to get the latest Grisham—I'd been meaning to pick it up for quite a while. It was also someplace to hang out until my lunch date."

"How long were you with this second client?"

"Not much more than an hour."

"And you were at Barnes & Noble until what time?"

Bruce shrugged. "About twelve-twenty, I guess it was. I'd made a reservation for twelve-thirty at the Union Square Cafe, which is practically around the corner. But it was a beautiful afternoon—or so I thought then—so I took a nice, leisurely walk over there." He ran his tongue over his lips now, and when he spoke again his voice was hoarse. "And after lunch I returned to my office, where two detectives were waiting to inform me that my wife . . . that my wife had been run over by a subway train."

"What time did it happen?" I asked softly.

"Around twelve, they said."

"At the West Fourth Street station, wasn't it?"

"That's right."

"Do you have any idea where Cheryl had been that morning—or where she was going?"

"I'm reasonably certain she'd been to see a friend."

"What friend was that? Do you know?"

"Well, not specifically, I'm afraid. Let me explain. . . .

"Two nights before her death, Cheryl and I were having dinner. She'd just returned from a flight to the Bahamas a few hours earlier, and as soon as we sat down to eat I could see that she was very disturbed about something. At first she refused to talk about it. But after a little persuading, I got her to tell me what was troubling her. I had the feeling that she was actually glad to unload, though; I think she was anxious for my take on things. But to go on . . . It seems that Cheryl witnessed something on that trip that led her to believe a good friend—someone she flies with—could be smuggling drugs into this country. And I'd make book that this is the person Cheryl went to visit the morning she died."

"She didn't say who the friend was?"

"She refused to give me the name. But I've narrowed the possibilities down to three people."

"Three people, huh?" I'd settle; it could have been worse. "Cheryl worked for American Airlines, I think Pat told me."

"Not anymore. She used to, back in Chicago. But she left her job a couple of months prior to coming here. She had a lot of personal matters to take care of, and she wanted to give herself plenty of time to wrap things up before making the move, which she'd scheduled for mid-February. But for quite a while she'd been toying with the idea of quitting, anyway; she wasn't sure she wanted to continue to fly."

"She apparently had a change of heart, though."

"That she did. Toward the end of March, about a week after

we got home from our honeymoon, Cheryl was talking to a friend of hers in Chicago—Suzanne Potts, her name is." With the word "honeymoon," Bruce had directed his gaze downward, imparting the remainder of the information to the parquet floor. It was another display of the sensitivity he'd revealed on the telephone—a sensitivity I'd have sworn he didn't possess. As before, however, it was hardly necessary. As far as I was concerned, Bruce Simon had happened to me in another lifetime.

He met my eyes again now. "Suzanne told Cheryl that a woman they both used to work with—Laura Downey—had been living in New York for almost two years and that she was a flight attendant with Royal Bahamian Air. They're a small outfit that flies New York to Miami to Nassau. Anyhow, Laura and Suzanne, it seems, were still in pretty frequent contact, and just a few nights earlier Laura had casually mentioned to Suzanne on the telephone that there was an opening at Bahamian. Well, it appears that all of a sudden Cheryl *was* sure she wanted to keep flying. Because she certainly didn't waste any time in getting herself an interview."

I'm positive I would have been curious even if Bruce's tone hadn't had a bit of an edge to it then. I mean, knowing Bruce, I would have thought he'd expect any wife of his to greet him at the door every night, a freshly baked cherry pie in hand. "You didn't object to Cheryl's being away from home so frequently?" I asked.

"I won't lie and say I was crazy about the idea," he admitted. "But it was something Cheryl really wanted to do, and in spite of what you might think of me—and for good reason, I know— I do try to be fair." He colored here, then added quickly, "Uh, about most things, anyway. But at any rate, Cheryl started at Bahamian at the beginning of April. She and Laura hadn't been that tight in Chicago, but now they really bonded. With an airline that size, the same people fly together all the time, you see. Anyway, almost instantly Cheryl also became very friendly with the other two flight attendants on her run. When she wasn't working, she'd often have lunch with one or more of them here in the city. And twice all four met for dinner."

I was astonished at this. Bruce is far, *far* from your laissez-faire kind of guy. And there he was with this brand-new wife who, if she wasn't jetting about in the clouds somewhere, was cutting out on him to pal around with her airline cronies. Even if those dinner things did only happen a couple of times, it was impossible to imagine his not voicing an objection—a very strenuous objection—to their happening at all. "You didn't mind?" I couldn't help it; nosiness is in my genes.

"Of course I minded!" he snapped. And for a moment the old Bruce was glaring at me out of those hazel eyes. Then he said sadly, "We had words about it, too. Several times. Actually, the only reason the group got together those evenings was because one of them was having problems of some sort—with a new lover, I believe it was. But I really put my foot down after that second dinner, and Cheryl agreed to do any future problem-solving during the day."

"So you think it was one of these three that Cheryl suspected was smuggling dope?" I asked to put us back on track.

"Yes, I do," he answered firmly.

"Just what did she say to give you that impression?"

"For starters, she told me it was a good friend. And she wasn't that close to anyone else in New York. Also, you have to understand about Cheryl. She was a very moral woman. Straight-laced, even, you might say. If the person in question wasn't someone for whom she had a special fondness, my wife would have reported what she'd seen *like that.*" He snapped his fingers.

"But she wasn't going to do any reporting now?"

"I believe she intended talking to whoever it was first."

"She didn't, by any chance, give you a clue as to what it was she saw that prompted her suspicions, did she?"

"As a matter of fact, she did. It was a couple of things. I have to preface them, though, by telling you what took place very soon after she'd started at Bahamian—maybe it even occurred on her first trip.

"Cheryl's plane had just landed in Nassau, and she was leaving the airline terminal with the pilot when he spotted this guy—a very large, very gross-looking man, according to Cheryl, with a face that was all covered with pockmarks. 'See him?' the pilot said to her. 'That's'—and he's said some name. 'They call him El Puerco, though—*the pig*. And he's famous. A big-cheese Colombian drug dealer.'

"All right. Now, a couple of weeks went by, and Cheryl was on layover in Nassau again. The whole crew was going over to the Atlantis casino on Paradise Island in the early afternoon—it was less than a thirty-minute ride from their hotel. But Cheryl had to pass. She'd developed a headache she just couldn't shake, and she wanted to try to sleep it off.

"But an hour or so after the others left she woke up, and the headache was gone. Well, she was fidgety, so she decided to take a bus into town for some shopping. Once she walked around in that heat for a while, though, the headache started to come back. She was a little off the main drag at that time—Cheryl always liked to explore—but there was this tiny luncheonette at the end of the street. She thought it might be a good idea to stop off to get a cold drink and take some aspirin. She was just about to go inside when this man came barreling out of the place. He almost knocked her over, too, with this big black bag that was slung over his shoulder. Cheryl was certain it was the same guy the pilot had pointed out at the airport. She said it would be hard to find *two* men that repulsive looking.

"Anyhow, when she goes in, Cheryl sees her friend sitting at the counter, having an iced tea."

"I assume you're referring to the friend she came to suspect."

"That's right. The friend said something about returning from Paradise Island a little earlier than the others in order to shop for a gift of some kind. A birthday gift, as I recall. In fact, after they left the luncheonette, the friend headed for the stores again."

"Cheryl didn't accompany this person?"

"No. Actually, she might have done some more shopping

herself—seems the aspirin helped—but she needed a bathroom, and she figured the best thing would be to go back to the hotel."

"She didn't want to use the facilities at the luncheonette?"

"They only had one rest room—it was for both men and women. And her friend warned her that the toilet was backed up."

"So the proximity of this other flight attendant to that Colombian is what first tipped your wife to the possibility they might be involved in some illegal activity together?"

"Oh, no. It never occurred to Cheryl there could be a connection between any buddy of hers and a notorious drug dealer. Not then." Suddenly Bruce got to his feet. "Look, are you sure I can't offer you a drink of something or other?"

"Positive, thanks."

"I'll be right back. I have to get myself a Pepsi; I'm parched."

A few minutes later, he returned, clutching a very tall, very full glass. "Running off at the mouth can make you pretty thirsty," he informed me jokingly just before taking a few healthy swallows. Then he set the near-empty glass on the coffee table. "Okay, so anyway—" But wrinkling his brow, he stopped, apparently to gather his thoughts.

"The luncheonette," I prompted.

"Yes, I know. But it's time we got out of there, Dez," he teased, eyes crinkling. And for a moment I glimpsed the charisma of the man, the appeal that had not that long ago charmed the pants off me. Literally, it pains me to say. "Let's fast-forward a few months to last week," he continued more soberly. "On that particular layover the crew members went to a hotel right there in Nassau for dinner and some casino action. I can't remember the name of the place, but it was maybe five minutes from where they were staying."

"They all went?"

"All six of them: the pilot, the copilot, and the four flight attendants. Anyway, almost immediately Cheryl lost most of her self-imposed limit in blackjack, so she decided she'd leave the tables for a while and go into the lounge for a glass of wine. And who does she spot as soon as she sets foot in there?"

"I can guess."

"And you'd be right. Cheryl's good buddy and this El Puerco are sitting at the bar on adjacent stools. Cheryl said that stopped her cold. It wasn't that she had any inkling the two of them might be together at this point—her buddy was laughing it up with the bartender, while El Puerco was hunched over his drink. But for a minute or so, seeing that drug-dealing creep again kind of threw her. At any rate, just as Cheryl is about to go over to the bar, her friend suddenly stands up, then reaches down for one of the two shoulder bags that had been lying there side by side between the bar stools." Bruce was looking at me intently now, and I had no doubt that he was about to impart something significant. *"The friend picked up the bag that was closest to El Puerco."* From the way he delivered this information, I almost expected a flourish of trumpets to follow. "Anyhow," he continued, "the friend heads for the rest room with the bag, and Cheryl takes off."

"Any chance your wife might have been seen?"

"I asked her about that. She told me no, that neither of them even glanced in her direction. And by the way, I just want to mention that as soon as she left the lounge, that business at the luncheonette flashed through Cheryl's mind. Only, as you can appreciate, she put a much different interpretation on it now."

"I'm surprised they kept meeting out in the open like that," I mused.

"But there wasn't any meeting. Not as far as anyone could tell. El Puerco and that flight attendant behaved as if they didn't know each other from Adam. Cheryl thought they were probably in that lounge just to switch bags, although she didn't quite say that. But she did say that from what she could make out, both bags looked to be black—or at least a very dark color—and about the same size and shape. While the room wasn't exactly brightly lit, it was bright enough to see that much, at least," Bruce clarified.

"And as for that luncheonette, Dez," he went on, "the place

was off on a side street—an alley, really, from what I gathered from Cheryl. Besides, I'm sure the dealer and Cheryl's friend didn't say boo to each other there, either." A brief pause followed, after which Bruce added somewhat tentatively, "Also, if they'd been spotted together at someplace *really* out of the way—some hole in the wall—that would have been a helluva lot harder to explain."

Well, the man did seem to be making sense. Although I wasn't exactly ecstatic about this. I mean, who was the detective here?

"Anyway, in spite of everything," he said then, both irritation and fondness in his tone, "would you believe that Cheryl still found it difficult to accept the truth? She kept trying to convince herself that there could be another explanation. I remember that later that night—the night she confided all this to me—she was still making these excuses: 'Maybe this friend of mine walked off with El Puerco's bag by mistake. Or maybe I'm the one who made the mistake,' she said, 'and it was the right bag after all.' I didn't even bother to respond; I knew she didn't actually believe either of those things to be true. And she verified this a couple of minutes later, too, because she mumbled—more to herself than to me, really—'But everything fits. Everything fits now.' That's just what she said."

" 'Everything fits now,' huh? Sounds to me like there was something else that contributed to her suspicions."

Bruce pondered this notion for a moment. "You may be right," he conceded. "But if there was anything more, Cheryl never mentioned it."

"One thing I don't understand, though. Since Cheryl revealed so much to you, why hold back on identifying the friend?"

"Because if those meetings—or whatever you want to call them—should turn out to have been completely innocent—" On seeing my expression, Bruce broke off, then shook his head. "I know, I know. But Cheryl was still holding out hope; she was just so anxious for those incidents not to be what she knew they were. What I started to say, though, was that she was afraid that even if she learned her friend had no connection at all with El Puerco, she'd never be able to convince me of that. She was certain I'd always have my doubts—she was constantly reminding me of how stubborn I am."

"And you say that your wife intended to go to her friend about what she'd seen? Didn't either of you realize this could be dangerous?"

Once again something of the old Bruce surfaced. "You must take me for a total moron," he snarled between barely open lips. "I pleaded with Cheryl not to do it. I advised her to talk to the police or somebody in authority at the airlines. I warned her that any confrontation could put her in jeopardy, and I tried to get her to promise that she'd give up on the idea. But all she'd say was that she'd think about it. It was my impression, though—although she denied it—that she'd already made up her mind to give her friend the chance to explain. She felt she had to."

He sighed deeply now. "And I'm just about positive it was this sense of loyalty that got my poor Cheryl killed."

Chapter 4

"Try to think," I urged. "Did Cheryl say anything else that could give us a handle on this mysterious friend of hers?"

"I have thought. I've gone over the conversation we had that night again and again. And I'm certain I've told you all of it. Look, Dez, Cheryl took great care to protect this person's identity. I can't even tell you whether it was a man or a woman."

A man? This possibility hadn't occurred to me, although I have no idea why not. "How well do you know these three friends of Cheryl's—or don't you?"

"I knew Laura casually when we were both living in Chicago; I dated her roommate for a short·time a few years back. And afterward I'd run into the two of them at cocktail parties every so often. I saw her again in New York—in May, I think it was—when she came over to the apartment for dinner. And then more recently Cheryl stopped in at the office with Laura and this other flight attendant, a woman named Donna Wolf."

"This Donna is also one of our suspects?"

"That's right. The third one's Herman—Hank Herman. I never had the pleasure there, but Cheryl said he was a faggot."

I winced. I absolutely hate that word! "That's what your wife called her friend—a faggot?"

"No. That's what I'm calling him. Listen, I'm sorry if this offends your sensibilities, but—" He broke off abruptly, evidently having reminded himself that he was counting on my help. "It's probably not the best term I could have used," he admitted, "but I didn't mean anything by it. My tough Chicago street background, I guess." And he grinned disarmingly.

I moved on. "I'm supposing you can give me the three telephone numbers. And I'd like the addresses, too, if you have them."

Reaching into his shirt pocket, Bruce pulled out a neatly folded piece of notepaper. "Everything's here," he said, handing it to me. "I figured you'd want to know those things, so I copied them out of Cheryl's address book before you came. They all live in Queens—in Forest Hills."

Unfolding the paper, I glanced down. Two of the addresses were exactly the same, while the other was just one digit off. "Do Hank and Laura share an apartment?"

"No, they each have a place of their own. They're a couple of floors apart, I think."

"And Donna's not more than a stone's throw away, I see."

"She lives in the building directly opposite theirs. Her last apartment was a real hellhole, Cheryl once told me. And the woman was paying a pretty high tariff, too, for the privilege of cohabiting with half the cockroaches in Flushing. So when Laura and Hank found out there was a vacancy across the street from them, Donna grabbed it."

"By the way," I brought up now, "there's something you haven't told me yet."

"What's that?"

"Why would the police think you had anything to do with Cheryl's death?"

"You won't believe this."

"Don't be so sure. I can be pretty gullible." *You can say that again.* I was reminded of my previous relationship with this man. He'd really lucked out with me, hadn't he? I'd been the perfect dupe—make that *dope.* I mean, even though he hadn't actually lied to me—not that I was aware of, anyway—he'd never allowed himself to be hampered by the truth, either. And in spite of his frequently questionable behavior, yours truly, I pointed out to myself disgustedly, hadn't suspected a thing.

This wasn't the time, however, to dwell on past hurts. I got the words out with an effort. "Go ahead, give me a try."

Bruce smiled ruefully. "To be honest, I can hardly believe it myself. You see, when these detectives told me how Cheryl had been killed, I said something like, 'She's been flying all over the world for years, and nothing ever happened to her. Then she moves to New York and gets run over by the A train."

Not always being as quick as I wish I were, I looked at him quizzically. "I don't understand."

"Well, it seems Cheryl really *was* killed by an A train. The police, though, hadn't been that specific."

And now I was even more perplexed. "What made you say that, then?"

"Lucky, I suppose," he answered petulantly. "Look, I could just as easily have made it the B or the C or the D—or any other letter in the alphabet. But this was the first one that came to mind. Probably because of 'Take the A Train.' You remember what a Duke Ellington fanatic I am, don't you?"

I wasn't sure that I did. But then, I couldn't swear that I didn't, either.

"I tried to explain this to the police," Bruce continued. And now with a halfhearted attempt at levity: "But I think this Sergeant Fielding had definite doubts about my veracity."

"Well, well. Tim Fielding," I murmured, a fond smile forming on my lips.

"You know him?"

"He's an old friend." *Most of the time, that is.*

"If that's the case, maybe you can convince him that it was just by chance I came up with the right train."

"I'll do my best," I said. "But, in any event, try not to worry about this. It could be you're just imagining Fielding's reaction. Besides, it's really no big deal. All it proves is that you're a damn good guesser."

"That's reassuring to hear, Desiree," Bruce responded—right before slipping me the zinger. "Uh, there's . . . uh . . . something more."

I steeled myself. "What?"

"Fielding came by to see me on Sunday. He wanted to know about this little argument Cheryl and I had."

The alarm in my head was ringing like crazy now. "How little?"

"Probably not that little, actually." He had the decency to look embarrassed, at least. "As I told you before, while I wasn't exactly thrilled about Cheryl's having gone back to flying, I realized—intellectually, anyway—how important it was for her to pursue her own career, her own interests. Emotionally, though, it was a different story, I'm sorry to say. At any rate, this one evening I'm afraid I sort of, well, lost it. I suppose what set me off was that I'd just had to attend an office function by myself because Cheryl wasn't in town. Anyway, we—Cheryl and I—were having something to eat at this coffee shop on the next block. I hadn't planned to open a discussion then. And that's the truth. But, I don't know, it just came out. I told her I wanted her to quit the damn job. And, of course, she wouldn't even consider it. So I . . . I, uh, pretty much let her have it."

"What did you say?"

Bruce's face reddened. "Things that I wish I hadn't."

"I think you'd better tell me. All of it."

"I put it to her that maybe our getting married had been a mistake, and she said if I wanted out, that was fine with her. And then I said swell, that I didn't know how I could have wound up with such a"—grimacing now, he stiffened and moved further back in his chair, as if recoiling from the words he was about to utter—". . . such a stupid bitch, anyway."

My expression was apparently not as noncommittal as I intended it to be, because Bruce found it necessary to justify himself. "It was the anger talking. Haven't you ever lost your temper and said things you regretted? At any rate, though, Cheryl started crying, and she told me that I wouldn't have to put up with her much longer. She'd be speaking to a lawyer in the morning, she said. And then she picked herself up and ran out of the restaurant."

"And there was a witness to your fi—argument?"

"A couple from our building—wouldn't you know it? I never even saw them come in. But they'd been sitting in the booth directly behind us."

"And they overheard all of this?"

"Enough. Listen, Desiree, I swear that Cheryl and I made up that same night. I really loved the woman, and if she was happy being a flight attendant, then I was willing to go along with it."

The thought that he probably wouldn't have been willing for very long popped into my head. But sadly, this had become a moot point. "Tell me something. Did you mention the drug smuggling to Fielding?"

"I couldn't."

"Why not, for heaven's sake?"

"Look, when the detectives first notified me about Cheryl's death, I was so numb I didn't think about that. It completely slipped my mind that she might have gone to confront this friend of hers that morning." His eyes were filling with tears now, and he was extracting a fistful of tissues from his pants pocket just as two large drops raced down his right cheek. After wiping away the wetness and then blowing his nose once or twice, he went on, his voice thick with grief. "It was hard enough for me to accept that Cheryl had met with a terrible accident, but *murder*? I couldn't even consider that. It—"

"And the police. Did they seem to believe that Cheryl was murdered? Initially, I mean."

"I'm not sure."

"Okay, sorry I interrupted. You were saying?"

"Well, later, once the shock wore off a little, the likelihood of a connection with the drug business began to dawn on me. Only while I was still working myself up to getting in touch with Fielding about that, he and this other cop came here with questions about the argument. And by then, of course, anything I said would have been regarded as an attempt to divert suspicion away from myself. That's why I need so badly for you to look into things for me."

"By the way, when was this argument?" I asked.

Bruce's response was barely above a whisper. "I'm afraid that's the trouble, Dez. It was just one week before Cheryl died."

Chapter 5

I swear there's something wrong with me.

My opinion of Bruce hadn't really become any more favorable in the last few hours. I still rated him a triple-A, gold-plated louse. Yet almost as soon as I was back in my own apartment I started blubbering in sympathy for the man. But I think I probably reacted that way because he *did* have such crummy character. I guess I should make that a little clearer—or try to, anyhow....

The thing is, you just never expect somebody like Bruce to shed a tear. Actually, until tonight it would have been difficult for me to imagine him even capable of genuine human emotion. So seeing him weep, I realized his anguish had to be truly overwhelming. And I couldn't help it; this touched me. In fact, being the prize weenie that I am, it had been all I could do not to part with a few tears myself right then and there.

Okay. So maybe lo these many months I had been engaging in a bit of fantasizing about witnessing the man in excruciating pain. But I'd concentrated exclusively on the physical variety. You know, four or five smashed ribs, dislodged fingernails, broken kneecaps, et cetera. But what he was going through now—well, I hate to see *anyone* in *that* kind of pain. Even Bruce. Nevertheless, I felt I should probably be committed for letting him get to me like this.

Of course, it was also possible I was crying mostly for *her,* for Cheryl. That would certainly make more sense, wouldn't it?—regardless of my never having set eyes on the victim. According to the very little Pat had told me about her, though, Cheryl had been a pretty nice person. And when you take into account that she and I had once—unbeknownst to either of us—been rivals for the same rotten stinker, and then you consider what a true-blue friend Pat is, you can be sure Pat thought it necessary to cut way back in her praise of the woman. I would put money on this. Which meant that, at the very least, Bruce's dead wife had to have been only a notch below Mother Teresa.

It was after I finally dried my eyes and there were just a few intermittent snuffles left in me that I admonished myself: *Oh, hell, why look for explanations? You cry at supermarket openings, for God's sake.*

When I got to the office Wednesday morning the first thing on my agenda was to phone the twelfth precinct—or the one-two, as the police like to refer to it. Tim Fielding, I was apprised, was off for the day.

I waited impatiently until ten-fifteen before making any of my other calls. At which point I took out the brief list I'd obtained from Bruce. I dialed the number at the top of the paper.

Laura Downey's telephone rang six or seven times, and I was just about to drop the receiver back in its cradle when someone picked up. There was a very faint "hello?" I had obviously pulled the woman out of a deep sleep.

"Ms. Downey?"

"Yes?"

"I'm sorry. I woke you, didn't I? I could call back later," I offered.

The voice became a little stronger. "No, that's okay. I'm up now. who is this?"

I introduced myself. "My name is Desiree Shapiro. I'm a private investigator, and Cheryl Simon's husband hired me to look into her death. Umm, there's been some speculation that Cheryl might have been murdered."

A horrified "Oh, no!" And then, after a brief silence: "That's not definite, though, is it?"

"No, but it's a possibility. And I wondered if I could stop by for a few minutes to talk to you."

"Yes. Of course. But I'm driving out to New Jersey a little later today to visit my aunt and uncle—they live in Morristown—and there's no telling when I'll be back. They've been known to hold me hostage once I get there." Her titter was practically musical. But almost at once her tone was serious again. "Would it be all right if we made it tomorrow?"

"No problem," I assured her. And we set up an appointment for one o'clock at her apartment.

I tried the second name on the list the instant we hung up.

This time the phone was answered on the first ring. "Hank here," announced a pleasant male voice.

I explained who I was and the purpose of my call.

"*Murdered? Cheryl?* You're kidding, aren't you? No, no, of course you're not." This was closely followed by an almost inaudible: "Lord."

"Well, as I told you, we aren't really certain what happened to her, not yet. But it appears that murder *is* an option."

"The police stopped in to question us on Friday, you know, right before our flight. They asked a few questions like did we have any idea if Cheryl was having trouble with anyone, did she seem happy on the job, were we aware of any problems at home—that sort of thing. They told us it was just routine, though. A couple of us even got the impression they were thinking suicide—which, if you knew Cheryl, is preposterous. But murder? Lord," he murmured again.

"I'd like to speak to you about Cheryl as soon as you can do it. Would it be okay if I came to see you this afternoon? I promise not to keep you too long."

"How's three o'clock? I should be back from the doctor's by then. My yearly checkup."

"I'll be there," I said.

And now there was one more call to go.

"This is Donna."

"Hi, Donna. My name is—" But it was as far as I got.

"I'm up, up, and away today," the voice chirped. *Damn! I'm conversing with a damn answering machine here.* "Leave a message and I'll get back to you, or else give me a call Thursday night. Thanks. And have a good day now, ya hear?"

At least I had the sense not to say, "You, too."

Chapter 6

I'd had the foresight to drive to work that morning. And at a little past two, I retrieved my Chevy from the garage around the corner and headed for Queens.

Fortunately the car's temperamental air conditioner was working for a change—although hardly at top efficiency. Still, it was cooling enough so that my blouse didn't wind up plastered to my back by the time I got to Forest Hills.

The address I was looking for belonged to a modest well-kept building on a block of modest well-kept buildings. Hank Herman buzzed me upstairs.

I stepped off the elevator on the fifth floor to find the doorway opposite me practically filled by a stockily built man of average height. He was dressed in light blue slacks and a crisp plaid sport shirt, the sleeves of which were neatly rolled up to the elbows. He couldn't be much over twenty, I decided with my characteristic perceptiveness. I was to learn at some point that he was well past thirty.

"Hi, I'm Hank. Come in," he said as he continued to block the entrance. Then flushing, he mumbled, "Excuse me," pushed back the door, and stepped aside. "I've been so upset since I spoke to you this morning that I hardly know what I'm doing." His round boyish face wore an expression of great concern.

Leading the way down a short hall, he spoke over his shoulder. "Cheryl and I were very close. I really loved that girl. She was just so . . . so *caring*."

We entered a good-sized living room, which was nicely, although far from luxuriously, furnished. "Sit anywhere," Hank instructed, gesturing. The choice, however, was somewhat limited, consisting of a narrow high-backed chair, a low-to-the-ground barrel chair (from which I'd have had to be hoisted by a crane), and a small modern sofa with a fat orange cat sprawled in the middle of it. (Who said cats were curious, anyway? This one hadn't even glanced at me.) I opted for the narrow chair—which barely managed to accommodate my very adequate backside.

"You're not allergic to cats, are you?" Hank asked. And before I could reply: "Because if you are, or if you just can't stand them, I can put Stan in the bedroom."

Stan opened one eye at the mention of his name and then promptly shut it again.

"No, I'm fine with cats," I said.

"You don't have to worry about Stan bothering you," Hank advised, taking a seat next to the cat and stroking the orange fur. "He's practically comatose."

"Is he sick?"

"Oh, no. Just the laziest creature God ever created." A loud snore gave added credence to this statement. "Instead of 'Stan,' my mother should have taken her cue from *Snow White and the Seven Dwarfs* and called him Sleepy. Or maybe Dopey." He smiled fondly down at the subject under discussion. "Old Bright Eyes here was a gift from Mother, so I guess she thought that entitled her to christening privileges. May I tell you why she picked the name Stan? I'm sure it was because when I was a little boy we had this mucho macho neighbor, Stan Frumkes." And now, looking up at me, Hank said with what seemed to be deliberate nonchalance, "My mother was no doubt hoping the name would be inspirational, that it would prompt me to go against my own basic nature. I've never told her I was gay, but I know she *knows*. And she's in denial."

I didn't have a clue as to the appropriate response to this, so I limited myself to an "Oh."

"When I get really nervous or upset, this is what I do—" Hank murmured apologetically, "talk a blue streak. So forgive me. You came here about Cheryl."

"Yes. As I indicated on the phone, the police think she might have met with foul play."

"You're not referring to a mugging or anything like that, I gather."

"No, I'm not, although that possibility hasn't been ruled out, either."

"Look, Desiree—it *is* all right to call you Desiree, isn't it?—I can't see anyone wanting to hurt Cheryl. She was the sweetest, the most—" Hank's pale blue eyes narrowed slightly. "What would make them suspect a thing like that, anyway?"

"Well, I'm not entirely familiar with their theory," I hedged, "but there's been some speculation"—I didn't say who was doing the speculating—"that Cheryl may have had some information regarding a drug-smuggling operation."

"And the cops think she was murdered to keep her quiet?"

I hedged some more. "Let's just say that this *could have been* the motive."

"Lord." Then, after he had a moment to absorb what I'd told him: "They can't believe someone at Bahamian Air is involved in the smuggling, can they?" His tone was incredulous.

"I'm not exactly certain what they believe. But you have to admit that airline personnel have a better opportunity to transport contraband into this country than your average citizen."

"But it's not as though we fly to Colombia or Mexico or anyplace like that. We go to *Nassau*," Hank protested.

"Yes, but from what I was told, this well-known Colombian drug dealer has been spotted in Nassau on a number of occasions. Apparently, he smuggles the drugs in there—or has another party smuggle them in—and then he gets someone to carry them into the States for him."

"This someone being with Bahamian Air."

"Maybe so."

Hank screwed up his face. "It's inconceivable to me that anyone I fly with would be into something like that. I really work with such a great bunch, Desiree."

"Have you ever heard the name El Puerco?"

"Never. He's the Colombian?"

"That's right. And his U.S. contact, well, I believe . . . uh . . . that is, there's a likelihood it's one of three Bahamian Air crew members." I fixed my gaze on the snoring orange lump stretched out on the sofa.

"And I'm one of the three? Is that why you can't look me in the eye?"

"Listen, there's something you should know." And I told Hank how Cheryl had confided to Bruce about twice spotting a good friend—who had to be one of her fellow flight attendants—in close proximity to the drug dealer. Then I laid out the rest of it: Cheryl's reluctance to go to the authorities without first advising this friend of her suspicions, and the conclusion that could easily be drawn from these things.

When I was through, Hank said with a small smile, "Naturally, I'm positive *I'm* not the smuggler. But I'd also be willing to swear for Laura and Donna. They're such decent people. Both of them."

"You may very well be right. Perhaps there's another explanation for what Cheryl saw, although, frankly, I have no idea what it could be. And maybe Cheryl's death *was* the result of a mugging or even an accident. But her husband is paying me to find out the truth—whatever it is. That's why I'm here."

Hank nodded. "I understand. Okay, how can I help you?"

"Do you recall one day—probably in late April or early May—when your whole crew went to Paradise Island to gamble?"

"We spent a few evenings over there around that time."

"This was during the afternoon."

"Oh, sure. I remember that."

"Well, one of your group left early and went back to Nassau, ostensibly to buy a birthday present. But actually to meet with this El Puerco."

"No. Can't be." Hank was shaking his head.

"Why do you say that?"

"Because we all returned to Nassau together."

"You're positive of this?"

"Uh-huh. We'd made up to leave the casino at six o'clock,

and I specifically remember having to drag Donna away from the poker machines to get her out of there. And as for Laura, I was just so annoyed with her on the way back to our hotel. She and Nick—he's our copilot—didn't stop bitching for a second about how much they'd lost at blackjack. If you're not prepared to lose, you shouldn't play, is what I always say."

"And that was the only time you went over to Paradise Island this spring? In the afternoon, I'm talking about."

"That was it."

"Is it possible the others went on another day, too—a day you didn't make the trip to Nassau?"

"Well, I *was* sick this one time. Still, if they did go then, most likely I'd have heard about it. But on the other hand, maybe not." It was a few seconds before the realization struck him. "Hey, that would let me off the hook, though, wouldn't it?"

"I suppose it would."

Hank leaned forward in his chair now, and his voice grew confidential. "Look, I don't know if I should be saying this, but are you positive Cheryl's husband has been leveling with you? The two of them were having some problems, you know. And while I'm not suggesting the man killed her, I'd believe that a lot quicker than I'd believe that either Laura or Donna had anything to do with her death."

I couldn't be sure he wasn't right. But on the other hand, it was difficult for me to accept that Bruce had concocted the entire El Puerco story—or that he himself had pushed Cheryl in front of that train. Well, I had a lot more work—and a lot more thinking—to do before I could hope to find any answers.

In fact, I even had a couple more points to go over with Hank right now.

"When was the last time you saw or spoke to Cheryl?"

"I saw her Tuesday—the Tuesday before she died—on the return flight from Nassau."

"You had no contact with her after this?"

"No, none," Hank murmured sadly.

"Speaking of that return flight, did Cheryl's manner toward

either Donna or Laura seem any different to you then? Different than usual, I mean."

"I didn't notice. We were booked solid that day, so there really wasn't much time for interaction. Plus right outside of Florida one of the passengers became ill—for a while I was afraid it might be a heart attack—and we were all pretty stressed out."

Which left just one more question. The one that was hardest to ask.

"Umm, I wonder if you could . . . that is, would you mind telling me where you were that Thursday morning Cheryl was killed?"

I must say he took it in stride. "No problem. I was here in the apartment until eleven-fifteen, eleven-thirty. And then I went out jogging for about a half hour. After that I stopped off for something to eat. I got home just before one." He grinned good-naturedly. "And, no, I didn't see anyone I knew. And I'd be totally floored if the waitress at the restaurant could alibi me; I'd never even been in there before. But, of course, you're welcome to give it a shot."

I didn't bother taking down the particulars. Let's say that by some chance the waitress did remember him after a week. How could she be certain just when he'd been in?

I said good-bye to Hank five minutes later. I also said good-bye to Stan, who didn't so much as bat an eye.

Chapter 7

What with traffic and everything I returned from Forest Hills later than I'd anticipated. And I was expecting my niece Ellen and her almost-fiancé for dinner tonight, too.

But, for once, I was not in my usual "company's coming" dither. I actually had things well in hand. They wouldn't be here much before nine, since Ellen—a buyer at Macy's—was working until eight-thirty this evening. And I'd prepared almost the entire meal a couple of days ago, including mushroom turnover appetizers, leek and potato soup, Boeuf Bourguignon, and a dessert both Ellen and Mike insist is the best they've ever eaten: my chilled lemon soufflé. Food-wise, the only things left to do were to fix the salad and then, a little while before I planned to serve the meat, boil up some noodles. Even the apartment was in decent shape; all it really required (if you didn't look too closely) was a few swipes with the feather duster—which I wielded as soon as I got home. I glanced at my watch then: five after six. Plenty of time for a leisurely bath.

Taking a book along for company, I relaxed in that tub for close to a half hour. And if I weren't so damn nosy, I would have been tempted to stay longer. The thing is, though, I'd heard the phone ring twice in the last few minutes, and I was anxious to find out what my answering machine had to say to me.

Toweling myself off perfunctorily, I threw on a robe, and with water still trickling down my legs, went into the living room to check my messages.

The first call was from Christie Wright.

Christie's an old and dear college friend who had lost her

husband in an automobile accident only ten months earlier. The machine informed me that she'd flown down from Minnesota this week to spend some time with her folks in Riverdale. "So far I've been tied up here with family-type doings," she explained. "But yesterday I decided that before heading back, I was going to treat myself to a couple of days' stay at a posh Manhattan hotel. I'm looking forward to some nonstop shopping at Saks, Bloomingdale's, Bergdorf's, and all the rest, and I would love to have dinner with you, if you're available. I booked a room at the Pierre for next Monday and Tuesday nights. I hope you're free one of those evenings. Give me a ring and let me know."

The second call was from Bruce.

"I realize I'm being premature," he said, "but I just had to ask if you'd gotten the chance to talk to any of Cheryl's friends today." I gritted my teeth. *Oh, shit! Don't tell me he was going to be one of those.* "Please get back to me as soon as you can," he concluded.

Right away I dialed the number Christie had left for me. We made arrangements to meet on Monday night at a French restaurant on West Sixty-third Street, a place that had been highly recommended by Christie's brother-in-law.

Bruce could wait.

At exactly nine o'clock, Ellen and Mike were buzzing my buzzer. The first thought I had on opening the door was *What a handsome couple they make!* But then that's invariably my first thought when I see them together.

And imagine. They might never have met if I hadn't had the good luck to pass out cold in the hallway of Mike's building at a time when Mike—a resident at St. Gregory's Hospital—was around to minister to me. Now, while I consider that this entitles me to most of the credit for the romance, I suppose that at least a small portion of it should also go to the vicious killer whose assault had precipitated that dead faint of mine.

I looked dotingly at the happy pair, who were now standing just this side of the threshold. Mike was helping Ellen off with the little waterproof jacket she was wearing—it had started drizzling about an hour earlier. Ellen said something at that moment—I don't remember what it was—and I wish you could see how Mike beamed down on her from his towering six feet whatever. And how adoringly she gazed up at him. In spite of the fact that my 10,000 B.T.U. air conditioner was on high, I suddenly felt a rush of warmth.

Following me into the kitchen, Mike opened the merlot they'd brought. Ellen, meanwhile, had ensconced herself on the sofa, undoubtedly to get a head start on the mushroom turnovers. As soon as Mike was out of my way (it's really a one-person kitchen), I put a very low flame under the soup and then joined them in the living room for a couple of minutes.

"How have you been, Dez?" Mike asked, pouring me a glass of the wine.

"Just fine, thanks, Mike."

"Any interesting cases lately?"

"Uh, only one. I'll tell you about it later. How are things at the hospital?" I put in quickly.

Ellen preempted his answer. "Mike's doing exceptionally well there, Aunt Dez. Dr. Beaver—that big cardiovascular sur-geon he works under—said he considers Mike one of the best young doc—"

"Ellen," Mike remonstrated gently. He was now practically the exact shade of my favorite lipstick.

I like modesty in a man. I also like Mike. Very much. Al-though whenever I was around him, I had to be careful that I didn't say what Ellen would strangle me for saying. But look, they'd been seeing each other regularly for over two years now, so I felt I'd been extremely patient with him. It really was time the man got off that nicely rounded little tush of his and mar-ried my niece. Don't you agree?

The meal was a huge success. Mike had second helpings of everything, and Ellen more than kept pace with him. She even had thirds of the salad. (And where that girl puts it all is one of life's true mysteries. I mean, my ballpoint pen is wider than

Ellen's hips.) Anyway, at the table, the three of us chatted about a whole variety of topics: current events, books, yoga, the concept of friendship—even what Liz Smith was saying lately. And then after we'd finished eating and were sitting around in more comfortable seats sipping anisette, Mike turned to me. "Listen, I know you don't like to discuss your work during dinner, so I've been biding my time waiting to hear about this new case of yours. Well, dinner's over now," he reminded me with a grin.

Marry my niece, and I'll tell you everything, I responded. But silently. Aloud, I was slightly more circumspect. "All right. To begin with, Bruce Simon has just become my client."

Ellen's *"Bruce Simon!"* and Mike's "Bruce Simon?" came out simultaneously.

"Don't you remember him, Mike?" Ellen said impatiently. "He's that . . . that despicable man who treated Aunt Dez so badly. The one with the secret fiancée back in Chicago."

Mike's eyes widened. *"Him?"*

The look I got from Ellen an instant later seemed to contain equal measures of astonishment and anger. "I can't understand how you can have anything to do with that . . . that rat," she scolded, frowning. "What kind of a case is it, anyway?"

"His wife was run over by a subway train last Thursday."

"Ohh. That's too bad," Ellen murmured, sheepish now. And then she added magnanimously, "I have nothing against *her,* of course."

"How decent of you."

She ignored my sarcasm. "He married that woman in Chicago, I suppose."

"That's right. In March. And Bruce and Cheryl—his wife—had had a pretty bitter argument the week before she was killed, and well, it appears that the police suspect he might have had something to do with her death."

"It wouldn't surprise me," Ellen pronounced.

Mike glanced at me inquiringly. "But you don't think he was responsible, Dez?"

"Frankly, no. I wouldn't give you two cents for the man, but I just don't believe he's a killer."

"Could it have been an accident then?"

"Possibly. Although there's another possibility, too."

Ellen pounced. "Which is—?"

"That Cheryl witnessed something she shouldn't have." And for the second time that day I provided a brief synopsis of Bruce's narrative about the link between El Puerco and the unknown flight attendant.

"And you think Cheryl was murdered by this person she worked with?" Mike wanted to know.

"It looks that way to me."

"Well, don't be too sure," Ellen cautioned. "I wouldn't put anything past that creepy ex of yours. And after how he acted with you, what made you agree to help him in the first place?"

Mike's expression asked the same question.

My reply was truthful, if not exactly informative. "I'm damned if I know," I said.

Chapter 8

I called Tim Fielding at nine-thirty the next morning. This tme he was at his desk.

"Sergeant Fielding."

"Hi, Tim."

"Desiree!" There was a real warmth in his greeting, which unless I catch him off guard like this, is something he takes pains to omit. At least that's how I choose to interpret the less-than-cordial receptions I'm accustomed to from him. "How have you been?" he asked.

"Pretty good. What about you?"

"Not too terrible for an arthritic old cop."

"Since when? The arthritis, I'm referring to."

"Since over a year ago. Got it in my neck."

"You mean we haven't spoken in a *year*?" I was genuinely surprised.

"It's been a lot longer than that." And then warily: "But why are you calling now, all of a sudden?"

"I just found out that we're working on the same case. It'll be like old times, huh?" I told him cheerily.

There was a loud groan. "Christ, I should have guessed." *This was more like my friend Tim.*

"It'll be nice to see *you* again, too," I responded tartly.

"Yeah, I'll bet. So which case of mine you sticking your nose into this time? Is it the decapitation thing?"

I gulped. "No. I'm investigating the death of Cheryl Simon. She was hit by—"

"I know who Cheryl Simon is," Fielding snapped. "Who hired you? The husband?"

"That's right."

"Well, good luck."

"You really think he had something to do with it?"

"I'd almost bet my pension on it."

"I'm glad you said 'almost.' Look, Tim, I thought maybe we could help each other out on this one. I was—"

"Can it, Shapiro. If memory serves me right—and I'm not *that* old yet—whenever you give me this 'maybe we could help each other out' crap, I'm the one who ends up doing the helping."

"Tim, Tim," I said softly. "Your memory *is* going, I'm afraid. Do you happen to recall those murders in my niece Ellen's building? And that's not the only instance where I—"

"Okay, so you got lucky once or twice. But I'd like to take a stab at handling this one myself, if you don't mind. It'll maybe be proof that the hundreds of other cases I solved without your assistance weren't a fluke."

"Just give me a few minute so we can compare notes, Tim," I wheedled. "I think you're going to find it worth your while."

He snorted. "A few minutes? That'll be the day! But, okay, you can have your few minutes. In fact, I'll give you fifteen of 'em. But that's all. And I mean it. Stop by tomorrow morning. Around ten. But call first, just to make sure I'm in."

"Thanks, Tim. I really appre—"

"Hold it. There's one condition. I expect you to pay something for my time."

"Pay?"

"The least you can do is spring for donuts. I'm particularly fond of the ones with the chocolate icing and the walnut sprinkles. And in the event it's slipped your mind, I take my coffee black, no sugar." He hung up then.

Sitting with that mute receiver in my hand, I smiled. I've known Tim Fielding going on forever. And I'm very fond of him. He and my deceased husband Ed had been good friends, too. In fact, once upon a time, before Ed left the force to become a P.I., the two men had worked out of the same precinct.

Well, I was looking forward to seeing Tim again. And I was

certain he felt the same way—even though he'd rather pull out his tongue than admit it.

The phone rang maybe ten seconds after I replaced the receiver. It was Bruce.

"I stayed home to wait for your call last night," he told me, trying not very successfully to conceal his annoyance.

"I was out for the evening," I lied.

"You could have gotten in touch with me this morning; you know where I work."

"The truth is, I couldn't think of the name of your company." Another lie.

"Look, Dez, I realize I'm being pesky, but I can't seem to help myself. I'm so damn anxious about everything."

I softened a little. "The only one of Cheryl's friends that I got to see yesterday was Hank Herman. I have an appointment with Laura Downey this afternoon. And Donna Wolf's out of town—I'll try her again tonight."

"Did Herman have anything important to contribute?"

"I can't tell yet. Not until I gather all the facts and start putting them together."

"Oh."

"I promise I'll keep you posted. Honestly."

"Thanks. I really need to know what's going on."

As soon as I finished talking to Bruce, I began to type up my notes on yesterday's visit with Hank Herman. I didn't get very far before the phone rang again.

Now, as I usually do when I schedule a meeting, I'd given Laura Downey both my office and home numbers—just in case. And apparently it had been a wise move.

"I'm so glad you're there," she told me. "It looks as if I'm going to have to cancel our appointment for this afternoon. I seem to have a virus of some kind, and my aunt wouldn't even hear of my driving home last night. In fact, she insisted I get right back in bed this morning, and I didn't wake up until a few minutes ago. I'm awfully sorry about this."

"Don't worry about it. I'm sorry you're not feeling well."

"Can we reschedule for Sunday afternoon? I'm working Friday and Saturday, and I've already made plans for Saturday night." Then she added halfheartedly, "Although I could change them, I suppose."

I assured her that Sunday would be fine.

"Is around two-thirty okay?"

I told her that two-thirty would also be fine, remembering to slip in a hasty "Hope you feel better" right before the call ended.

I'd intended to eat in that day so I could transcribe the rest of the Hank Herman notes. But at eleven o'clock Jackie poked her head in my cubbyhole. "You free lunchtime?" she asked.

"Yes and no."

"Could you explain that?"

"I don't have any plans, but I don't want to go out, either."

"Oh, c'mon, Dez. You've gotta to do me a favor. I've been invited to this wedding—a second cousin's and pretty fancy. Anyhow, it's in a couple of weeks, and I don't have a dress yet. I've been looking around on my own, but I can't seem to find anything. And I always have such good luck when I'm with you."

"There's some work I'm anxious to finish this afternoon. And besides, it's too hot to schlepp around the city today. Why don't we make it tomorrow?" I suggested. "It's supposed to be cooler then."

"Please, Dez," Jackie said plaintively. "Elliot and Pat will be in court all afternoon, so I can take a little extra time now. Please," she said again. "We'll only go to one or two stores, okay?"

Well, in addition to being my secretary, Jackie is also my very good friend. And a friend in need, and all that stuff . . . Anyhow, I said okay. Something I would soon have reason to regret.

Jackie dragged me into four of the neighborhood boutiques, trying on a total of six dresses. After this she practically shoved me into a cab—without air conditioning, naturally (which is supposed to be illegal in New York City)—and we headed across town to Lord & Taylor's.

"I shopped there last night," she explained on the way over, "and I saw two dresses I kind of liked. But since I couldn't make up my mind between them, I decided that maybe neither one was that great. I could have been wrong, though; I really want your opinion."

When we got to the store, Jackie had no trouble locating one of the dresses—a two-piece peach silk. Thrusting it into my hands, she continued her search. "The gray was in this department, too. Right on this same rack, in fact," she mumbled, going through the rack a second time and then—very quickly— a third. Her face seemed to fall a little further with every dress she pushed aside. Convinced at last that she hadn't overlooked anything, she hurried over to the nearest salesperson, a small, olive-skinned woman with meticulously coiffed silver hair.

Trotting after her, I heard Jackie say almost tearfully, "I was here after work yesterday, and I couldn't decide between these two dresses—I was probably too tired to make a choice then. Anyway, I thought I'd come back and take another look at them both today. But one of the dresses seems to be gone."

The woman—Ms. Simms, as the little nameplate she wore proclaimed—regarded Jackie with a superior expression. "You should have requested that someone put them aside for you." From her tone, she might just as well have added, *you dope.* (No question about it; we had ourselves a real sweetheart here.) "What was the dress like, dear?" she asked, producing an ex- aggerated sigh.

"It was gray silk, with a round neck and a chiffon skirt and—"

"Little covered buttons?"

"That's right."

"Oh, this *is* a shame. I *do* wish you'd gotten here just a tad sooner. I sold that dress not ten minutes ago. It was the last one like that, too. A size fourteen, right?" And then, as if poor Jackie weren't depressed enough: "I suppose you know that it was on sale—fifty percent off."

"Would you mind calling some of your branch stores to see if they still have it?" I suggested curtly.

"I wouldn't mind at all, although I hardly expect that they will," Ms. Simms informed me condescendingly. And now her eyes traveled slowly up and down Jackie's substantial, large-boned torso. "The fourteen wasn't a little snug on you, dear?" she demanded of my rapidly reddening friend.

I fielded the stinging question before Jackie had to deal with it. "Not one bit," I pronounced emphatically. Then glancing at my watch—which revealed that it was after one-thirty—I said, "While you're checking on that dress, we'll be in the fitting room, Ms. Simms."

Well, all I can tell you is that when Jackie tried on the peach two-piece, I was delighted. It was perfect on her. Even the color was great, very flattering to her complexion and blondish-brown hair.

She was standing there, checking herself out in the full-length mirror, when through the door we heard: "Ladies? It's Ms. Simms. We're out of luck on that gray size fourteen, I'm afraid; I couldn't locate one anywhere. I'm terribly sorry." I didn't believe her "sorry" for a minute.

"It doesn't matter," I assured Jackie. "The gray couldn't be any nicer on you than this is."

"Oh, I don't know. You really think so?" She was turning her body this way and that.

"Absolutely."

"You're not just saying it because I can't get the gray any-more, are you?"

"I wouldn't do a thing like that."

"You don't think this kind of skirt makes my hips look bigger?" she asked as she continued to appraise her gyrating reflection.

"I think it makes them look smaller."

"Honestly?"

"Honestly."

"I'm not that crazy about the color, though."

"It does a lot for you."

"Really?" There was a prolonged pause before Jackie declared, "You're right. I'm going to take it."

Hallelujah!

But later, as Miss Simms was ringing up her purchase, Jackie took hold of my arm. "Uh, Dez? About the style . . ."

"What about it?"

"I was just wondering if maybe it isn't a little too youthful for me."

Now, I'm not what you'd call a drinking woman, one glass of wine being my normal limit. At that moment, however, I could have made quick work of an entire bottle.

Chapter 9

I realize I should have expected to hear from Bruce that night. For some silly reason, though, I figured he'd give me a little breathing space, at least.

Well, about a half hour after I'd made an appointment with Donna Wolf for Saturday evening, guess who called?

"Hi, Dez. I hope you don't mind my checking in with you again today"—I knew he didn't care if I did mind—"but I couldn't wait to find out what Laura told you this afternoon."

"She didn't tell me anything, Bruce. She wasn't feeling well, so we had to postpone our talk."

"Uh-*huh*." After a few moments he put to me tentatively, "You don't think that means anything, do you?"

"Means anything?"

"I just wonder if it's possible she's not very anxious to meet with you. Maybe the woman has something to hide."

"I hardly think that's why she canceled out. We've already rescheduled for Sunday."

"Then I suppose that takes care of that." But Bruce wasn't quite ready to abandon his theory, because practically on the heels of this he said, "Uh, was it at your suggestion—the rescheduling?"

"No. At Laura's."

"Oh." He sounded let down. (The man hated to be wrong.) "At any rate, you can see now why I need you," he told me, chuckling. "I'd make a pretty lousy P.I."

And then the conversation was more or less over.

*   *   *

Just before nine on Friday morning I phoned Tim Fielding to verify that he'd be available for our ten o'clock get-together.

"Yeah, you can come ahead; I'll be in." He didn't sound exactly overjoyed by the prospect of our little reunion. But, like I said, he deliberately downplays his feelings. I really am sure of it.

Anyhow, I walked into the station house armed with half a dozen donuts—four with chocolate icing and walnut sprinkles—and two containers of coffee.

Fielding glanced up when I approached his desk, and I swear that for an instant I spotted a smile flitting around the corners of his mouth. He rose to greet me, which whether he liked it or not (*not,* as it turned out), provided me with the opportunity of giving him an enthusiastic one-armed hug (the other arm being weighed down with all those calorie- and cholesterol-laden goodies). "Hey, cool it, Shapiro," he grumbled, losing no time in extricating himself from my clutch. "You want these characters here to think I play around?" And he checked behind him to see if any of the other eight or nine poeple in the room were watching us.

"How *is* Jo Ann?" I asked, placing the white paper bag on his desk.

"Still a lousy cook with a terrible temper. But she's not a bad poker player. For a wife, I mean." He regarded me thoughtfully for a couple of seconds. "Well, you've been holding your own against the ravages of time and life in the big city, I see."

"So have you." The nice, familiar face was still topped by a full head of wiry, close-cropped salt-and-pepper hair. He hadn't gained or lost a pound, either, I decided, quickly appraising the short, muscular body that resembles nothing so much as a fire-plug.

"Sit down." Fielding indicated the chair alongside his desk before taking a seat himself. And then he picked up the paper bag and peered into it, scowling. "There'd better be something here with chocolate icing and walnut sprinkles," he warned, digging in determinedly.

"Hey, I come in peace. I got four of those."

"You know, Shapiro," he told me, grinning as he spotted what he was looking for, "sometimes I have this idea that I could grow almost fond of you. If you weren't a pain-in-the-ass P.I., that is." And he removed a donut, along with the Styrofoam cup that had a "B" marked on the lid. "Feel free to join me," he said, passing the bag to me. I helped myself to a jelly donut and the other Styrofoam cup.

"Don't think I haven't noticed that you've been looking around for Corcoran every few seconds," he remarked with a straight face, just before biting into his donut.

"That'll be the day," I muttered, just before biting into mine. We were referring to Tim's partner, Walter Corcoran, with whom I have a long-standing hate/hate relationship.

"I'll save you from getting eyestrain. Walt's on vacation. In Paris, no less."

"That's nice." *Maybe he'll fall into the Seine.*

"Don't kid me. You're probably hoping he'll topple off the Eiffel Tower," Tim accused, coming remarkably close to reading my mind. "But enough with this chitchat. What are you going to do for me on the Simon case?"

"For starters, I'm going to show you that you're making a big mistake with your investigation."

"You don't say. And what mistake would that be?"

"You're assuming that my client is guilty."

"Now, in the first place, I'm not assuming anything. But Simon's a viable suspect, if I ever saw one."

"Why? Because he happened to mention something about his wife being run over by an A train? That was just a good guess. You see—"

"A very good guess, I'd call it."

"Look, you remember Duke Ellington's 'Take the A Train,' don't you? Well, Bruce is a big Duke Ellington fan. A fanatic, you might call him."

"So he told me."

"That's why the A popped into his head. I mean, you have to admit that if he knew it really *was* the A train, he'd have to be a total moron to say a thing like that."

"Listen," Tim retorted, "a guy does something like ice his wife, he's gotta be at least a little nervous that maybe we'll catch on to him—unless he happens to be completely off his trolley, that is. And when people are nervous they're liable to ramble on and give us a lot more than they intend to. I've seen it happen time and time again. And so have you." Here, Tim took another bite of donut, following it with a few gulps of the coffee, while I thought uncomfortably about Hank Herman and his lengthy narrative about Stan, the cat—which had, by Hank's own admission, been prompted by his nervousness. "Hell, how do you think we manage to nail so many of these scuzzbags?" Tim demanded. "Besides, Simon may have thought we'd already said what train it was."

"But he—"

"Let's assume you're right about the train thing, though. That's the least of what we've got on your client."

I tried to sound unconcerned. "So you heard he had an argument with his wife. Big deal."

"A particularly nasty argument."

"Listen, if every man who argued with his wife went on to murder her, we'd have to start building jails on the moon for enough space to accommodate all of them." I bent to my coffee.

"Maybe. But whenever I come across a guy who's that jealous, I take a good, long look at him if the lady ends up dead."

"Jealous?" I said sharply, depositing the Styrofoam container on the desk. "You mean of her job?"

"No, Desiree," Tim corrected. "I mean of her pilot." And then he shook his head slowly from side to side, after which he murmured with mock pity, "Don't tell me ol' Brucey didn't mention that he suspected his wife of fooling around with another member of the flight crew? He sure as hell didn't keep it a secret from the people in that coffee shop."

Well, apparently my client had been considerably less forthcoming with me. I swear, if he had been there at that moment, I'd have stabbed him with Fielding's jade-handled letter opener. I made a pathetic attempt at some face saving. "Uh, we haven't had time to go over the specifics of what was said yet. But I'm sure Bruce will explain everything when we do."

"Of course he will. I imagine he'll also tell you that the police back in Chicago still believe he may have had something to do with the death of his first wife."

I opened my mouth to speak. Only nothing would come out. It was as if someone were pressing down hard on my chest. I don't know how long it took before I was finally able to squeak, "What was that again?"

"I didn't *think* he'd want to bore you with anything so trivial. But allow me to do the boring.

"After we checked Simon out and learned that his former wife had committed suicide, I contacted the Chicago police. One of the detectives involved in that investigation said that while the woman's fingerprints were on the razor—her wrists had been slit, in case you don't know—there were these suspicious bruises on her wrists and hands. The speculation being that the abrasions might have been caused by someone's grabbing both her wrists with one hand while slashing them with the other. Mrs. Simon number one had very tiny wrists, by the way, and your client has very large hands. Of course," Tim concluded, "it goes without saying that under those circumstances the perp would have wiped his own fingerprints off the razor and replaced them with the victim's."

"And the perp you're talking about is supposed to be Bruce?" I put to Tim, my voice shaking.

"He was there the afternoon of the woman's alleged"—and Fielding really came down hard on the *alleged*—"suicide. Only a week, for your information, after the divorce became final. Simon didn't deny he was at the apartment, either—he was obviously aware that both the doorman and one of the tenants had seen him leaving the place. Eventually he even admitted to being responsible for the bruises. His story was that he went to visit his very recent ex at her request. He's with her just a short while, however, when she tells him she has no desire to continue living now that their marriage is kaput. He must have been one helluva husband, huh? At any rate, to show him she means business, the former Mrs. Simon then rushes into the bathroom and comes out with a large bottle of tranquilizers, saying she intends to swallow the whole bottleful the minute he leaves. But your boy, hero that he is, grapples with her for the pills and finally gets her to loosen her grip on the bottle. Oh, incidentally, Dez, there were scratches on Simon's hands and traces of his skin tissue under the fingernails of the deceased."

"That would certainly be consistent with Bruce's version of what happened," I pointed out weakly, being still a little numb from these revelations. "And so would the bruises on the woman's wrists and hands."

"I'll grant you that. But let me ask you this. If you were visiting someone who threatened to commit suicide as soon as you waltzed out the door, would you just pick up and go? Uh-uh. You'd contact a member of that person's family or maybe a close friend and possibly also her doctor to make sure she didn't get another prescription."

Fielding went on before I could come up with a response. "But Simon didn't do anything of the sort. And, naturally, the Chicago police were bothered by that, even though your client insisted that he didn't believe his ex was really serious about killing herself. He said she had a flair for the dramatic, and he thought she was only grandstanding to make him feel guilty about the bust-up. But, nevertheless, he stayed at the apartment for about an hour to talk things out, he said. And he held on to the pills, disposing of them when he got home. His former wife was just fine when he left her that day—he claimed." Fielding's tone became almost sympathetic here. "Simon didn't mention a word to you about any of this, did he?"

"No," I admitted dejectedly. And then I was struck by the obvious, and all at once, the pressure on my chest lifted. "But there was really no reason for him to go into that," I countered. "His ex's suicide has absolutely nothing to do with this new tragedy in his life. And now I've got a question for you: What motive could he have had for killing his first wife, anyway? He was already free of her."

"Thta I can't say. And neither could the Chicago police. This was apparently a stumbling block for them, particularly since there wasn't even any alimony involved. But I can give you a few 'maybes'—you know, those things you're so fond of throwing at me whenever you're trying to push a particular scenario."

"Like—?"

"Like maybe she had something on him and was trying her luck at a little blackmail. After all, she'd been married to the man for a number of years, so if there were any skeletons around, she'd be in a pretty good position to know where they were buried. Hey, she might have learned that he was an embezzler or a forger or a bigamist or, say, the offspring of a couple of ax murderers. Another possibility: Maybe your boy had become interested in someone else, and this former wife of his was threatening to make trouble. Or maybe—"

"Okay, enough." *The offspring of ax murderers. Really!* "There's absolutely no basis for any of this. The only thing I can buy into is that you have an active imagination."

Fielding grinned. "I'll have to keep those words in mind the next time *you* try 'maybeing' *me* to death." And now in another, softer voice, he said, "Incidentally, there's something puzzling me, Dez."

He seemed to be waiting for some kind of encouragement, so I obliged. "What's that?"

"I'm going to concede that it's possible your client isn't guilty. Not likely, but possible. Still, he's a sleaze of the first order. You want the truth? The guy makes the hairs on the back of my neck stand up."

"And because of some neck hairs you've decided he's a killer?" I demanded shrilly.

"Don't be ridiculous," Fielding retorted. And then jokingly: "Although my neck hairs do have a damned impressive indictment record." This time, though, I've decided to trust the facts. I—" He stopped abruptly. "But I think I've gotten a little far afield here. What I started out to say is that I can't understand how you could ever have agreed to work for a jerk like that."

Well, while I'd found myself momentarily taken aback by

Fielding's hostility toward Bruce, I should have expected that the man wouldn't exactly endear himself to the police. His tendency to resort to sarcasm when challenged was almost reflexive, so how long would he have been able to restrain himself? But at any rate, I'd sooner have foregone Häagen Dazs for the rest of my natural life than admit to Fielding that I was involved in the case because I'd known Bruce before. (And in the biblical sense, too!) I mean, I wouldn't own up to even a casual friendship considering Fielding's opinion of him—which, however, was no doubt a rung above my own. (You'll notice that I didn't take any exception whatsoever to the less than flattering descriptives of my client.) All I was willing to offer by way of explanation—and it happened to be at least partially true—was "I'm self-supporting, remember?"

Fielding eyed me skeptically. "Granted. But I can't see you putting up with a lot of guff from someone just because he's paying a few of your bills. And from what your Mr. Simon's showed me so far, he has himself quite an attitude, guilty or not."

"Look, I—"

"Hey, wait a second," he commanded, checking his watch. "This talk of ours was only supposed to last fifteen minutes. And not only that, but *you* were supposed to enlighten *me*. 'It's going to be worth your while,' " he mimicked, raising his voice a few octaves. (It was, I thought, a really pitiful imitation of me.) "Isn't that what you said on the phone?"

"Yes, I did. And it is. And now I'm going to tell you why you're so wrong about my client." Simultaneously we reached for the donut bag, with Fielding beating me to the punch by about a millisecond. "Before I go into that, though, I'd just like to know one more thing."

Now, I anticipated an argument here or a growl or, at the very minimum, one of Tim's practiced black looks that are meant to initimidate but rarely make it. My old friend was just sitting there calmly, though, taking a bite of donut and waiting for the question. Either he'd mellowed considerably since I'd last seen him or those walnut sprinkles were sheer magic.

"Why don't you believe Cheryl Simon's death was an accident? Is it because you have a witness?" I asked.

Fielding snorted. "Are you kidding? The subway stations are a zoo at lunchtime. Nobody pays any attention to what's going on around them; everyone's too busy pushing and shoving everyone else. It's a wonder more people don't wind up on the tracks."

"Exactly. Then why are you so sure that this was murder?"

"Haven't you been listening?" he said, suddenly testy. "From where I sit, I've just given you some damned good reasons. And, anyhow, *sure*'s the wrong word. Let's put it that I have a very strong suspicion Cheryl Simon met with foul play." And now Fielding placed both palms on the desktop and leaned forward, as if preparing to rise. "But I'm through answering questions, Shapiro. Either get on with it, or get going."

"All right. All right." I inched my chair a little closer to his. "There's something you don't know," I told him firmly. "Something crucial." But in spite of my attempt to sound confident, at that moment Bruce's smuggling story appeared to be on pretty shaky ground.

Chapter 10

"Two nights before she died," I began, "Cheryl Simon told her husband about some . . . well, some knowledge she had. And I'm all but convinced that it was the possession of this knowledge that got her killed." I paused for maybe two seconds to polish off what was left of a strawberry donut.

"Go on," Fielding prodded impatiently. (Lucky for me he didn't have a whip.)

"The victim," I continued (after taking my time swallowing), "was a witness to certain incidents involving one of her fellow flight attendants on Bahamian Air and a notorious Colombian drug dealer called El Puerco. You've heard of him, I suppose."

" 'Fraid not. So this Colombian did her in. Is that what you're saying?"

"No. It was her *friend,* the one she spotted with El Puerco, who killed her. Because Cheryl felt compelled, out of loyalty, to speak to this person about what she'd seen before going to the authorities."

Fielding picked up a pencil and reached for his notepad. "This person's name?"

"Umm, that's just it," I responded meekly. "Cheryl never said."

Now Fielding's expression went from skeptical to out-and-out disbelieving.

"Listen for a few minutes, okay?" I told him. And I proceeded to detail the El Puerco incidents.

"Let me make sure I have this straight. On two separate occasions the victim *just happened* to come across her friend and this dealer in very close proximity." He waited for verification.

"Yes, that's right."

"And you're the one who doesn't believe in coincidences," Fielding scoffed.

"It isn't as much of a coincidence as you seem to think. We're not talking about a big, sprawling metropolis here. We're talking about a small island in the Bahamas. And besides, it's not as though these things took place one day after another. The two instances when she saw them together—or more or less together, anyway—were months apart. And besides *that,* even in Manhattan you run into people you know, for God's sake."

"Yeah? When was the last time for you? Outside of your own neighborhood, I'm talking about." And before I could answer: "But as long as we're on the subject of coincidences again, why don't we recap just how many of those we're dealing with here?" And tilting back in his chair, hands behind his head, Fielding proceeded to enumerate.

"There's your client's remark about the A train, which I'll call coincidence number two."

"I explained about that," I said irritably.

"Sure. Duke Ellington." (Was this a smirk I was now seeing on my good friend's face?) "And let's not forget coincidence number three."

"And what's that?" I asked, mentally wincing.

"Both of the man's wives came to violent ends. Now, this is slightly above the law of averages, as I'm certain you'll agree."

"Hold on a second. The first Mrs. Simon was already an ex at the time of her death. Plus you can't even compare the tragedies; they were totally dissimilar."

"Fine. I'll move on to coincidence number four, then. Both women died only a week after a traumatic occurrence involving your client. With wife number one, it was the official dissolution of the marriage. While in the case of the more recent Mrs. Simon, it was a bitter public argument."

"You're attempting to draw some kind of parallel between an actual divorce and merely having a few harsh words? Oh, please! You can't tell me you and Jo Ann never raise your voices with one another."

"Not like that, we don't, and not in any damn coffee shops," Fielding retorted, righting his chair. "But I just want to make sure you realize that for someone who's always insisted she doesn't believe in coincidences, you're willing to accept any number of them now. And I've even got another one for you."

I braced myself. "Go ahead."

"The morning Cheryl Simon was run over by that train, her husband was in the same vicinity. At a bookstore on Seventeenth, he told us. Which would be no more than a five- or ten-minute cab ride away from the West Fourth Street station."

"But still, it *is* a cab ride away."

"Oh, it's in easy walking distance, too," Fielding informed me, a smile in his voice. "I mentioned a cab becuse I know it's easier for you to relate to that."

I chose to ignore this implied criticism of my long-standing reluctance to overtax my lower limbs. "Okay, so shoot the man because after seeing a client in that area, he needed to kill some time before his lunch date. And, anyway, it's not like he was right across the street from the station or anything."

"We have five coincidences," Fielding maintained stubbornly. "But let's not argue about that now; I'd like you to play this thing out for me." He gave me my cue: "Mrs. Simon goes to have a talk with her buddy the smuggler. . . ."

"Yes, well, I'm assuming she went to the home of whoever it was, since it's the kind of discussion you'd undoubtedly want to have in private. And then after the meeting was over, the perp most likely followed her to the subway and—"

"This would be the station at Seventy-first and Continental."

"Uh, I suppose so, if that's the one in Forest Hills."

"In case you're interested, there's more than one subway stop in Forest Hills," Fielding told me dryly.

Okay. So maybe I know next to nothing about the New York City transit system. (In all the years I've lived in Manhattan, the times I've traveled by subway could probably be counted on both hands—with a couple of fingers left over.) But, believe me, I'd have gotten around to educating myself when I began to trace the victim's movements—which had most certainly been on my agenda. I mean, don't forget Fielding had had almost a week's head start on me. "Uh, you've been out there to see Cheryl's friends, then?"

Fielding shook his head. "We questioned everyone briefly when they reported for work the day after she died, and I made note of all the home addresses. I happen to be familiar with the area where the three flight attendants have their apartments," he explained. "And they're only a couple of blocks from the station at Seventh-first Street and Continental Avenue. But continue."

"As I said, the perp could have tailed her and then gotten on the train without her knowledge, taking it to West Fourth Street, too. Or it might even be," I theorized, "that Cheryl convinced him or her to come into the city for some reason—to consult with a lawyer, maybe—and that they were actually traveling together."

"Your turn for the 'maybes' now, huh?" Fielding pointed out with a grin. "But let's say for the moment that the woman wasn't hustling her killer over to a lawyer's office. Why do you suppose she got off at West Fourth Street?"

From the look on his face when he put the question to me, I had the strong impression Fielding was hinting at something. But if so, I wasn't smart enough to figure it out. "She might have been on her way home," I offered.

"We know she wasn't. There was a conductor on the platform at the time she left the train, and she asked him where she could get the A, C, or E to Canal Street. He remembered her, he said, because she was so good-looking. Besides, this wouldn't have been her normal stop."

"Did the conductor notice if she was alone or not?"

"He wasn't sure. But, at any rate, maybe you can clear something up for a thick-headed cop. If Cheryl got on the subway at Continental Avenue, she could have taken either the E or the F train to Manhattan. And obviously she took the F, which—"

"Why 'obviously'?"

My friend spoke very deliberately now, as though attempting to make himself understood by one who is mentally challenged. "Because, Desiree, she was looking to *transfer* to the E."

"Oh." I wondered if my stupidity was reflected in my expression.

"Also"—and his eyes were twinkling here—"the conductor happened to see her actually get off. He directed her to the upper level, which is where she was run over. But what I want to know from you is why she didn't take the E to begin with."

"Well, one possibility is that she decided to head down to Canal once she was already on the train." I thought a moment longer. "Or else," I suggested—surprising even myself with this one—"maybe the F came along first, and she figured it didn't pay to wait for the E. After all, once she got to West Fourth, she'd have a choice of *three* trains to Canal Street."

"Spoken with the reasoning of a bona fide commuter," Fielding responded with what seemed to be reluctant admiration. "And to think you've never even been aboard one of those big ugly things."

"That's not true. I've traveled by subway lots of times."

There was a loud guffaw. "Yeah. About as often as I've traveled by stretch limo."

I gave him a dirty look, then said, "Tell me, do you have any ideas about why Cheryl might have been going to Canal Street?"

"A couple." Naturally, I was expecting something to follow right after this, but Fielding took his sweet time before continuing. He sat there for about ten seconds just tapping a pencil on the desktop.

I waited him out in silence. (But it wasn't easy.)

"To start with," he said at last, "I asked your client who in his wife's circle of friends lives in that neighborhood. It was with great reluctance that he parted with the information: Chet Byrnes."

"Chet Byrnes?"

"Oh, I forgot. You don't know the name of Cheryl's pilot sweetie, do you? Or, until this morning, that she even had a

pilot sweetie—and that her relationship with him was destroy-
ing the marriage. Or so your client insisted. And at the top of
his lungs, too. Anyhow, the bone of contention—Byrnes—has
an apartment on Vandam Street, which is just off Canal."

"So you think—"

"I don't think anything yet. Byrnes claims he wasn't expecting her. And there are lots of other places just off Canal—
stores, restaurants . . ." *Was it my imagination or had Fielding
put a little something extra into the word "restaurants"? And I
could swear he had that same peculiar look again, too!*

"Would you mind giving me Byrnes's phone number?" I
asked.

"Why not?" And picking up one of three manila folders on
his desk, Fielding thumbed through it quickly. "Here we go,"
he mumbled a short while later. He jotted down the number on
his notepad, after which he ripped off the page with a flourish
and handed it to me. "Now that you've got everything I've got,
I can finally rest easy. In fact, I should really be leaving for a
week's vacation this minute. I'm sure you'd have the whole
case wrapped up by the time I came back."

"You're probably right. And I would feel privileged, too," I
told him, sounding like my tongue had been dipped in saccha-
rine, "if I could remove this burden from your weary round
shoulders.

"Anyway," I proclaimed, grinning and sitting a little taller in
my seat, "at least now we know that Cheryl took the train from
Continental Avenue. Which backs up what I've been trying to
tell you—about the drugs, that is. You want the proof?" I
didn't even pause for breath. "Has any of the three admitted to
being with her that day?"

"No," Fielding conceded.

"So I think we can be pretty damn positive she wasn't in the
neighborhood for a social visit." I was really pleased with myself at that instant, maybe even a bit smug—until Fielding stuck
a pin in my balloon.

"There's only one tiny, practically infinitesimal flaw in your
reasoning," he pointed out. "There is absolutely no evidence

the victim got on that train in Forest Hills. Do you have any idea how many other stops the F makes in Manhattan and Queens?"

I was groping for a response, but he spoke again, letting me off the hook. "Seriously, Dez, I wouldn't put too much stock in this drug business," he said, not unkindly.

"It's so logical, though. After all," I reminded him, "Cheryl died only two days after she talked about confronting her friend."

"She had definitely decided to do this?"

"Well, I certainly believe that was her intention."

"I guess the real question, though, should be: How do you know there even *was* a smuggler?"

Just in time, I stopped myself from answering. But Fielding caught my expression.

"Bingo." He held my eyes with his own. "There's only your client's word that his wife ever said anything at all about any drug smuggling. And, frankly, I wouldn't believe that guy even if he sat here and told me I was making a pig of myself this morning."

And with this, he reached into the bag for another donut.

Chapter 11

That "explain something to a thick-headed cop" crap! Honestly! I was walking down the block now, conducting a postmortem on my just-over meeting with Fielding.

It was obvious he'd been trying to convince me that Cheryl didn't get on that F train at Continental Avenue as I believed. But I thought I'd handled things pretty neatly, don't you? I mean, both the reasons I'd suggested as to why the victim could have taken the train from Continental and then decided to change at West Fourth for Canal Street made perfect sense. In fact, if Fielding weren't so prejudiced against Bruce, they might have induced him to open up his own thinking a bit.

There seemed to be something else on his mind, too, though. What were those little hints of his all about? Maybe I should have called him on them, but I just hadn't wanted to give him the satisfaction. Well, it was possible that I was mistaken, anyway, that it was only my imagination in overdrive.

There was a pay phone at the corner that showed some promise of being in working order. I mean, it was intact, at least.

I put in a quarter, heard a dial tone, and tried Bruce—the bastard!

He was out of the office, and they didn't expect him back. Which was probably for the best; I had a lot of cooling off to do where he was concerned. I'd call him at home tonight. Maybe by then this lust for his blood would have dissipated.

But it didn't. Not so you could notice, anyway.

* * *

I dialed Bruce's apartment at around seven, right after a delicious omelet and immediately preceding two scoops of Häagen Dazs macadamia brittle. On the fifth ring I was greeted by the answering machine. I responded with a very unfriendly few words: "It's Desiree. Call me." Hanging up, I became aware that I was clenching my left fist and that my nails had been digging into my palm.

For that entire evening I waited to hear from my client. I thought I'd read this new book to help the time pass more quickly—one of those "how to make a million dollars without investing a dime" guides that I'd never been the least bit tempted to even look at before. I have no idea why I ever bought it, except that I was getting tired of receiving so many bills lately with SECOND NOTICE prominently stamped in red. Besides, it was on sale.

In case you're interested, though, I never did benefit from my purchase, because it was such a problem reading that damn thing. And this was only partially due to the trouble I had in concentrating—thanks, of course, to my low-life client. The major difficulty was the author's premise, which was pretty incomprehensible, if you ask me. It wasn't even necessary to finish the first chapter to decide that I didn't care to be rich, after all. Not if it meant attempting to make sense of those entire two hundred and fifty-three pages. In fact, the very next day I passed the book on to my neighbor Barbara Gleason, who, being a teacher, might also be able to use the extra cash. But maybe she couldn't manage to plow through all that gibberish, either. Because so far I haven't noticed any giant improvement in her lifestyle.

Anyway, it was well after midnight when I went to bed, still fuming at Bruce.

I was much calmer when I got up on Saturday, however. Not that it was my intention now to go easy on him. It was just that I was no longer bent on tearing his lying throat out. Listen, looking at things rationally, what did I expect from Bruce— *honestly,* all of a sudden?

I thought about a couple of the matters he'd neglected to

mention to me. Matters like his practically brand-new bride's alleged love affair with a coworker. And the suspicions surrounding the demise of wife number one. Knowing Bruce, though, how could I even have been surprised at his omitting such inconsequential little items?

I wondered then what else he hadn't told me. And how much of what he had told me was the truth. But strangely enough, I found that, in spite of everything, I still had some faith in that smuggling story of his. Probably the result of my not being wrapped too tight. I mean, if I were in my right mind, would I ever have gotten involved with Bruce Simon again—even on a professional level?

At any rate, at eleven o'clock that morning I took another stab at reaching him. He wasn't in, so I left a second message. Only—the edge off my anger now—this one was more cordial. "It's Desiree," I said. "I've been trying to get in touch with you because there's something I'd like to speak to you about. So please give me a call when you come in." Following this, I had myself a fresh cup of coffee, threw on some clothes, and went out to do a little grocery shopping.

The minute I returned I dumped my bundles and pressed the playback on my machine. And there, at last, was Bruce.

"Hi, Dez." He was sounding contrite. "I'm sorry I didn't get back to you before this, but I haven't been home. I had an all-day business meeting in Westchester yesterday, and from there I drove straight over to Pat and Burton's for dinner. I'm afraid I drank a little more than I should have, too—I passed out on their sofa. And I didn't wake up until ten a.m.

"Look, I'm going to take a quick shower and change my clothes, and then I'll be having lunch with Cheryl's brother and sister-in-law—they're in town for the weekend. I should be here until about quarter to one. But if I don't hear from you before I leave, I'll give you a call as soon as I come in."

I checked my watch: 1:05. I tried him anyway, but, of course, he'd already gone out.

*   *   *

It was close to four, and I was just starting to dress for my appointment with Donna that evening, when Bruce and I finally made contact.

"Hope you didn't give up on me," he said. "It was a very long lunch—we had a lot to talk over. I kept thinking of what you might have to tell me, though, and I could hardly wait to check in with you. Have you learned anything?" he asked eagerly.

Well, I couldn't risk a prolonged discussion, since I had to be in Forest Hills at seven, and I don't exactly move at the rate of a speeding bullet. The fact is, it takes me a year and a day just to coerce my glorious hennaed hair into behaving with a little class. So this was certainly no time to even hint at what was on my mind. "Nothing really important. I—"

"But there's *something,* isn't there?"

Boy, did he have a surprise coming to him! "There were just a couple of minor points that I felt we should sit down and go over in person, that's all," I answered—and quite civilly, too.

"I'm free tonight," I was informed.

"But I'm not." I didn't for a second consider supplying the reason I was unavailable. The last thing I needed was to find Bruce waiting on my doorstep for the report when I got home. And I'd feel that way even if I didn't hold him in such sub-basement regard at present.

"Tomorrow afternoon?" he suggested.

"That's no good for me, either." I also chose not to mention that I'd be seeing Laura Downey then. "Can you make it tomorrow night?"

"Damn! Jack and Sheila—Cheryl's brother and sister-in-law—are only here for these two days, and I've invited them out to dinner Sunday. They insisted on picking up the tab for our lunch, and I wanted to reciprocate. Can it wait until Monday?" And then uncertainly: "You did say it wasn't anything important, didn't you?"

"Yes, I did. Monday would be fine." Now that I wasn't quite as gung ho about socking it to Bruce, I was actually pretty flexible. And, anyway, I didn't see how postponing our little showdown another day could have any real impact on my investigation. Unless, that is, he wound up confessing that all of this drug stuff was just so much made-up garbage. But the chance of this happening I put at far less than the chance of a collision of the planets.

"Then what about lunch?" Bruce was asking.

"On Monday? I'm afraid I've already got a lunch date." A small untruth. But the conversation on my agenda wasn't one I'd be very comfortable having in a restaurant.

"Well, why don't we do it at dinner, then? Or later on, if that's better for you."

I was about to recommend we meet at his place around nine when I remembered I had plans with Christie—my friend from Minnesota—for Monday evening. Should I check with her to see if we could get together Tuesday instead? I instantly vetoed the idea. Why bother? There was no reason I couldn't wait the extra twenty-four hours to have it out with my client.

So we finally made arrangements for Tuesday night.

Bruce didn't realize it, of course, but this was his lucky day. He'd gotten himself a reprieve.

Chapter 12

At a little past seven that evening I was sitting in Donna Wolf's cozy yellow-and-white kitchen having my fifth cup of coffee for the day and just the tiniest sliver of Sara Lee cheesecake so as not to offend my hostess. (That *was* the reason I was indulging, honestly; I'd just finished a very generous slice of pecan pie before driving out here.)

This second of the victim's good friends was short, a little on the chunky side, and wore what appeared to be a perpetual smile. She had on torn jeans, red vinyl thongs, and a blue-and-white-striped T-shirt. There were rose-tinted aviator-style glasses perched atop the short, curly, orangy hair—which was almost the exact shade of Stan, the cat. I figured her to be in her mid-twenties, but, as in the case of Hank, I later learned that I'd underestimated her age by close to ten years.

Seated with Donna and me, a couple of feet back from the table and strapped into a high chair, was a happy, chubby-cheeked child with the same orangy hair. He was wearing these little white pajamas with red- and blue-bowed teddy bears all over them and eating a banana, most of which was decorating his face. Rusty—given name Charles—was seven months old, his mother informed me.

"I hope you don't mind Rusty's being here, too, but I just can't bring myself to put him to sleep yet. I just missed him *so* much. Didn't Mommy miss oo, lovey?" Donna cooed, half rising and then stretching way over in order to plant a kiss on one of the chubby cheeks. "I was away practically this entire week," she explained when she drew back—the top of her head now covered with what little was left of the banana.

"I thought you, Laura, and Hank flew together," I said, puzzled since the others had been in town at least part of that time.

"Oh, we do. But my sister in Pittsburgh just had a baby, and I also spent a couple of days out there with her. And then yesterday and today I was working. Today's flight was delayed, too, and I didn't get home until almost five."

A deep frown replaced Donna's smile now. "Hank told me what you said to him—about why the police suspect that Cheryl might have been murdered. And I just can't go along with that. We all loved Cheryl. And even if she did know something incriminating about one of us, we couldn't do what they . . . that is, none of us would have been capable of—"

I broke in hastily, afraid she was about to cry. "Well, that's only a possibility. It's also possible your friend had an accident."

"Oh, do you really think so?" Donna demanded anxiously.

"Well, it certainly could have happened that way."

"I *do* hope so. Not that that isn't horrible, too," she murmured, shuddering. "But it's certainly preferable to the . . . to the alternative."

"Yes, it is," I agreed.

I saw the beginning of a smile, and I was about to put a question to her when a large purple grape plopped into Donna's coffee cup. She turned to her progeny, who was, at present, threatening to destroy my sanity with his nerve-shattering squeals of delight. "Please don't throw things, Rusty, and stop your screeching or Mommy will have to put you to bed," she admonished in a nice, even tone. Rusty continued expressing his glee at the same unbearable volume, which was, I had to admit—but only to myself—sort of understandable. I mean, wouldn't you carry on if you'd just had such a lucky shot—and most likely your first ever, at that?

The kid immediately began exercising his pitching arm again. And before long his entire grape supply was exhausted, all but one of this new barrage now dotting the kitchen floor. That one, I am pleased to report, somehow caromed off the tray of the high chair and ended up hitting an astonished Rusty on the nose. The wail that followed this unlikely bull's-eye made every other sound that had emanated from the boy's mouth thus far seem like so many whispers.

Donna calmly stood up at this point. Then briskly lifting the child out of his high chair with her right hand, she bent to pick the fruit up off the vinyl tiles with her left. She accomplished this so quickly that by the time I rose to assist her, my assistance was no longer needed. And now, a squalling, flailing Rusty tucked under her arm, she walked from the room, calling to me over her shoulder, "I'll be right back. My son is going beddy-bye."

I breathed a sigh of gratitude.

Returning a couple of minutes later, Donna closed the door behind her. But we could still hear Rusty loudly voicing his objections to the banishment. "Don't worry," his mother assured me. "He'll be asleep in a few minutes. He takes after his father that way. Do you know Billy even fell asleep on me a couple of times when we were talking on the phone? Can you imagine?"

"How long have you been married?" I inquired conversationally.

"Oh, Billy and I aren't married. I haven't heard word one from the stinker since before Rusty was born." The amazing thing was that this was said completely without rancor. I'd never in my life met anyone with a disposition like this. I had to wonder if Donna Wolf was for real.

"It must be hard having to deal with all this responsibility by yourself," I said at once, anxious to move past what I considered a faux pas on my part. Which was hardly necessary, since it was obvious that I was the only one here who'd been made at all uncomfortable by my question.

"I have plenty of help," Donna informed me. "Thank goodness for my mother; she looks after Rusty when I'm working. She also pitches in a lot of other times, too. How do you think I was able to go to Pittsburgh? Actually, my mother would rather take care of her grandson than do anything else. I think that's why she encourages me to keep flying. Not because she knows I love my job—which I do. But mainly because she wants me out of the way." The grin on Donna's face now stretched almost to her earlobes. "Oh. Would you like more coffee?"

"No, thanks. I still have some," I answered, noting then that the level of the sounds coming from the other room had already lowered considerably. "But I wanted to talk to you about a few things, and I guess we should get started."

"Sure."

"As you're already aware, the reason there's a suspicion of foul play is because Cheryl appears to have had knowledge of a drug operation involving a fellow crew member."

Donna nodded. "Hank explained everything to me."

"Have you yourself seen anything that could conceivably tie in with drug smuggling? Anything at all?"

"No, I haven't. And I find this whole thing really hard to believe, too."

"Listen, even though you've already heard the entire story from Hank, just to be certain he got all the facts straight, let me summarize for you exactly what it was Cheryl confided to her husband only two days before she died."

And I proceeded to do just that.

When I was through, Donna said, "This is pretty much what Hank told me. And if it's true—if Bruce didn't make the whole thing up—that would mean one of us, Laura or Hank or I—" Breaking off here, she looked at me intently. "And I don't believe that. I definitely don't."

I attempted to be reassuring. Or as reassuring as possible, anyway, given the circumstances. "Remember, Donna, nothing's certain yet. Maybe we'll eventually find out that Cheryl was shoved off that platform by a crazy person. Or that she was pushed off by accident. Or she might suddenly have felt faint and lost her balance and fallen off on her own. Right now I'm only trying to gather whatever facts I can."

"I understand. But I'm just not able to help you. I don't know anything about any drugs."

"Are you familiar with the name El Puerco?"

"No, I never heard of him, not until Hank mentioned him the

other day—although I'm not sure Hank got the name exactly right. I think he called the guy El Puerto," she said, grinning. "Which, unless I'm mistaken, means 'the door.'"

I laughed. "You could be right." And then immediately getting back to business again: "But anyhow, on Cheryl's last trip to Nassau—the return trip, I mean—did you, by some chance, notice a change in her behavior? Did she appear to be different in any way?"

"She was the same as always. Or that's how it seemed to me."

"She didn't act even a shade cooler maybe to either Hank or Laura?"

"Not that I was aware of. We were exceptionally busy that day, though. The plane was completely full, and then on top of that, one of the passengers took sick."

"Did you see Cheryl again after the flight?"

"No. That was the last time," Donna answered. And in a tremulous voice: "The very last time." Her eyes, I saw, were glistening now.

I had the feeling there was very little chance of staving off the tears just then. But still, I gave it a try. "How about the telephone?" I put in hastily. "Did you speak to each other once you were home?"

"No," Donna murmured, brushing at her eyes with the back of her hand. "I was thinking of calling her to have lunch on Thursday, but I don't know, I just didn't. Maybe if I had . . ." And placing both arms on the table, Donna buried her head in them and began to sob.

I patted her awkwardly on the shoulder because I didn't know what else to do. And then I opened my pocketbook and shoved a pack of tissues under her hand. She mumbled something unintelligible—probably "Thank you"—before putting them to use.

It couldn't have been more than a couple of minutes later that she lifted her head, blew her nose, and told me she was sorry.

"Don't be silly," I responded, choked up myself. (Predictably, on seeing Donna break down like that, it had been a real effort to keep from shedding some tears of my own—and behaving like a major idiot while I was at it.) I cursed this ridiculous weakness of mine, and following that, I swallowed once or twice. "It's very understandable—your feeling this way. I'm aware of how close the two of you were."

"You just never imagine this kind of thing happening to someone you love, you know?" And she snuffled a little and blew her nose again, after which she said quietly, "What else did you want to ask me?"

"Are you sure you're up to it?"

"Yes, I'm fine now. Really."

"All right. What can you tell me about the afternoon the group of you went to the Atlantis?—everyone but Cheryl, that is. Do you know if either Hank or Laura left the casino early?"

"That's the part that doesn't make sense," Donna answered thoughtfully. "How could Cheryl have claimed she saw one of us in a luncheonette in Nassau that day? We all left for Paradise Island together. We all had lunch over there at the same table. We all gambled for a few hours. And then we all—all five of us—returned to Nassau in the early evening."

"Did your crew spend more than one afternoon on Paradise Island this spring?"

"No. It was only that once that we went during the day. The bunch of us, anyway. Chet and Nick—our pilot and copilot—head over by themselves pretty often, though. They love the Atlantis. Have you ever been?"

I shook my head. "Not so far."

"It's quite a place. They have a fabulous aquarium right on the premises. Plus there are all sorts of restaurants, a beautiful beach, and most important—from Nick's point of view, anyhow—a nice big casino. The largest in the Caribbean, I understand. You really ought to go there sometime."

"Maybe I will," I said abstractedly, thinking now about how to phrase my next question. I mean, sooner or later I had to get it over with. And it was already way past sooner. As usual, though, the words didn't come easily. "Do you . . . I mean, would you mind telling me where you were on the Thursday morning Cheryl died?"

I lucked out again. Like Hank, Donna didn't appear to be the least bit offended by my asking. "We did some grocery shopping that morning, I remember—Rusty and I. And then we drove over to my mother's; she lives in Kew Gardens. We had supper there and stayed until around seven."

"What time did you leave your apartment? Do you recall?"

"Not exactly. On my days off I hardly pay any attention to the clock. I think it might have been around ten. Maybe ten-thirty. But it could have been a little later. Or maybe even a little earlier." She gave me a small, apologetic smile here. Which made me realize that it had been a while now since she'd done any smiling at all.

"While you were out shopping, did you happen to run into anyone you knew?"

Donna concentrated for a few seconds. "I don't think so."

I was down to one final question. And I wasn't any too happy about having to ask this one, either.

"Uh, someone mentioned to me that there might have been some romantic feelings between Cheryl and the pilot—this Chet. Were you aware of anything like that?"

At this, Donna seemed to step completely out of character. She was incensed. "Who told you that—Bruce? He's crazy! Cheryl would never—Besides, she was practically a newly-wed," I was reminded.

"Yes, but sometimes things like that happen."

"Well, this wasn't one of those times."

"You sound pretty positive."

"I am. Because I know—I knew—Cheryl."

"I don't really doubt that you're right," I said in all honesty. "But I had to check. Was Cheryl especially close to either the pilot or the copilot, though? I'm referring to a friendship now— a *platonic* friendship," I clarified quickly. It had struck me just seconds earlier that perhaps Bruce was wrong in not extending that list of his wife's circle of intimates—and therefore, possible murderers—to include the remainder of the crew.

"Not really. She got a kick out of Nick, our copilot—he has a great sense of humor. But the guy's a genuine stud. Also, a pretty big gambler. We all indulge once in a while when we're in Nassau—as you know. But we don't do it that often, and believe me, the rest of us aren't in Nick's class. We can't afford to be. Actually, neither can he, though. And one of these days he's liable to end up with a couple of broken kneecaps."

"He plays blackjack, I understand."

"That's right. And so does Laura. But when Laura sits down and plays, it's at a table with a five-dollar minimum bet. It was the same with Cheryl—blackjack was her game, too. Only Cheryl was a much better sport than Laura, who carries on like crazy if she doesn't win. Anyway, Nick wouldn't be caught dead at a five- or ten-dollar table."

"You yourself like the poker machines, I understand."

"I *love* them. Especially the ones with lots of wild cards." And once more the smile was at full wattage.

"Do the others play the machines, too?"

"Hank does—he's always at the slots when we're in the casinos. Chet shoots craps. But he doesn't lose more than he can afford to. When the dice get cold on him, he'll walk away and go have a bite or a drink or something. But what I started to say before was that while Cheryl liked Nick, she didn't exactly approve of him. Neither do I, and I'm fond of him, too."

"How did Cheryl feel about Chet?"

"She respected him. Chet's, well, he's a very solid kind of person. Somebody you can depend on. But he and Cheryl weren't exactly pals or anything, if that's what you want to know."

It was. But more than this, I wanted to know how Cheryl Simon had ended up under the wheels of a train.

And I was suddenly very concerned that I might never find out.

Chapter 13

It could have been such a simple case.

For a brief while it seemed that all I would have to do is find out which of the flight attendants hadn't left the Atlantis casino with the rest of the crew that day—and I'd have my killer.

Well, as has been hammered home to me time and time again—and which a person with any smarts would certainly have absorbed by now—life is never that simple.

Tonight Donna had verified Hank's assertion that the entire group returned to Nassau from the Atlantis together. Which I suppose I knew that she would—only I hadn't even let myself consider the import of this until now.

If nobody had skipped out early, then Cheryl couldn't have run into anyone in that luncheonette. Which shot Bruce's entire drug-smuggling story to pieces.

No wonder I was clenching the wheel, gnashing my teeth, and muttering under my breath on the drive back from Donna's.

And then all at once, when I was less than fifteen minutes from my apartment, the fog in my brain just seemed to evaporate.

What a numbskull I'd been!

I took my right hand from the wheel so I could apply a well-deserved fist to my forehead—and flinching from the blow, I almost rammed the car alongside me.

The perpetrator *had* gone back to Nassau with the others—*and* rendezvoused with El Puerco, as well.

And it had been ridiculously easy, too.

Think about it. The perp sneaks out of the casino, takes a

taxi into Nassau for the meeting, and then right after leaving Cheryl in that luncheonette—ostensibly to do some shopping—returns to Paradise Island to resume his/her play at the tables or machines or whatever. I mean, with everyone so intent on their own game, who'd even be aware of the absence of one of their number for what was probably around an hour and a half—if that. I imagine it's not at all uncommon to lose someone in a casino for a while—and this, according to Donna, was a particularly large casino, to boot. Even if, by any chance, someone went on a serious hunt for this missing crew member, there was a plausible explanation available. In fact, a bunch of them:

"I took a break and got myself some pie and coffee." Or "I was feeling a little light-headed so I thought I'd go out for a bit of fresh air." Or "I went and sat by the pool for a few minutes." Or . . . But you get the idea. And hadn't Donna just told me their pilot did more or less the same kind of thing on a regular basis?

Bruce's story, it seemed, lived, after all.

And now I had another thought. What if Cheryl had mentioned to the others that she'd run into this friend in town that afternoon? But almost as soon as I posed the question to myself, I came up with a reasonable answer. In that event, I presumed the killer would just have owned up to sneaking into Nassau—say, in order to buy this gift that he/she had just remembered urgently needed buying. I even supplied the perp with some sample dialogue so I could see how it would play out:

"I knew you'd all give me the business for forgetting my mother's" (father's? lover's? best friend's? sister's? . . .) "birthday to start with. And then you'd think I was definitely off the wall for running back and forth like that, so I made up my mind not to say a word to any of you."

I found myself nodding. Yes, that—or something along those lines—should certainly do it.

Anyhow, now that I was satisfied that the killer could have seemingly been in two places at the same time, you'd think I'd have been able to relax during what remained of the drive home, wouldn't you? But I refused to let myself. *Why did it take me so long to realize this?* I groused.

And much more important, exactly who is this killer whose alibi I've just destroyed?

It was about seven-thirty when I woke up on Sunday morning. And after trying to fall back to sleep for over an hour, I threw in the towel and crawled out of bed. I fixed myself a quick breakfast—some dry cereal, a corn muffin, and coffee—and then went into the living room and plunked myself down on the sofa. There was a Robert Redford movie on AMC that I'd been anxious to see (for the fourth time), and I wouldn't be meeting with Laura Downey until two-thirty, so this was my chance.

Reaching for the remote, I switched on the TV—and got a screen full of white flakes and static. This had happened often enough in the past so that I was fairly certain the cable was out. I decided to call the cable company to find out how long they anticipated it would take them to fix the trouble, whatever it was *this* time. The company's number is in this peach-and-blue address book I keep on the counter right by the kitchen telephone, and I'd just opened the book to C when my downstairs buzzer sounded, startling me. (I tell you, I have nerves of marshmallow.) The book damn near fell out of my hands, but I managed to grab hold of a corner of it. However, since it was now upside down, some of the countless little slips of paper that I wedge in right after the Zs because they don't merit permanent entry came loose and fluttered to the floor.

I let them lie there for a few moments while I demanded "Who is it?" of my intercom half a dozen times—without receiving the courtesy of a reply. *Probably some punks who want to gain entry to the building,* I speculated. Anyway, I returned to the kitchen and scooped up all the errant pieces of paper. I had just started to shove them in the back of the book again with the other unworthies when I noted the name scrawled on the messiest of the slips: AL BONAVENTURE. There was a barely legible—but still decipherable—phone number underneath it.

Now, Al Bonaventure is both dentist and friend to Derwin, Jackie's significant other. And after learning Bruce and I were kaput, Jackie—over my loud, strong, and crystal-clear objections—had persuaded Derwin to have this Al person phone me. It took him a while to call, but it took even longer for me to put that extremely unpleasant Bruce thing behind me. I mean, at that point, I was still having trouble tolerating a member of Bruce's gender in my line of vision—much less in my life. And so I declined Al's dinner invitation, explaining that I was tied up in a murder investigation—which was true. And then when he suggested I get in touch with him once the case was over, I agreed that I would—only this was not true. In fact, almost immediately after I scribbled his number down—which I did automatically, the pen and notepad being right there at my elbow—I ripped off the page and tossed it into the garbage. But later that evening I told myself that this was not at all a nice thing to do, and so I retrieved the crumpled-up paper— covered with coffee grinds by then—straightened it out as best I could, brushed it off, and exiled it to that dark place behind the Zs.

Looking at that paper now, I had an impulse to call Al Bonaventure. For the first time since all that angst with Bruce, I suddenly felt that it would be nice to go to dinner with a man again. And who knows? There was even a chance it could lead to a normal, healthy relationship. I mean, maybe this guy would turn out to be among what I estimate is the .001 percentile of single, heterosexual males in New York City who *are* normal and healthy.

I checked my watch. Nine forty-five. It wasn't too early to call on a Sunday, was it? But then lifting the receiver—and ignoring my own indolent tendencies—I decided that if Al Bonaventure was still sleeping at this hour, I'd just as soon find out about it now.

* * *

The man's "hello" didn't sound sleepy in the least.

"Uh, hi. Is this Al?" I asked.

"That's right. And who is this?" Al inquired cordially.

"Uh, Desiree Shapiro. I don't know if you recall the name, but—"

"Sure I do. Derwin—and Jackie."

"You have a pretty good memory."

"Not bad. Say, that must have been a real marathon of a case you were working on." And he laughed.

"Yes, well, it . . . uh . . . lasted longer than I'd anticipated." There was a pause, and I knew I should be the one to fill it— after all, I'd initiated the contact. *Oh, why hadn't I at least planned what I intended to say to this man?* Do I actually ask him out? Or should I put it that I'm available now and let him take it from there? What if I just tell him that I'd like to meet him? I realized then that I'd been born a little too soon to be comfortable with any of these approaches. Which made me feel like something of a dinosaur—and deservedly so. It finally occurred to me that it would have been wise to consider the situation a bit more carefully before picking up the phone in the first place. But unfortunately, this blinding revelation came abut two minutes too late.

"The reason I called," I ventured, my voice not as steady as I would have liked it to be, "is that now that I've been freed up—I mean from that case—I wondered if you would still be interested in having dinner sometime."

"Absolutely."

What next? Was I supposed to suggest a particular evening —or was he? While I was still struggling with this aspect of our arrangement, Al said, "When would you like to make it?"

"How would next Friday be?" I suggested for no particular reason—except that this is what came out of my mouth.

Friday, I was told, would be perfect. And we made plans to meet at seven-thirty at a new Chinese restaurant Al knew of in Chelsea.

By the time we hung up, my hands were like ice. But it wasn't until later in the day, when I was driving out to Laura

Downey's, that I realized I'd never even considered the possibility some woman might have stayed over at Al's on Saturday night. And not only that, but she could have been the one to answer the phone this morning.

And my hands were like ice again.

Chapter 14

Laura Downey wasn't exactly pretty. But she wasn't exactly *not* pretty, either—if that makes any sense.

In her thirties, probably (I had no idea just *where* in her thirties), and maybe five six, Laura had the kind of figure my late husband Ed would have described as zaftig. I mean, you wouldn't call her heavy, but her curves were definitely ample—and then some. She had thick, shoulder-length brown hair, highlighted by glints of auburn, which she was wearing in a ponytail—very likely in deference to the heat. (Although it was comfortable enough in here, the temperature outside was well over ninety this afternoon.) Her nose was short and straight, her lips, full and pouty. And while her eyes were kind of small and her face was kind of large and her cheekbones were definitely no match for Cindy Crawford's, the total effect was still rather striking.

She also boasted an absolutely gorgeous tan (the woman obviously didn't give a fig for all those warnings you hear about the sun), and, what's more, her clothes appeared to have been selected to show that beautiful bronze skin of hers to its best advantage. Unfortunately, however, the very brief white A-line skirt—which she'd paired with a white sleeveless blouse—also called attention to the shape of her legs. And these, unlike the rest of her, were skinny and stick-straight.

Laura's living room—which was all I was able to see of the apartment—was done in a crisp green-and-white color scheme, accented with yellow and furnished with good-looking traditional pieces. Although I, personally, lean toward the contemporary, I had to admit that my hostess had excellent taste. At any rate, I settled myself in one of the mahogany Queen Anne-style chairs. And after excusing herself for a short time to fetch a pitcher of lemonade, Laura took a seat on the plush velvet sofa opposite me, her legs tucked under her.

Opening the conversation now, she commented, "It's a shame you had to come out to Forest Hills so many times, Ms. Shapiro. And in all this heat, too. I wish the three of us—Hank and Donna and I—had been available on the same day."

Now, I had been grumbling about this very thing on the way over here, but I flashed the woman my sweetest, phoniest smile. "Oh, I don't mind at all. As a matter of fact, I enjoy driving. And please. Call me Desiree."

"Fine," she told me, "and I'm Laura."

"I suppose your friends have filled you in on my visits," I said, just prior to draining half the lemonade from my glass. (I'd worked up quite a thirst in the car, the air conditioning being even more ineffectual today than it usually was.)

Laura took three or four small, ladylike sips before responding. "Yes, they have." And then she murmured sadly, "Poor Cheryl. My poor, poor Cheryl." Her mouth began to quiver at this juncture, and I dreaded the full-fledged crying jag I figured would commence at any moment. I imagine my expression reflected my apprehension, too, because Laura eked out something very like a grin. "You don't have to worry," she assured me. "I'm really pretty much cried out by now." And a couple of seconds later: "There's still nothing definite, though, is there? What I mean is, the police haven't definitely established that Cheryl was . . . that Cheryl was murdered, have they?"

"No, as I told you on the phone—and I said the same thing to your friends—foul play is only one possibility."

"Maybe it's silly—after all, Cheryl is gone no matter how it happened—but murder is just so hard for me to accept. And Hank and Donna feel the same way. Plus for the police to suspect that it could be one of us, well—" Breaking off, she pressed her lips together and stared into space for a brief time before she spoke again. "Listen, I had nothing to do with smuggling drugs. But I suppose you'd expect me to say that, wouldn't you?" She went on at once, obviously not looking for a reply. "And I don't for a single minute believe that Hank or Donna was involved in anything like that, either. But let's just pretend that one of them *had* somehow gotten into that kind of a mess, and Cheryl found out about it. It wouldn't even have occurred to them—to either of them—to kill her to keep her quiet. That much I can swear to you."

I bit back the words about no one really being able to swear for anyone else. Instead I said, "I have no doubt that by now you're very familiar with the incidents Cheryl happened on in Nassau, but I want to make sure your friends gave you an accurate recap. So let me go through them quickly, anyway. You never know, maybe something will ring a bell for you."

And I recounted what I'd heard from Bruce—which I could probably do in my sleep by this time. And afterward I downed what was left of my lemonade.

"That's pretty much the way I heard it from Hank," Laura informed me, immediately picking up the pitcher and refilling my glass. "And with some very minor variations, it's not that different from Donna's version, either." She tittered now—a pleasant, lilting sound that I recalled from our first telephone conversation. "Actually, I'm surprised she got it that straight; Donna has a notoriously bad memory."

"You yourself never witnessed one of your friends in any situation that might be regarded as suspicious?"

The response was as firm as it was fast. "Never."

"And how about this El Puerco? Had you ever heard of him before the tragedy with Cheryl?"

"No, I hadn't."

"Tell me this. During her last flight from Nassau, did Cheryl seem to be at all troubled? Or preoccupied? Maybe not like her usual self in some way?"

Laura reflected on the question for a few moments. "Well, maybe she was a little quieter than I was used to seeing her. In fact, I remember asking her at one point if everything was okay."

"What was her answer?"

"She said she was just frazzled. We were very busy that day, and then one of the passengers became ill. I suppose we were all a little uptight. I really don't think it meant anything."

"How did Cheryl act toward Hank and Donna?"

"On that particular flight, you mean?"

"Yes."

"The same as always."

"You're sure?" I pressed.

"As far as I know, she didn't behave any differently toward them than she had on any other trip."

"Did you see or speak to Cheryl again before she died?"

Laura looked at me dispiritedly. "No. I intended to phone her on Wednesday night just to chat, but then my—" She hesitated here. "Damn, I never know what to call him—my special friend, let's say—dropped in unexpectedly, and I didn't get the chance. I wish now that I'd *made* the chance."

"I don't think your speaking to Cheryl could have changed what happened, Laura," I told her softly.

"Oh, I realize that. But I would have had that one more time to talk to her before she . . . before she left us."

"You two had known each other back in Chicago, hadn't you? You even worked for the same airline for a while, I understand."

"Yes, but we weren't particularly buddy-buddy then. It wasn't that we didn't get along or anything," she added quickly. "It's just that we didn't have that much to do with each other. Once Cheryl came to Bahamian, though, and we were on the same schedule and everything, we got to be . . . well, very, very close friends."

"Look, I hope this doesn't offend you," I put to her at this point, "but there's something I have to ask you. Something I have to ask everyone."

"Yes?"

"Would you mind telling me where you were on the Thursday Cheryl died?"

For a brief time Laura just sat there scowling. And then she protested, her voice rising, "I would never have harmed Cheryl.

Not for anything in the world!" I was about to try and placate
her when she said, more calmly now, "Sorry. I know you're
only doing your job. Anyway, I was right here in the apartment."

"All day?"

"Most of the day. I went out to pick up a container of milk in
the early afternoon. Around one, it must have been."

"Did you see anyone you knew?"

"No. I was only gone for around fifteen minutes. Maybe
less."

"How about before that—in the morning? Did you talk on
the telephone at all?"

"I spoke to my cousin Ruthie for a while."

"What time was that?"

"At nine. I remember because I was watching television
then, and the Regis and Kathie Lee show was just going on
when the phone rang."

"And how long did the call last? Any idea?"

"Not more than five or ten minutes."

Well, this still would have afforded her plenty of time to take
that train into Manhattan and push Cheryl off the platform by
twelve.

Laura had evidently been thinking along these same lines because she said, a touch of irony in her voice, "That's not much
of an alibi, is it?"

I considered this a rhetorical question. Even if it wasn't,
however, I thought it best to ignore it. "I'd like to ask you one
thing more," I brought up here. "It's about Cheryl and your
captain. According to Bruce—" I didn't have to say anything
further.

Jumping right in, Laura was adamant in her defense of her
friend. "There was absolutely nothing between the two of them.
No affair. No anything. Whatever was going on between
Cheryl and Chet was just a product of Bruce's sick imagination."

"You know about the accusations, I gather."

"I know he and Cheryl had a big blowup over Chet about a week before she died."

"She must have been furious with him."

"You're wrong there," Laura asserted. "She *had* been initially, of course. But she pretty much forgave him that same night. All it took was for Bruce to make nicey-nice, the way he usually did after he'd pulled something crappy. You have no conception of how that man could play her."

Oh, haven't I? "Why would Cheryl even mention the incident to you, then?" I asked.

"Because she was still terribly hurt. She didn't understand how Bruce could even have gotten an idea like that in his head—the woman was really crazy about him for some reason that I could never fathom. Anyway, I guess she just had to talk it out."

"I'm getting the impression you don't think that much of Bruce."

"You're right, I don't. I didn't know him very well in Chicago. I'd bump into him at parties once in a while; that was pretty much the extent of it. But I didn't particularly care for him then, either. If you want the truth, I can't see how Cheryl ever came to marry him."

Laura tilted her head to one side. "You want to know something else?"

She waited politely for my nod.

"If Cheryl *was* murdered and it wasn't a mugging and it wasn't one of the subway crazies who did it, then it was Bruce."

"But—"

"You'll see," she pronounced.

"Listen, I agree that Bruce is far from a saint. Still, he would never—"

But uncurling her legs and getting to her feet now, Laura drowned out my protest. "And let me tell you this: If Bruce did push her off that platform, it was for some twisted reason existing only in his twisted mind."

Less than five minutes later Laura was showing me out. She opened the door, and there, on the other side of the threshold—staring me right in the face—was a truly sinister looking character. I mean, I came *that close* to screaming.

He was young—probably in his late twenties or early thirties—and thin, with a kind of Fu Manchu mustache. His dark hair—which didn't look as if it had been washed in months—was pulled back in a ponytail. And he had an unhealthy pallor, besides. The fact that he wore a sweat-soaked black T-shirt with his tight-fitting black jeans and was badly in need of a shave didn't do much for his image, either.

But then he smiled benignly enough. And I saw that Laura was smiling, too.

She introduced him to me as her friend Bobby Lomax. (The chances were, I thought cynically, that this wasn't even his real name.) And I presumed by the sappy way the two of them were gazing at each other that he was the *special* friend she'd referred to earlier. Well, I supposed it was possible some women might find him attractive—although it was tough to figure out how.

Now, I realize it's not fair to judge someone on appearance. But I just didn't feel any too comfortable in this man's presence.

The thing is, though—as I was quick to remind myself—when it comes to forming impressions of people, my track record isn't something I can point to with very much pride. Or putting it a little more bluntly, in countless instances, my judgment has proved to be nothing short of atrocious.

So it really wouldn't have been all that surprising if I eventually learned that the guy was a brain surgeon. Or maybe even a man of the cloth.

Chapter 15

Recognizing my fallibility in assessing people still didn't stop me from speculating as to Bobby Lomax's involvement with drugs. I mean, his looks practically demanded it, that's all.

Maybe he was El Puerco's U.S. connection, I mused on the drive home that afternoon, *and he was paying this visit to Laura to pick up the latest shipment she'd smuggled into the country. Yes. This was certainly possible.*

Hold it. Why would he show up on the very day Laura had an appointment with a P.I.? It didn't make any sense. And if he'd come over unexpectedly, which I considered unlikely, I'd have been bound to notice signs of awkwardness—particularly on Laura's part. Besides—and this was really the clincher— you'd have to be blind not to see that there was something going on between the two of them. Something of a man/woman nature, I'm talking about.

So I finally had to concede that it was highly improbable Lomax's presence at Laura's had anything to do with smuggling. Laura Downey, I concluded, was no more—or less—apt to be a murderer than Hank or Donna were. In spite of her taste in men.

After dropping off my car at the garage, I stopped in at Jerome's, this coffee shop right near my building. Now, I practically always walk into the place with my mind made up to having, say, a Cobb salad. Or maybe the grilled vegetable platter. But then Felix, this sweet, elderly waiter, will shuffle over to the table, and before I can get a word out, he'll hold up his hand. "Wait. Don't tell me," he'll insist. Following which he'll

recite the first order I ever gave him. "You want the cheese-
burger deluxe. Well-done, right? The French fries, they also
gotta be well-done. And you'll have a Coke with that, only not
before I bring you the burger, God forbid."

With the man taking such pride in his memory, I just can't
bring myself to disappoint him. And so I invariably set aside
my more sensible choices. Not today, though. Today I didn't
have the slightest intention of eating any dumb, boring veggies
to begin with.

I no sooner returned to my apartment than I phoned Chet
Byrnes at the number Fielding had given me. I reached the
pilot's answering machine (doesn't anyone ever stay in these
days?), ignoring the directive about leaving a message. At eight
o'clock I tried again—and getting the answering machine
again, disobeyed its instruction a second time. My last attempt
was shortly after nine, at which point the machine finally won
out.

"My name is Desiree Shapiro, and I'm a private detective," I
said. "I'm looking into the death of Cheryl Simon, and I'm hoping you may be able to help me. I'd appreciate it if you could
call me as soon as possible." I provided both my office and
home numbers.

It was around nine-thirty when I walked into the office Monday morning. As soon as I made it through the door Jackie
waved a piece of pink notepaper in front of me. "You'd better
get back to this guy right away," she advised. "Here's where
you can contact him." She pointed somewhere toward the bottom of the slip before handing it to me. "He told me his flight
had been delayed, but they'd probably be taking off soon. Say,
who is he, anyway? Someone to do with that new case?"

But I was already hurrying down the hall by then. "I'll tell
you later," I called out, irritated.

I assume it showed, too, because Jackie shouted in response,
"Well, I didn't mean for you to tell me *this instant*!"

I dialed Chet Byrnes the second I got to my cubbyhole, even

before sitting down. Introducing myself, I said that I'd been hired by Cheryl Simon's husband to investigate the circumstances of the tragedy and that there were of couple of things I wanted to ask him.

"You caught me just in time, Ms. Shapiro," he informed me. "I should be boarding the plane very shortly. But what is it you'd like to know?"

"Uh, well, actually, it's a little difficult to do this on the telephone. I think it might be a good idea if we could get together. It won't take more than a few minutes," I was liar enough to promise—never having taken only a few minutes to question anyone in my life.

"I'll be glad to meet with you if you feel I can help in some way. But I'm not available today, of course. I'll be back tomorrow, but I've already made a commitment for then, so I'm afraid that's out, too. Is Wednesday night convenient for you?"

It was very convenient, I told him.

He explained that he had plans to have dinner with his daughter in the early part of the evening. "You wouldn't by any chance be located anywhere near Eighty-sixth Street, would you? That's where the restaurant is, also my ex-wife's place—on East Eighty-sixth."

"As it happens, I live on East Eighty-second Street."

"Great! Okay if I stop in at your apartment, then? I could be there by eight-thirty, right after I drop Megan at her mother's."

"Whenever you get here is fine," I assured him.

After the call ended I immediately began to transcribe my notes on the conversations I'd had with both Donna and Laura that weekend. Hopefully, when I was through, I'd be able to spot something in print that I hadn't picked up on in person. I was really determined to have everything typed up by five. Which was fine. I mean, I'd be finished way before then. I was still certain of this even after taking a half-hour phone break around ten-thirty to accommodate Pat Martucci, who was anxious for an update on the case, and then taking a slightly longer break right after that to be sociable with Ellen, who just wanted to chat. But at twelve-twenty I happened to glance at my watch.

They were having this one-day earring sale at Chez Lisa's, which—in spite of the fact that earrings are a very major weakness of mine—I'd had every intention of passing up. But now, face-to-face with the prospect of losing out on what could turn out to be the bargain of the decade, I *had* to get over there.

I was so disgusted with my lack of willpower, though, that I practically skulked out of the office and down the few blocks to the boutique. And while skulking, I imposed a limit on myself: I could buy only one pair of earrings today—no matter what. This edict being handed out partially as a punishment and partially because my finances demanded it.

Well, as you can imagine, with this kind of restriction, it took me forever to make up my mind. I finally settled on a pair of large silver disks, although believe me, there were tears in my eyes at having to leave those stunning gold door-knockers behind. But after all, how many times in a single day can you be a disappointment to yourself?

Anyhow, what with the hour spent at the store, plus the fifteen minutes or so I required to have a sandwich at my desk, I barely managed to meet my deadline regarding those notes. It was 4:56 when I typed the last sentence into the computer.

I printed out all of the work, then shut down my Mac and headed for the ladies' room. I'd have to step on it now.

Christie Wright (my friend from Minnesota) and I were meeting at Claudine's on West Sixty-third Street at six-thirty, which—considering how long it would take to get there with the traffic at this hour—didn't give me nearly enough time to make any decent repairs to myself.

Well, I supposed I would have to do the best I could.

Jackie walked in just as I was completing a pretty slapdash job of applying fresh makeup, while simultaneously priming myself for a fierce battle with that thoroughly impossible hair of mine.

"Hi," I said pleasantly.

There was a few seconds' silence. "Yeah. Hi, yourself," Jackie grumbled when she deigned to respond.

"Is something wrong?" I inquired naively of the lipstick-wielding reflection now next to mine in the mirror.

"I ask you a simple question, and you make it sound like I expect you to drop everything and answer me right then and there. That was not my intention, I assure you; I knew you were in a rush. Listen, wasn't I the one who told you to hurry?"

I immediately ceased ministering to my image in order to smooth Jackie's ruffled—for some reason—feathers. "Yes, you were," I said soothingly, not having the vaguest idea what she was even referring to. And then it hit me: *The call from Chet Byrnes!* I turned away from the mirror to address her scowling flesh-and-blood profile. "I'm sorry if I was a little brusque, Jackie. It's only that I was so anxious to get back to the man before he left."

The apology was obviously not sufficient, because Jackie, with only her upper lip colored, purposefully put her lipstick down on the sink, placed both hands on her hips, and spun around to confront me. "I think I deserve a little more credit than you were giving me, don't you?" she demanded, fastening on my face with frosty eyes.

"Yes, you do," I agreed.

Her gaze softened somewhat. "All right. Let's just forget it." And a moment later: "Well?"

I was thoroughly confused again. "Uh, well what?" I asked meekly.

"Who's the guy—the one on the phone?"

"He's a member of the crew that Cheryl Simon normally flew with—the pilot."

"Oh. It *is* business." She sounded dejected. "That's what I was afraid of. I was really hoping you'd met someone. Someone you could be interested in on a *personal* level." (I've told you, haven't I, that as much of a pain-in-the-whoosis as she might be on occasion, Jackie does have my best interests at heart.)

We spoke for a few minutes after this, with Jackie availing herself of the opportunity to let me know—as she had several times previously—what a wuss I was for agreeing to take Bruce on as a client. Then she asked about my plans for the evening and I asked about hers—she was meeting a friend at the theater later—and by the time we said good night, she seemed to be more or less favorably disposed toward me.

This newest reminder of Jackie's very thin skin got me to thinking, though, that I might be making a mistake in not telling her about my forthcoming date with Al Bonaventure. But I just didn't want to make a big deal of the thing by trumpeting it in advance. Which is why I'd opted to wait until Al and I had already been out together.

Still, what with Al's double role as both golfing buddy and dentist to Jackie's boyfriend, I was a little concerned. Suppose Al should mention something to Derwin and Jackie learned about our plans that way? God! if she thought I was trying to keep this from her, she'd have me eating crow into the next millennium.

I made up my mind I'd take my chances, anyway. Which I regard as one of my braver decisions.

Chapter 16

Thanks to that Jackie business and everything, I got to Claudine's a little late. Fortunately, though, I managed to make it there well before seven when the prices went up—and through the ceiling.

Christie was already seated in the restaurant, with a glass of white wine in hand, when I arrived. She rose as soon as she spotted me, a broad smile lighting her face.

"It's so wonderful to see you, Desiree!" She hastily put down the glass so she could hug me. I braced myself. Christie's hugs are surprisingly vigorous. I mean, the woman isn't much taller than I am and has a lot less flesh on her bones, besides.

"Same here." I meant it, too. Christie's a lovely person—sincere, generous, funny, bright—and all sorts of other nice adjectives.

Stepping back and holding me at arm's length, she gave me a quick once over before nodding solemnly. "Lookin' good, Shapiro. Lookin' real good."

"So are you." She was thinner now than I remembered—maybe a little too thin. And these days there were probably a few more lines in her forehead and around her mouth, along with the hint of a double chin that I didn't recall having seen before. But none of these things could really detract from that glowingly healthy complexion of hers or those shiny, electric-blue eyes. She appeared to be cheerful and composed tonight, too. But I knew how close Christie and Jim had been and how much she'd grieved for him, how much she still must be grieving for him.

Our appraisals of one another completed, we sat down at the

table, and I took stock of our surroundings. The wallpaper was peeling, the carpeting worn, and the dark green needlepoint chairs positively pleading for an upholsterer. Which is why Christie and I agreed that the food had to be truly outstanding. I mean, the ambience certainly couldn't have contributed to the astronomical prices—the after-seven prices, I'm talking about. Plus, according to Christie, her brother-in-law had been extremely enthusiastic about the place. "And Judd," she assured me, "has a very sophisticated palate."

We were to discover that the service wasn't exactly in the four-star category, either. We waited interminably for our orders to be taken and twice as long as that to be served. But under the circumstances, neither of us was too disturbed by this; there was a lot of catching up to do.

We started off by trading a few "Guess who I bumped into?"s, then segued into a whole bunch of "Do you remember?"s before the captain finally put in an appearance. Once we'd made our selections and we were alone again, though, the conversation took a more serious turn.

"Umm, how are you managing?" I said tentatively.

"I'm managing okay. Actually, better than okay, I think. I don't believe I told you this, but I'm going back to school in the fall to get my teaching credits."

"That's great!" I enthused, extremely gratified to learn that after the kick in the pants life had bestowed on her ten months ago, my old friend had not only picked herself up off the ground but was reaching for new goals, as well. "Tell me, do you still have that same nanny—what was her name, Marie?— for the girls?"

Christie came close to doubling up with laughter. "Of course not," she answered at last, dabbing at her eyes with her napkin. "The 'girls' are young women now—Sara's eighteen and Jodie's nineteen. They're both in college."

"I can't believe it! Has it been that long since I've seen them?"

"Sara's taller than I am now, so it must be," she informed me, grinning. I scrounged up a smile—a very weak smile. I don't think I'll ever stop feeling guilty about not attending Jim's funeral. I was sick in bed—really sick—with an ear infection at the time. Naturally, I called frequently, but still, it bothered me terribly that I wasn't there for Christie. And it does to this day. I attempted to make what must have been my hundredth-plus apology, but Christie cut me short.

"I haven't a doubt in my mind, Desiree, that you would have come to Minneapolis if it were at all possible. So don't you dare mention another word about it. Do you hear me?"

"All right." She closed her hand over mine for an instant. "How are the girls?" I said then. "And I don't care what *you* call them, they're still girls to me."

"They're doing fairly well. They were both very close to Jim, so of course they took his death hard, especially Sara. But they're adjusting. I'm very grateful for that. And incidentally, Sara's the reason I didn't let you know in advance that I planned on coming to New York. She was having some boyfriend trouble recently, and she was terribly down. I didn't want to leave while she was upset like that, so for a time the trip was really up in the air. But then Sara and Win made up—as I should have realized they would. The two of them started going together in seventh grade, and they've been breaking up and making up on a fairly regular basis ever since. At any rate, here I am."

"I'm really glad you made it, Christie. I'll bet Mr. Bloomingdale is, too. To say nothing of Mr. Saks and Mr. Lord and Mr. Taylor, et cetera. Well? How's the shopping been, anyway? Bought out all the New York stores yet?"

Christie laughed. "Not quite. I left a couple of things for you. But I did get a great pair of black patent leather pumps on sale. Also, a couple of Oscar de la Renta scarves for Sara and Jodie. They were on sale, too. And look." Reaching down next to her chair now, she picked up her handbag—a white leather Dooney & Bourke with tan trim, the trim almost the exact shade of her short-sleeved linen dress. "Like it?" she said, handing it across the table for my inspection. "I had to pay full price—which will probably cause me to break out in hives—but I just couldn't resist."

As I was admiring her purchase, our drinks arrived at last, the dour waiter setting them in front of us almost resentfully. It was Christie's second glass of wine and my first. She took a couple of sips before asking what had happened to "that man Bruce you were seeing."

And so I presented her with an abbreviated update of that ridiculous and ill-fated affair, during which she shook her head intermittently and made faces constantly.

"What a bastard," she muttered when the recitation was over. And then I told her I'd taken on the job of investigating his wife's death. She stared at me in disbelief but refrained from commenting. Almost immediately, though, she began questioning me about the case. When she felt that she was sufficiently informed—having been pretty much filled in on everything I knew by this time—she provided a stern warning. "Be careful, Desiree. Don't take anything for granted."

"I don't," I assured her.

"Good. But just keep in mind the possibility that the conversation Bruce supposedly had with Cheryl may never have taken place. It's not inconceivable that he hired you for the sole purpose of spreading around that smuggling story—and diverting suspicion from himself."

"Of course, that could be why he came to me," I acknowledged. "But for some reason, I don't really think so."

"Well, just be careful," Christie reiterated. "That's all I ask."

The food at Claudine's—when it finally materialized—turned out to be even worse than the service. Since we weren't through eating until almost nine-thirty, you can pretty well guess at the quality of the cuisine. Anyway, I was really tired by that time, and as much as I'd enjoyed being with Christie again, I was prepared to call it a night.

We were standing outside the restaurant when, just as I was about to envelop her in a good-bye hug, my friend asked plaintively, "Can we drop in somewhere for a drink? I really dread going back to my hotel room."

I eyed her quizzically.

"I suppose I shouldn't have made a reservation at the Pierre," she explained. "Jim and I used to stop there whenever we stayed over in Manhattan. But we hadn't done that in years, so I didn't think it would bother me—being there again. The truth is, though, I'm not as together yet as I thought I was. Or as I've been trying to get you to believe I am." Her smile was so twisted it momentarily distorted her face.

I was very sad for Christie—but certainly not surprised. In spite of the positive steps she'd taken to restructure her life, you don't get over the death of someone you love in a matter of months. Or even years. That much I knew firsthand.

"Listen, why don't you sleep at my place tonight?" I suggested. "The sofa opens up, and it's actually pretty comfortable."

"Thanks anyway, but I can't. I changed my plane reservations; I'll be leaving for home tomorrow morning. Look, even I can have my fill of shopping," she quipped, trying to make light of the situation. "At any rate, I've got a nine-thirty flight, and I have to pack before I leave and settle my bill and all."

"Maybe you could take care of those things now. I'll come back to the hotel with you and give you a hand," I offered.

Christie declined with a shake of her head. "I appreciate that, Dez, honestly. But I'll be okay. All I need is a little fortification."

I didn't feel I should mention that she'd had three glasses of fortification already.

"It would only be for one drink." And then the electric-blue eyes pleading with me: "Okay?"

"Okay," I said.

Well, what would you have said?

Silhouette was a small cocktail lounge not far from Claudine's that looked pretty nice and wasn't overly crowded. At least, not when we first walked in. We sat down at the long, curved bar, which at this point boasted only four or five other customers. I asked for an anisette and Christie had the bartender mix her a martini—a little risky, I thought, in view of all that wine she'd consumed at dinner. But foolishly I kept my concern to myself. In retrospect, though, I realize I should have given it a voice. (Who can say? She might even have listened to me.)

At any rate, almost at once the room started to really fill up. We soon learned that every Monday was ladies' night at Silhouette, and women imbibers paid only half price for their drinks. The inducement for the men, I suppose, being the promise of a larger-than-usual female turnout, along with the free hors d'oeuvres the event apparently merited.

Now, my capacity for liquor being what it is, I was still concentrating on that one anisette when Christie—politely vetoing my strong recommendation that we leave—downed another martini. And then—before I realized she'd even ordered it—most of another.

By this time the lounge was mobbed, I was feeling trapped, and Christie was very obviously feeling nothing at all. I couldn't get her to go, and, of course, my conscience wouldn't let me abandon her.

It wasn't until not a single drop of that third martini remained that I was at last able to coax her into vacating the bar stool. I propelled her resolutely toward the exit, the two of us getting pushed, pulled, and elbowed every step of the way. Some joker—I have no idea which one he was—even pinched my bottom.

The fact that the place was bursting at the seams actually turned out to be a blessing, however. Because when, in the middle of our little trek, my friend Christie suddenly passed out, there were all these bodies to break her fall.

Chapter 17

With the assistance of two sympathetic and able-bodied gentlemen I eventually got Christie out of the bar and into a cab. I even managed to schlepp her up to the twentieth floor of the Pierre somehow. As soon as we entered her room, however—and before I could stop her—she made a beeline for the bed. This would never do; she had to be in shape to catch that nine-thirty plane in the morning. But she threw herself down on the diagonal and lay there without moving so much as an eyelash until room service delivered the coffee I ordered. And then I had the job of propping her up and inducing her to swallow—which took all the urging, wheedling, and threats I could muster. Afterward, though, I was able to help her out of her clothes and maneuver her into a cold shower.

By the time we returned to the bedroom Christie had sobered up considerably. I sat her in a chair, then plopped down on the edge of the bed. Christie was on her feet almost at once. She stood there awkwardly, facing in my general direction, but her eyes were downcast. "I've never consumed so much liquor in my life," she mumbled, fidgeting absently with the ties of her terry cloth robe. "I— Uh-oh." Suddenly her hand flew to her mouth, and she took off as though the fires of hell were lapping at her heels. She barely made it to the bathroom, and I swear they must have heard her retching all the way down in the lobby. I mean, these were epic eruptions.

When she came back into the room a few minutes later, she looked green and sheepish. "I am so-o-o sorry." She sank into the chair she'd vacated. "I've given you quite a night, haven't I?"

"I admit I've had better," I cracked. "But never mind that. How about if I order up some tea? Or a Coke, maybe?"

"No, nothing. I couldn't handle a thing right now." And then she grinned. "Well, at least I no longer have that lead veal chop lying in my stomach." And a moment later: "I can't wait to come East again so I can treat that brother-in-law of mine to dinner at Claudine's. Him and his recommendations! But listen, it's late; you'd better get going." ·

"Only if you're okay."

"I'm a lot more okay than I was five minutes ago, I'll say that. Please. Go home. I feel guilty enough about tonight as it is."

"Stop that." After which I asked hesitantly, "You're sure you're all right?"

"Yes, I'm sure."

I stood up now, and Christie did, too. Then closing the short distance between us, she threw her arms around my neck. "Anyway, I *am* glad we got to see each other."

"So am I. Very glad. Next time, though, you're drinking Shirley Temples."

"Amen."

And we both laughed.

I left a couple of minutes later. But not before arranging a wake-up call for Christie at six-thirty the next morning. *This* morning, I mean. It was already one-ten when I walked out of that room.

I couldn't remember when I'd been so exhausted. Ministering to drunken friends is no picnic, believe me. As soon as I was back in my apartment I had this urge to pull a Christie and just make a lunge for the bed. But I have these habits of many years' standing—never mind just how many years' standing— that kept me from indulging my inclination. So after playing back the only message on my answering machine—it was from Bruce, who was once again requesting a progress report—I followed my usual, time-consuming routine. This included meticulously removing every last trace of makeup (who wanted clogged pores?) and then brushing with my Braun electric toothbrush until the red light finally started flickering two minutes later (it always feels more like ten) and even swishing my mouthwash around for a while (although you might very well question why I had to be concerned about bad breath just now). Anyway, when I was finally ready for bed, I reset my alarm to six-thirty. I considered myself duty-bound to see to it that Christie made her plane.

I fought it for all I was worth, but eventually the insistent bzzzz wrenched me away from my lovely dream. Stretching out my arm, I groped for the clock on the night table next to the bed. I felt around for the alarm lever, pushed it in, and then forcing one eye open, checked the time: six-thirty.

Six-thirty?

But an instant later I remembered. Christie.

Swinging my legs off the bed, I picked up the telephone—which sits right next to the clock. I had to dial Information first for the number of the Pierre.

"Hello?" Christie said weakly when I was put through to her.

"How are you feeling this morning?"

"Who is—? Dez?"

"That's me."

"Oh, I'm kinda' queasy, but it's not too bad. Not as bad as I deserve. I don't know what got into me, drinking like that. Listen, I can't thank you enough or apologize enough for what happened last night."

"Please, Christie. No more thanks or apologies—and I mean it. I'm phoning because it occurred to me you might turn right over and drop off again after you got your wake-up call. I did that once," I admitted.

She clucked her tongue. "Tied one on yourself, did you? Well, as it happens I've even started to get dressed. But seriously, Dez, I really appreciate your—"

"Cool it, Wright," I ordered with mock severity. "Have a safe flight, and I'll talk to you soon."

Then gently replacing the receiver in its cradle, I sat there dangling my feet and contemplating my options.

It was too early to get up, I decided. But on the other hand, I had to concede that it was probably too late to crawl back under the covers for any quality sleep time. And after all, I did have things to do at work today. Besides, it might be worth an hour's sleep to see the look on Jackie's face when I marched into the office at nine a.m.

Shocked might be too strong a word to describe her reaction. But not by much. Jackie's eyes were almost huge enough to reach her hairline when I made my entrance at nine. (Okay, 9:03, if you're that much of a purist.)

"What's with you?" she asked sharply.

"I couldn't sleep." It seemed the easiest way to explain things. Also, in a way, it was true. I mean, I *couldn't* sleep— not past six-thirty, anyway, if I was going to call Christie then.

Jackie eyed me skeptically. "I suppose there's a first time for everything," she remarked, shrugging.

"My coming in early is not a first," I contested.

"Maybe not. But if it happens even once a year, then I'm a two-headed giraffe."

"Well, see you later, Stretch." And giggling, I turned away. "Or," I tossed over my shoulder, "should I say, 'Double Stretch'?"

I was still giggling at this inanity of mine back in my cubbyhole. But I suppose that's what happens when you go against nature and drag yourself out of bed at the crack of dawn: Your brain malfunctions.

At this juncture it was obvious my mind required some stimulating if it was to be of any use to me today. So before getting out my typewritten notes on Donna Wolf and Laura Downey, I paid a visit to the coffee machine down the hall. But maybe the caffeine just didn't do its job. Because after going over my conversations with the two women again and again and then carefully studying the entire file, I was no more enlightened than I'd been before.

Of course, it was possible that there was nothing enlightening to be found there. I mean, who says a killer has to be considerate enough to provide you with a clue of some kind? Or, for that matter, that it was one of the women who'd killed Cheryl?

The only thing I knew for sure was that in my search for Cheryl Simon's murderer, I would continue to focus on her fellow flight attendants. Because regardless of the opinions of Fielding and Ellen and Christie and anybody else, I just couldn't buy the alternative.

Chapter 18

Okay. So I didn't believe Bruce had murdered his wife. But I still had a few matters to settle with the man. And once I was home from the office on Tuesday, the anticipation of reaming him out in just a few hours had my adrenaline working over-time. Even my appetite was affected. All I fixed myself for sup-per that night was a chicken salad sandwich. And I had trouble getting that down—that, and those two measly little Enten-mann's chocolate chip cookies.

While I was in the shower and then later when I was dress-ing, I kept rehearsing just what I would say to him—something I'd been doing on and off since Fielding first apprised me of Bruce's treachery.

And yes, as far as I was concerned, it *was* treachery. As Robert Louis Stevenson put it: "The cruelest lies are often told in silence."

Well, that was exactly what Bruce had done—lied to me in silence. And how are you supposed to do your job, I'd like to know, when your client refuses to level with you?

Bruce didn't greet me any too warmly. "How are you, Dez?" he said, his face expressionless. He smiled an instant later, but you could tell he didn't mean it. And then when we were seated in the living room he let me know the reason for his displea-sure. "I called you last night. Didn't you check your machine?"

"Yes, but I was out until late."

"What about this morning? You could have gotten back to me then." And now sarcastically: "Don't tell me you forgot the name of my company again."

How do you like that! I'd come here to confront him, and he was the one doing the confronting.

I retaliated with some sarcasm of my own. "It happens that I was rather busy today following up on a couple of matters concerning your wife's death—and, incidentally, trying to clear *you* of suspicion." In spite of my tone, I felt I was showing remarkable restraint—considering that just then there was nothing on earth I wanted so much as to punch my client in his smirking mouth. "And anyway, I expected to be seeing you tonight. Besides, if there'd been something to report—something of substance—*I* would have phoned *you*."

"Yes, I'm sure you would have. But what I can't seem to be able to impress on you is that even if you don't have what could be considered *information,* I need to know what's going on. Cheryl was my wife, for Christ's sake, and I loved her. I just can't take being kept in the dark like this, don't you understand?" He shifted gears now without missing a beat. "In any event, have you met with Donna yet?"

"I was there Saturday evening. And then I paid a visit to Laura on Sunday. But I still have no idea which of her three friends Cheryl suspected."

Bruce nodded, after which he returned to the source of the current friction between us—this time, though, employing a more conciliatory voice. "Uh, about this calling business, you did give me your word last week that you'd make contact a little more often." And when I didn't immediately respond: "Is that too much to ask, Dez?"

"I suppose not," I conceded none too graciously.

"I'd appreciate it." He flashed me the kind of grin that was meant to declare, *And don't forget what a charmer I am.*

It didn't make it. "You know, Bruce, I think it might be a good idea if you found yourself another investigator. That's why I wanted to see you—to tell you that."

Now, to be honest, this was mostly a bluff. Once I've taken on a case, I feel committed to seeing it through. And that was especially true in this instance. The way I looked at it, anyone who was willing to give a friend the benefit of the doubt the

way Cheryl Simon did shouldn't be made to pay for her loyalty
with her life. And I was determined to nail her killer—whether
I was compensated for it or not.

"Don't say that, Dez. Please. I'm depending on you. I
promise to cool it about the phone calls. I didn't know it irritated you that much."

"This isn't about the calls, Bruce. It's because I can't work
with a client who lies to me."

"*Lies* to you? I haven't told you a single lie. Not one," Bruce
protested stridently.

I hit him with a slightly bastardized version of Robert Louis
Stevenson. "You told me a lie in silence." Even now, I take a
certain pride in the fact that I refrained from tacking on, "Just
as you did when we were going out together."

"I told you a lie in silence? What's that supposed to mean,
anyway?" But a telltale flush was creeping up his neck, so I had
no doubt he already knew the answer. Nevertheless, I was only
too happy to lay everything out for him.

"For one thing, you neglected to mention the real reason you
and Cheryl argued so bitterly in that coffee shop."

"Real reason?" The flush had spread to his cheeks, which
were flame-red now.

"It was because you suspected her of having an affair with
her pilot, wasn't it?"

"That cop Fielding tell you this?"

"It doesn't make any difference who told me."

"Listen, Dez," Bruce said softly, looking down at his hands.
"I didn't say anything to you about that because I was too
ashamed."

"Clarify this for me, will you?" I instructed testily.

"Well, here I am, practically a newlywed, and I accuse my
wife of taking up with another man. It makes me sound so
damn insecure. I just couldn't have you, of all people, regarding me as if I were a total wimp."

I had to admit the "of all people" was a pretty nice touch.
Bruce embellished it an instant later, too. "I can't help it. What
you think of me really matters, Dez."

I-ignored the obvious pandering. "No. What really matters is the effect your withholding information of any kind could have on this investigation."

"I don't see that applying—not in this instance," Bruce contended stubbornly. "Cheryl and I had a terrible argument. I told you that. And it was because I wanted her to give up flying. I told you that, too. The thing about the affair, well, I was only shooting my mouth off."

"Let me explain why it does apply. When I heard from the police that you'd accused your wife of carrying on with another man, I was so dumbfounded I wasn't even able to open my mouth. If I'd known about it beforehand I could have attempted to minimize it. 'Oh, Bruce told me all about that,' I might have said offhandedly. 'It doesn't mean a thing. He knew there was nothing but friendship between Cheryl and that pilot. But he was mad at her, so he wanted to bug her.' Something like that, anyhow." I looked at him curiously now. "And what do you mean you were just shooting your mouth off?"

"Well, you see, Cheryl would make a comment about this Byrnes every so often, about what a good person he was and how thoughtful, what an excellent pilot he was—innocuous remarks like that. And he was supposed to be nice-looking, too, from what one of her friends once said. At any rate, that night in the coffee shop when Cheryl and I were going at each other about her continuing to fly, I became pretty hot. And all of a sudden I just popped off and accused her of having a *thing* with Byrnes. I didn't for a second believe it, though. It's just as you said a couple of seconds ago. I threw that in to bug her. Or maybe to put her on the defensive. Possibly in the back of my mind I was even hoping she'd quit her job to reassure me. If you want the truth, I can't really tell you what my motive was—I'm not clear on it myself. But I repeat: I didn't actually think Cheryl was cheating on me. I swear to you, I didn't."

"Fine. The point is, though, that it was obvious I was taken by surprise when the police informed me about your accusation. And from their point of view, your neglecting to mention it to me only gives it added weight. Can't you see that?"

"But that wasn't the main thrust of the argument. It was really about her flying, as I've been telling you from the beginning."

It was apparent I hadn't gotten through to Bruce—at least, not completely. And I felt that it was fruitless to continue this particular discussion. "All right," I said wearily, "let's talk about your first wife, then. Why didn't you ever let me know there was some question about the circumstances of her death?"

"Because I didn't think it had anything to do with what happened to Cheryl. I still don't."

Of course, in a way, I agreed with this. Hadn't I said pretty much the same thing to Fielding? Still, I couldn't afford to let Bruce off the hook. I had to make him appreciate how crucial it was that he be totally up front with me.

"Besides, that was pretty much straightened out at the time," he added.

"Not according to the authorities back in Chicago, it wasn't."

"Look, my ex-wife slit her own wrists, plain and simple. Naturally, in retrospect, I realize that when she said she intended to do away with herself, I should have taken it more seriously. But you didn't know Gerry. The woman was always 'on'—sometimes I used to think I was living with Bette Davis. Regardless of this, though, I'll never forgive myself for putting her threat down to playacting. That, however, was the extent of my complicity in her death. And if you can see how this could have any bearing on Cheryl's being pushed in front of a train, please explain it to me."

"Figure it out, Bruce," I responded, my tone almost sympathetic here. "When a man's two wives *both* die violently, there's bound to be speculation as to his involvement."

"Well, all I can say is that I cooperated fully with the Chicago police. I even gave them skin samples—knowing it was a match to the skin they'd found under Gerry's fingernails. Are you aware of that?"

"Yes," I answered. "But this still doesn't excuse your not telling me you'd been under suspicion. I was stunned to learn about it. If I'd only been forewarned, I could have argued the irrelevance of Gerry's suicide with a little more conviction."

"But that was years ago, Desiree. It never even occurred to me the police would dredge up all of that now."

"I just don't like surprises," I said firmly. "They put us both at a disadvantage." And eyeing him warily: "There wouldn't be anything else you've been keeping from me, would there?"

"No. And that's the God's honest truth."

"All right."

"You'll remain on the case, then?"

"I'll remain. But if I find out you're hiding something . . ." I left it at that. "Well, as long as I'm still working for you, there's something I've been meaning to ask you about."

"Okay. But how about a drink first?"

"Does the offer include coffee?"

"You bet."

"Milk and—"

"—one sugar," Bruce finished for me.

"Ahhh, you remembered," I joked.

"I remember many things about you" was the response. And it was accompanied by the requisite poignant smile.

Now, if this was supposed to endear him to me, it met with even less success than his earlier attempts that evening. *Yeah?* I thought bitterly. *Well, I remember a lot of things about you, too, buster.*

But by the time Bruce came back with my coffee, along with a soft drink for himself, I'd managed once again to submerge his past transgressions—and the hostility that bubbled up in me whenever I was reminded of them.

He handed me the mug, then took a seat. "Go ahead, fire away."

"The day after Cheryl spoke to you about those instances in Nassau, did you ask if she'd reached any decision on how she intended handling things?" I had a sip of the coffee now. It was very close to being as horrendous as my own. *No,* I concluded with my second—and final—sip. *It was worse.*

"Yes, of course," Bruce answered. "Cheryl insisted she still hadn't made up her mind. But as I think I told you before, I'm almost certain she planned to talk to her friend right from the start. She just didn't want to admit it to me because she knew I didn't approve of the idea. Or it's possible she wasn't that sure yet of what she was going to do—even though *I* was."

I set the nearly full coffee mug unobtrusively—I hoped—on one of the coasters that sat on the glass-topped table in front of me. "Well, this would explain why she waited that extra day to take action."

"No, not really," Bruce countered. "Even if she'd been a hundred percent positive she was going to speak to whoever it was, she'd most likely have had to work up to it. It was the sort of thing that would have been extremely difficult for Cheryl. For anyone, probably."

This made sense.

"What else did you want to ask me?"

"That about does it," I said. "If I think of something, though, I'll phone you. And speaking of that . . ."

"I know." Bruce grinned. *"Don't call me; I'll call you."*

Chapter 19

It was close to twelve when I got home that night. Immediately after turning on the air conditioner, I dialed my friend Christie.

Now, even if there hadn't been this one-hour time difference between New York and Minnesota, it would have been perfectly okay to call Christie at that hour. The woman just starts revving up at midnight.

Nevertheless, as soon as she answered, I found myself saying as if by rote, "It's Dez. I hope I didn't wake you."

"Are you kidding? This is me—Christie. Remember? I've been sitting here trying to decide whether I should pick myself up off the sofa and do a load of wash—which really needs doing at this point. Or maybe bake a carrot cake—I have this new recipe that's supposed to be fabulous."

"You are seriously crazy, do you know that? But anyway, I wanted to find out how your flight was this morning."

"It's really nice of you to call, Dez. I planned on giving you a ring later in the week. In answer to your question, the flight was great. I slept from practically the minute we took off until the minute we landed."

"And you're, uh, feeling okay?"

"No, I am *not*."

"What's wrong?" I asked nervously.

"I'm too damn sober." She laughed. "Just kidding. I'm not sure if you mean am I physically okay—or emotionally okay. But in either case, the answer is 'I'm fine.' And listen, I know you don't want to hear this, but I can't tell you how much I appreciate—"

"If you say even one more word about that, I'm taking out a

contract on you. So consider yourself forewarned, Besides, not possessed of your superhuman stamina, I intend to hang up now anyway. I have to get to bed."

"Okay, but really, thanks for all—"

I broke in before she could come out with another syllable. "Keep well, and I'll talk to you soon." Then, very gently, I put down the receiver.

Well, it's one thing to go to bed. But falling asleep is an altogether different story.

As soon as I hit the pillow, my mind began to do me dirty.

It began by focusing on Bruce and his phone calls.

Maybe I'd been a little hard on him about that, I decided. Sure, his calling so frequently drove me slightly crazy. But that was actually *my* problem. The man was entitled to be filled in on any and all developments. He was the one who was keeping me in Häagen Dazs at the moment, wasn't he? And besides, his anxiety was totally understandable.

Well, the next time he phoned—I didn't for a second expect that he'd keep his promise not to—I'd be more patient with him. And if I wasn't in when he called, I'd get back to him. And I wouldn't take a year and a day to do it, either.

Satisfied, I rolled onto my stomach. "Now go to sleep," I commanded.

But before I could stop it, that totally undisciplined mind I'm burdened with had wandered onto the subject of coincidences.

You remember, don't you, how Fielding had enumerated five examples of what he'd facetiously labeled coincidence in this case? And then he'd reminded me of how often—and unequivocally—I'd declared in the past that I didn't believe there was any such thing. According to him, though, I'd now done an about-face on the subject because it was of benefit to my client.

Could Fielding be right? Was I willing to depart from this conviction of mine when it suited me?

I went through the list, mostly reaffirming for myself pretty much what I'd told Fielding at the time.

He'd accused me of accepting as coincidence the fact that Cheryl had spotted her friend and El Puerco together on two separate occasions. But really. How unlikely was it that this would happen on a small island—especially over a period of months?

And as for Bruce's being *in the vicinity* of the West Fourth Street subway station at the approximate time of Cheryl's death, well, it wasn't as if he were there at the scene or anything. According to Fielding himself, Bruce was a taxi ride away, for crying out loud. Some vicinity!

Uh-uh. I didn't see any coincidence here, either. And besides, if *I* wanted to do away with someone, I'd try to make it appear as though I were on the other side of town at the time of the murder. And I had to acknowledge that—as far-fetched as you might find this—it was very possible that Bruce was every bit as clever as I am.

I decided then that there was another thing, too, that shot down Fielding's theory here. Something that hadn't occurred to me before—although I probably shouldn't even admit it. How could Bruce have known just when Cheryl's train would pull into the West Fourth Street station, though? And for that matter, that she'd be changing to another train on the upper level?

And suddenly it hit me. This was what Fielding had been hinting at! This was why he'd asked me to speculate about the victim's purpose in getting off at West Fourth! He had the idea Bruce had induced Cheryl to meet him there, presumably so they could travel downtown together—say, for lunch. No wonder Fielding had emphasized "restaurants" when he suggested a few reasons Cheryl might have been headed for the Canal Street area.

Well, I didn't accept this for a minute. Let Tim have his stupid theory, though. Oh, how I was going to enjoy proving him wrong!

I proceeded to another so-called coincidence: the fact that both of Bruce's wives came to a violent end. *Forget it,* I instructed myself. One was a suicide, the other an apparent murder victim.

And with regard to that business about each of the women dying a week after some sort of—what was it Fielding had called it—"traumatic occurrence" involving my client? Where did he come off even including this one in the mix? What's coincidental about Bruce's current wife being murdered close on the heels of an argument and his ex killing herself soon after a divorce? I mean an argument and a divorce! Fielding had to have some kind of chutzpah to even equate the two.

Lastly, there was Bruce's remark about the A train. Well, that was certainly a lucky guess. Or, as it turned out, an *un*lucky guess. Okay, in this instance we probably did have what could qualify as a bona fide coincidence. The only other explanation being the one Fielding had attempted to palm off on me: that Bruce, after giving his wife a fatal shove, was so nervous when questioned by the police that he blurted out an extremely damning truth. The flaw in this proposition, though, was that it was completely out of character for the man. Bruce was far too controlled to make that kind of mistake.

So what did we have here? A single genuine coincidence in the entire bunch. But still, there was no question in my mind that it *was* a coincidence.

I had to concede at this juncture that I'd maybe been a little too rigid in my thinking until now. After all, how much in life is an absolute? From here on, I'd just have to revise my opinions to accommodate the fact that once in a while—albeit a very great while—coincidences *do* occur.

I could live with that.

Chapter 20

The last thing I remembered before drifting off to sleep was the hint of daylight creeping in under the shades. So when the alarm clock rang at seven-thirty I woke up just long enough to reset it. It didn't go off again until nine-thirty. I phoned Jackie at once.

"I won't be in today," I said. "I'll be working at home."

Thank God I called when she was busy on another line and, therefore, able to manage only a very abbreviated interrogation. I was actually permitted to hang up in less than a minute—an all-time record for a Jackie communication of this sort.

Anyway, I figured that an additional hour or so of sleep wouldn't hurt me, but I just couldn't drop off again. And after a while I gave up and dragged myself out of bed.

Once I'd eaten some breakfast and skimmed through the newspaper I hadn't had a chance to even open last night, I pushed myself into conceding that I was up to a little house-cleaning. As you can gather, I wouldn't be tackling my chores with any great relish. But the thing is, I was home anyway, and with Chet Byrnes coming by tonight . . . well, the apartment *was* a definite embarrassment. I hadn't dusted in—I'm ashamed to tell you how many days. And it was at least two weeks since I'd gotten out the vacuum cleaner. Plus the kitchen floor looked like an army had tramped through there—an army with muddy feet.

At any rate, while I didn't take on any of the heavy stuff—I always have to work on myself a lot longer for that—I managed to make the place look pretty good on the surface. And really, I felt I could be fairly confident that Byrnes would never check inside the oven—which still offered samples of the last company meal I'd prepared. Nor was he likely to peek behind the shower curtain—where the tiles over the tub were a study in grunge.

All in all, I decided, I'd done an admirable job of camouflaging the fact that I'm not the world's premier housekeeper.

And now I attempted to shove the vacuum cleaner back into an already overcrowded closet—where the recently vacated space seemed to have immediately been gobbled up by the closet's remaining occupants. After an exhausting struggle I was finally able to make room for the vacuum. Although I had to push against the door with all of my strength in order to close it.

But flushed with my cleaning accomplishments at this instant, I promised myself I was even going to straighten out that closet one of these days.

The man standing on my threshold that night was casually dressed in a pair of cream-colored slacks, brown moccasins, and a short-sleeved sport shirt striped in blue, green, and brown. He was of medium build and about six feet tall, with soft brown eyes, an aquiline nose, and a pleasant smile. His hair, which was just beginning to recede at the temples, was quite gray, giving him a look of maturity that was not in the least unflattering.

"Come in, Captain Byrnes."

The smile broadened. "Chet."

He followed me the few yards into the living room and sat down in one of the club chairs.

I hovered over him for a moment. "Can I get you some coffee? Iced coffee, if you like. Or a glass of wine? A coke? What?"

"Nothing, thanks. I just had two cups of coffee at dinner."

I settled myself on the sofa. "Help yourself to some fruit," I instructed, waving at the large crystal bowl on the cocktail table, into which I'd piled apples, pears, plums, nectarines, a couple of bananas, and two kinds of grapes. And, oh yes, even a kiwi.

"Thanks. I'll do that." And he obediently reached for a few grapes. (But I got the impression it was a pity reach—what I mean is, he'd have preferred to abstain, but he didn't want to hurt my feelings.)

"I don't quite know where to start," I said. "Uh, let me see. . . ."

Rather than taking this statement at face value—I really *didn't* know where to start—Chet misinterpreted my hesitancy as a reluctance to delve into his private life. "Maybe I can help you out. You want to ask if I was aware that Cheryl's husband had accused her of having an affair with me. The answer is yes, I heard all about that. And you want to know if it was true— about the affair. And the answer to that is no, it was not." Pleased with his astuteness, he sat up a little straighter in his chair now. "So how did I do? That is what you were going to ask me, isn't it?"

I grinned. "Well, not exactly. I was already certain there'd been no affair; Bruce Simon admitted to me that he made it up."

"Oh?" Chet lifted an eyebrow. "Well, then I guess that shows *me*. Why don't I just let you ask your own questions from now on, huh?"

"All right." Of course, my questions should have been more or less in order in my head before Chet Byrnes even showed up here tonight—but they weren't. (Sometimes I wonder if I could possibly be *less* buttoned up.) Anyhow, I began with, "There's been some speculation that Cheryl was on her way to see you the morning she died." Which seemed as good a jumping-off point as any.

"Yes, so I've been told. And I suppose that's possible, but it's highly unlikely. The whole crew is aware that I spend quite a lot of time with my daughter when I'm in town—her mother and I are divorced. As it happens I was home that day. But Cheryl wouldn't have had any way of knowing this, not unless she called first. And she didn't call."

"Had Cheryl ever dropped in on you before?"

Chet shook his head. "Never."

"I see. What can you tell me about the other three flight attendants? You must know them pretty well."

"I'm not quite sure what you're after," he responded, regarding me uneasily.

"What are they really like? What kind of lives do they lead? What sort of problems do they have? Anything you can think of. It's impossible to figure at this stage of the investigation what could wind up being helpful."

"Listen, Desiree, I'll be happy to answer whatever you want to ask about me personally. But I'm afraid I don't feel comfortable discussing my crew—my *friends,* actually."

"I'm not just being a busybody here, Chet; I'm trying to catch a killer," I retorted—probably a little more harshly than was necessary to get my message across.

"But I can't believe that any of these people would have harmed Cheryl. They're all so . . . so *decent.*"

"Look, I suppose you've heard that Cheryl spoke to Bruce about some drug smuggling only two nights before she was killed."

"No. I heard Bruce *claims* Cheryl spoke to him about that."

"I have reason to believe he's telling the truth."

"Why? He lied before, didn't he?—when he made up that story about the affair."

"Yes. He did. But he felt he had to say that at the time." (Now what this was supposed to mean, I had no idea. But fortunately, no explanation was requested.)

"Your client hardly inspires confidence, you know," Chet muttered.

I didn't appear to be getting anywhere, so it seemed an appropriate moment to toss out a little reminder. "Didn't you yourself spot El Puerco at the Nassau airport and point him out to Cheryl?"

"Yes, that's perfectly true. And it's very likely she mentioned it to her husband and that this is what inspired him to come up with the whole far-fetched tale."

"I think you should be aware that there's been some independent verification of Bruce's story." (Look, I was a desperate woman, okay?)

Chet was silent for a minute. And then he asked, "Is it possible you could be a little more specific?"

"I can't," I told him regretfully. "I wish I could. But it might mean trouble for a very honest cop if it was ever discovered that this information had been passed on to me." I must say I sounded completely sincere. I swear, if you didn't know I was lying, you'd never have known I was lying.

Evidently I convinced Chet Byrnes, too, because his next words were, "All right. I'll tell you whatever I can about the three. I'm afraid it's not very much, though. We're friends, as I said, but it's primarily a working relationship. We don't see one another too often outside the job, and I'm not what you'd call a confidante to any of them." And now looking almost grim, he moved forward in his chair, his hands on his knees.

"Donna, well, she's a sweet person," he began, his tone matter-of-fact. "She's hardworking. Crazy about flying. And almost invariably cheerful. She's also raising a son by herself—the father skipped even before the boy was born. Donna's mother is very supportive, though; gives her a hand all the time—too much of a hand, I suspect. And I have a feeling Donna may have come to the same conclusion, although she's never let on. At least, not to me."

"What do you mean—'too much of a hand'?"

"I think the mother would like to raise the boy herself. She's always encouraging Donna to go out with her friends, take a vacation, visit her sister in Pittsburgh for a few days—anything so Donna will have to leave Rusty in her care. At first, everyone considered the mother such a treasure to help out like that. But a couple of people have seen Mrs. Wolf in action, and she's very controlling. She tends to take charge of the child even when Donna's right there in the room."

"Donna seems like such a happy person, though."

"Yes, I know. But don't let her fool you. That's just the face she puts on for the world. From what I understand, she was all broken up when Billy—the boy's father—cut out. At any rate,

I think she's beginning to be aware that if she wants to have any say in bringing up her own son, she may have to trade in her career for something that doesn't deposit her in the Bahamas twice a week. And for Donna, that would really be tragic. She loves to fly. More than any of the others, I believe."

"What else do you know about her?"

"That pretty much covers it."

"How about Laura, then?"

"Well, Laura's a very bright lady, very stylish. Also, easy to get along with. But I probably know even less about her than I do about Donna. She's been with us about a year and a half, maybe two years. But I was grounded with sciatica a good part of that time and then she was on sick leave for quite a while, too."

"What was wrong with her?"

"She broke her leg. And it was a pretty bad break, apparently."

"How did she do that?"

"Laura used to go riding almost every weekend at some stable over in New Jersey. This one particular morning, though, something evidently happened, and the horse threw her—Laura insists he must have been spooked by a snake or some type of small animal. At any rate, Laura's mother is married to this Canadian millionaire, and the mother flew in that same day to cart her daughter off to Toronto in a private plane so she could look after her."

"The leg seems to have healed all right. I mean, Laura looked fine when I saw her."

"She is fine. The accident was back in September or October. Besides, her mother made certain Laura had the best doctors—*and* got plenty of nourishment." He chuckled now.

"What?"

"Well, when she first came to work for Bahamian, Laura was on the thin side. *Very much* on the thin side. Nick—my copilot—used to tease her almost unmercifully about that; he said they could probably fit two Lauras in her uniform. But after she returned from Canada, she was maybe fifteen pounds heavier."

"I take it her mother's a pretty good cook."

"That's what one of the others—Hank, I think it was—said to her. But Laura thought that was extremely funny. 'It's my mother's cook who's a good cook,' she told him."

"Have you ever met this friend of Laura's—his name's Bobby Lomax?"

"I've never actually *met* the man. I've just seen him from a distance a couple of times when he came to pick her up at the airport."

"Would you happen to have any idea what he does for a living?"

"He's a teacher, I believe. A high school teacher."

Bobby Lomax? A high school teacher? I almost said, "You're kidding!" But I clamped down on my tongue before it could run away with itself.

"Laura seems to be pretty interested in Lomax, too."

"I had the same impression."

There was a lengthy pause before Chet spoke again. "Sorry, but I really can't think of anything else to tell you about Laura. Would you like me to go on to Hank now?"

"Please."

"A really nice guy. Always ready to do his share—and more. He has a good sense of humor, too, once you get to know him. He's probably a little oversensitive sometimes, but that's understandable. Other than that, though—"

"Whoa. Back up a second, Chet. What do you mean, 'that's understandable'?"

"I suppose you're aware that Hank's gay?"

"Yes."

"Well, coming out hasn't been easy for him, that's all. His mother tries not to acknowledge the fact, his brother won't even speak to him, his father's disowned him, and he's gotten flak from some of the people at the airline, too. So every so often he takes offense when none is intended."

"How about his personal life?"

"He was seeing someone for a while, and they lived together for a few months. But then the other fellow met somebody else—an older man with a lot of money, I heard—and just took off."

"How did Hank react?"

"He was terribly upset; that much was apparent. But he seems to have recovered okay."

"When was all this?"

"I'd say it's been about a year since the guy left."

"Is Hank seeing anyone now?"

"I wouldn't really know. But Hank talks to my copilot about things like that. Have you met with Nick yet?"

"No. But I intend to do that soon."

Chet went home just a short time after this, leaving me with the copilot's phone number—and the promise he'd call if anything else should occur to him.

But something he'd said during my questioning had struck a chord . . . something that reminded me I'd been remiss.

Only damned if I had the slightest inkling of what it was.

Chapter 21

When I woke up on Thursday morning, it was with the same uneasy feeling of having left something undone.

I was completely frustrated. Whatever it was that Chet Byrnes had said was stored in some deep recess of my brain—where it apparently intended to remain.

Well, I'd be transcribing my notes on last night's meeting as soon as I got to the office. Hopefully, Byrnes's words would ring a bell again. But then, I fretted, you never can tell about things like that. I mean, suppose they made no impression on me at all this second time?

As soon as I was ensconced in my cubbyhole, I took out my file, turned on the computer, and started to work. To my great relief, not even five minutes into the typing I came across the phrase that had been eluding me. And a lightbulb went on!

Cheryl wouldn't have had any way of knowing he'd even be home, Chet Byrnes had told me. Not unless she called first.

Don't you see?

The same would be true with regard to the killer. What I'm trying to say is that Cheryl would most likely have phoned the perpetrator before trekking out to Forest Hills that morning. Otherwise, there was no way to be sure she'd find him or her in.

I was sorely tempted to bang my head on the desk. I mean, how could I have overlooked anything so obvious? And even if, for some reason, Cheryl hadn't made that call, it was certainly one of the first things I should have checked.

Shoving aside my notes, I dialed this contact I have at the telephone company.

I asked Val to go over the Simon phone records on the morning of Cheryl's death, as well as on the day immediately preceding it. "I need to know if there were any calls made to Forest Hills."

"No problem," Val assured me. "I'll get back to you in a couple of minutes."

And she did.

Just as I figured, on the Wednesday before Cheryl was killed, a phone call had been placed to Forest Hills from the Simon apartment. A shiver of anticipation ran down my spine. The call, Val told me, was made at three-twelve p.m. and lasted seven minutes. The number?

It turned out to be Laura Downey's.

Good God! Had I actually uncovered the killer by making this simple inquiry?

It certainly seemed that way. After all, Laura was the only one of her fellow flight attendants that Cheryl had contacted during those final two days of her life. And what's more, Laura had deliberately lied to me, claiming she hadn't seen or heard from Cheryl since they'd gotten back to New York on Tuesday.

I picked up the receiver. I had to hear how the woman could possibly attempt to explain these things away.

She sounded out of breath when she answered the phone. "Oh, you just caught me, Desiree. I'm about to leave for the city to meet a friend for lunch."

"I have to see you, Laura. As long as you'll be in Manhattan, would it be possible for us to meet somewhere?"

"I could stop in at your office," she offered.

"I'd appreciate that." I gave her the address.

"Three o'clock okay?" she asked.

"Whenever you can get here."

After this I went back to typing up my notes. But I was barely able to concentrate now, and I wound up making one typo after another.

It was exactly three when Laura arrived, dressed in a short, tight, black sheath, which would have been a lot more becoming if it had been one or two sizes larger or Laura had been ten or fifteen pounds smaller. Still, she looked damned attractive. Her thick auburn hair was pulled back into an elaborate chignon today, and that beautiful tan of hers was accentuated by bright coral lipstick and stark white jewelry—including a fabulous pair of triangle-shaped drop earrings that I'd have preferred to see dangling from my own ears.

Taking a seat alongside my desk, Laura appeared to study my face for a moment, as if trying to gauge my mood. Then she asked softly, "Has something come up—about Cheryl?"

"Why didn't you tell me she called you the day before she died?"

The woman didn't even seem particularly disturbed by the question. "Oh, you found out about that."

"Yes, I did. And you told me you hadn't spoken to her after your last flight together."

"I know. And I'm sorry. But I did have my reasons."

"You even lamented not phoning her that Wednesday night," I reminded Laura sarcastically. "It would have given you the chance to speak to Cheryl one last time, you claimed."

"That happens to be true. You see, her call to me was—I'm not quite sure how to describe it—*stilted*, I guess. She wanted to consult with me about something, but she was very careful to reveal only as much as she absolutely had to. You see, she was concerned about causing trouble for someone who could turn out to be completely innocent." There was a slight but meaningful emphasis to the next words. "And so was I."

"You're talking about the smuggling now, I assume."

"That's right," Laura admitted reluctantly.

"What was it Cheryl *did* say?"

"Well . . . I suppose it was bound to come out sooner or later. She told me she believed that a friend might be involved in a drug smuggling operation and that she intended to confront whoever it was. She wouldn't give me any of the details, though, and she even refused to say who it was she was talking about. But from something she let slip I realized she had to be referring to either Donna or Hank. And when I put this to her, she didn't deny it. Anyhow, she asked if I thought she should get in touch with this person in advance to say she was coming over, and I said probably not. I told her that if the party was guilty—and I really didn't believe either Donna or Hank *could* be; I still don't—the very fact she was making the trip out to Queens would put them on the alert and allow time for making up a story of some sort."

"And did Cheryl agree with you?"

"She'd been leaning that way, too. She figured a surprise visit was most likely the best way to handle it. And it became more practical, too, after I said that if whoever she suspected wasn't in when she got there, she could wait in my apartment until he or she came home."

"Tell me, Laura. When you heard that Cheryl was dead, didn't it occur to you that this was the time to come forward with what you knew?"

"Listen, whatever it was that happened to Cheryl took place in Manhattan. So I assumed that she never even got to Forest Hills on Thursday morning. And later, when I realized there was speculation that she did go out there and might have been followed back to the city, I have to admit I didn't find that very believable. We've been over this before, Desiree. And as I told you then, although it's highly unlikely that Donna or Hank would be involved in transporting drugs, I suppose it's not entirely out of the question. Murder, though? Never in a million years. And besides," she pointed out, "you did say that it hadn't been established yet how Cheryl wound up on those tracks."

"Is it your thinking that Cheryl was hallucinating about what she'd seen?"

"She never told me she'd actually *seen* anything. She just alluded to her suspicions. And it is possible she misinterpreted whatever it was that prompted them."

"Did you ever speak to either of the others about your conversation with Cheryl? After she was killed, I mean."

"No. I decided I'd just bide my time until the investigation turned up something, something that I felt was bound to implicate someone else."

Lowering her eyes now, Laura chewed on her bottom lip for a few seconds. "I suppose I should have let you know about that phone call from Cheryl," she murmured. "But I wanted to protect my friends. You can appreciate that, can't you?"

An instant later, however, she looked at me directly and, chin thrust out almost belligerently, insisted, "I don't care what anyone says, though. I'm positive that neither Donna or Hank had anything to do with Cheryl's death. There's another explanation. There has to be."

Alone in my office a few minutes later, I sat at my desk thinking for a long, long while.

Could Laura actually have been telling the truth? Or was she merely the best little actress this side of Broadway?

That phone call lasted seven minutes, I ruminated. But this really didn't prove a thing. It would have been enough time for Cheryl to give this highly condensed synopsis of her problem and for Laura to provide her advice. On the other hand, though, it wouldn't have been an inordinate amount of time for Cheryl to inquire as to whether Laura intended to be home on Thursday so that she could come by to see *her.* Not if there'd been some innocuous preamble beforehand.

Oh, hell! I was right back where I started! I sighed so loudly then that I'm surprised no one came sprinting down the corridor to see if I'd just emitted a death rattle.

Well, I'd never really counted on that call to the phone company solving my case for me. I mean, here was still further proof that absolutely nothing is that easy.

But wouldn't it have been nice, I posed to myself, if just this once, it was?

Chapter 22

I was wrong, of course. It didn't immediately penetrate, but I finally recognized that I wasn't back where I started at all. Laura had just verified my client's story!

Hooray!

You see? I hadn't actually lied to Chet Byrnes—not really—when I told him I had confirmation Bruce was telling the truth. It was more as if I'd been clairvoyant or something. At least, that's how I chose to regard it.

I felt justified now, too, in my faith that Bruce had been straight with me about this (if not about much else). And to my way of thinking, it was also a virtual certainty at this point that Cheryl had been killed by one of her dearest friends.

I briefly considered calling Tim Fielding to apprise him that I had proof of my client's veracity. But then I changed my mind. Knowing Tim as I did, it would take a lot more than that to rid him of the firmly embedded notion that Bruce Simon had murdered his wife.

Anyhow, it was after four when I went back to transcribing my notes, simultaneously attempting to study them as I worked. The result was that I was only able to absorb about two percent of what I read, while the typing progressed at the breakneck speed of about twelve words per minute. Regardless, I intended to stay right where I was until I completed the job.

The one time I took a break that evening—other than to have a bite of supper at my desk or visit the ladies' room, that is—was at a little past seven, when I tried reaching Nick Michaels. He wasn't at home—surprise!—so I left my usual message on his machine.

As soon as I was back at the computer again, something struck me—and I have no idea what triggered it, either.

I'd never given a single thought to motive in this case, and that's normally a critical factor in an investigation. But in the present instance, since I had always accepted Bruce's version of things, I hadn't considered motive to even be relevant. I mean, it was obvious that Cheryl Simon was shoved onto those train tracks because someone decided to prevent her from talking about what she'd witnessed in Nassau. It occurred to me now, however, that it might make sense to poke a bit deeper—and look into why the perpetrator might have gotten involved in drug trafficking in the first place.

Suppose the smuggler was Donna. According to what Chet Byrnes had told me, she could certainly use a little windfall in order to hire someone to care for her son.

I had to wonder just when Donna had begun to appreciate that her mother's willingness to Rusty-sit wasn't all that altruistic. And in conjunction with this, how long the perp had been into transporting drugs. But it wasn't too likely I'd have either answer until Cheryl's murder was solved—and maybe not even then.

I had another puzzler for myself, too. If Donna was the one hooked up with El Puerco, why hadn't she brought in someone to look after Rusty yet?

Here, though, a couple of reasons occurred to me at once. Perhaps the assignments weren't that steady, and she still didn't have the money for live-in help. Or could be she was waiting to accumulate the kind of bankroll that would allow her to relocate—and remove Rusty from his grandmother's clutches altogether.

Okay. Now let's suppose Hank is my man. If he was still hung up on his former lover, he could certainly benefit from a lucrative part-time enterprise. It appeared to be his one hope— if there *was* any hope—of luring that mercenary creep away from his current partner.

But if Hank was the perpetrator, how come he hadn't done anything about reuniting with his ex?

Wait a second. How did I know he hadn't? It was possible he'd made the attempt and been rejected. It was also possible that plans were in the works to cohabit again once there was no longer an active investigation into Cheryl's death.

And lastly, suppose it was Laura doing the smuggling. Well, in her case, there was no specific necessity for additional cash—not that I was aware of, at any rate. But since when does an actual *need* for money have that much to do with the desire to acquire it? Besides, the woman liked nice things; this was certainly obvious from my visit to her place.

I conjured up the furniture in that apartment for a few moments. Perhaps sitting among all of those fine reproductions was a genuine Chippendale commode. Or a Louis XVI armchair, circa 1775. *I* certainly wouldn't know the real Louis from the faux. How many people would?

Anyway, one thing was clear. I'd have to have a talk with Hank's erstwhile lover. But first, of course, I needed to find out who the hell he was.

It was after nine before I finally got through all of my notes. By then my eyes were bleary, my back was killing me, and I was all supposed out.

The answering machine had a message for me when I came home. It was from Bruce.

"Listen, I'm just calling to make certain you're aware that, true to my word, I haven't called you. Not even once in the last two days. Well, hope you're having a pleasant evening."

I had to smile. I mean, it *was* kind of cute in a way. And once again—but for a very brief time, believe me—I was reminded of what had attracted me to the man to begin with.

Chapter 23

When I got to the office on Friday I immediately phoned my client.

"I have news for you," I told him, "big news."

"You've learned who killed Cheryl?" It was put out tentatively, as if too much to hope for. Which, unfortunately, it was.

"Well, no. But it's the next best thing. Your story's been corroborated."

"What do you mean? What's happened?"

"The day before she was killed, Cheryl had a conversation with Laura in which—according to Laura—your wife spoke about confronting this friend who was smuggling drugs."

"How did you find out?"

I filled him in on my call to the telephone company and my subsequent meeting with Laura Downey.

"Thank God," Bruce murmured when he'd heard me out. And after a moment: "Do you believe Laura? About Cheryl's only calling her for advice, I mean."

"I'm not really sure. Could be. Or could be the woman's just a quick thinker. To say nothing of being a very gifted performer."

"Have you told your detective buddy about this?"

"Fielding? No, not yet. He can be pretty hardheaded at times. I'm fairly certain even confirmation wouldn't be enough to convince him your hands are clean."

"Why, for Christ's sake?"

"There's still your accusation that Cheryl and Chet were lovers and the A train remark and—"

"All right, enough said. But I wish there were a way to get

him to back off a little. He's been interrogating my boss, also the friend I had lunch with that Thursday, also my neighbors, and no doubt a lot of other people, too. His checking up on me like that isn't exactly enhancing my reputation, you know."

"I don't think the people he's talked to would take his questions as any reflection on you. It's to be expected that the police would gather all the information they could in a situation like this. Besides, he's probably already spoken to everyone on his list."

"Yeah. Well, maybe." There was a few seconds' pause before Bruce spoke again. "Look, don't you think that Fielding's learning I've been telling the truth about this smuggling business would lead him to at least *consider* that he might have made a mistake about me?"

"Umm, I wouldn't depend on it. Sergeant Fielding's a fair and intelligent man. But sometimes it takes a little doing to disabuse him of an idea once he's latched on to it. Hang in there, though," I instructed, wishing I had the conviction of my words. "We'll prove to him that you're innocent. I don't know how yet, but we will."

"What you're really saying is that before he's willing to concede that he's been barking up the wrong suspect, you'll have to hand him Cheryl's murderer on a silver platter. Am I right?"

"I'm afraid it could very well come down to that," I conceded.

"Well, don't be—afraid, that is. I have every confidence in you, Dez."

I was no closer to putting a face to Cheryl Simon's killer than I'd been at the outset, yet here was Bruce still showing all this faith in me. So I don't think it's hard to understand why, under the circumstances, I was more than a little anxious to meet with Nick Michaels. As far as I could see, he was my best hope for any new leads in the case.

Waiting for the copilot to get back to me that morning, I engaged in a little positive thinking. It was very possible, I told myself, that Michaels would know something. Most likely something he wasn't even aware that he knew. I mean, how often had I encountered that kind of thing in the past? I crossed my fingers—literally—at this reassuring thought. And then just not to take any unnecessary chances, I also crossed my legs. (But in a ladylike manner, of course—at the ankles.) And if you want the truth, I'd done such a fine job of brainwashing myself that I'd even have crossed my eyes if I had the least idea of how to go about it.

At any rate, I tried studying my notes for a while, especially the more recent entries, but I was too focused on the telephone to make much headway. I found myself rereading the same paragraphs again and again. When the phone finally rang at around ten-thirty, I pounced on it. But it was only my neighbor Barbara Gleason inquiring if I was free for dinner that night. I wasn't. (Al Bonaventure, remember?)

There was another call only minutes later. This time, though, it was my gynecologist's nurse. Was I aware, she asked in this irritating, nasal voice, that I had a twelve o'clock appointment with Doctor—she said the word with a capital "D"—on Tuesday? I was.

I let another half hour go by before I finally decided I'd been patient with Nick Michaels long enough. Or as patient as I knew how to be, anyway. My hand was already on the receiver when it occurred to me that all three flight attendants had mentioned something about working on a Friday. Most probably, I realized, the crew followed a set schedule. The copilot was no doubt a few thousand feet in the air just then—if he hadn't already landed in Nassau, that is. But to make certain, I dialed his number. Seconds later I slammed down the phone in frustration. His answering machine had merely stated the obvious— that Nick Michaels wasn't at home. Still and all, though, I concluded that he must be flying today. And I resigned myself to waiting until Saturday, at the very earliest, to talk to him. With this more or less settled in my mind now, I took another stab at my notes.

I'd been bent over the file for close to an hour when Jackie buzzed to ask what I was doing for lunch. I told her I was meeting with a client out of the office.

Well, all right, so this wasn't precisely the truth. But there was just no way that I could sit across the table from her knowing I was concealing the fact of my date that very evening with Derwin's friend. Maybe I'd do some browsing at lunchtime and then pay a visit to Little Angie's, where I'd try burying my angst (with regard to the murder) and my conscience (with regard to Jackie) in tomato sauce, anchovies, and mozzarella served on top of the thinnest, crispiest pizza crust in the five boroughs.

Once I got a load of myself in the ladies' room mirror a short time afterward, however, I immediately revised my agenda.

I suppose I should have realized I wasn't at my most attractive that morning, since I seemed to be getting some rather peculiar looks from just about everyone who walked by my cubicle. Pat Sullivan actually did a double take. And Ben Seaton, one of the senior members of the firm, smiled weakly and—when he thought he was out of eyesight range—raised his eyebrows about three inches. Plus this young punk of a law clerk out-and-out smirked at me.

Face-to-face now with what had prompted these reactions, I recoiled. My head looked like it had about a dozen pipe cleaners sticking out all over it. It didn't take any giant brain to figure out that during the course of my nonproductive reading, I'd been unconsciously plaiting my hair—a brand-new habit that would immediately and forevermore be dispensed with, I assure you.

At any rate, I put in an emergency phone call now to Emaline, my hairdresser, whose one recommendation is that her shop is only a few blocks from the office. After a couple of heart-wrenching pleas, instantly followed by some unremitting wheedling, I finally got her to agree to squeeze me in between her "dye job from Long Island" and her "haircut from Edison, New Jersey." Which customer designations, by the way, I have long suspected of being Emaline's version of name-dropping. Ten to one, neither woman even had to travel from the West

Side to avail herself of Emaline's less than inspired ministrations.

"You can come in at twelve-forty. But don't be late," she cautioned, "or I might not be able to do you at all. I'm really booked solid today. I even have a couple of ladies coming in from—"

"I'll be there," I told her.

Emaline didn't do such a hot job, and I ended up with a head full of these *things* that kind of resembled corkscrews. And while this was a definite improvement over the pipe cleaner look, it was nonetheless obvious that I'd need plenty of time to work on myself before my seven-thirty date tonight. So at quarter to four I was ready to leave for home.

I wasn't too thrilled about having to pass Jackie's desk on the way out, but thank goodness she was on the phone, deep in conversation.

"Have a nice weekend," I mouthed, attempting to hurry by.

Jackie, however, stopped me in my tracks. "One second, Dez." Then: "Hold it, Derwin," she said, putting her hand over the mouthpiece. And now she turned her attention to me again. "Through for the day?"

"Yes, I've got a couple of . . . quite a few errands to run."

She eyed my new "do" expressionlessly. "You went to the beauty parlor at lunchtime?"

"Uh, yes, my client canceled at the last minute, and my hair was just a mess so . . ." I hunched my shoulders.

"You got anything special going on this weekend?"

I didn't dare answer this directly. "My hair was just a mess," I repeated.

"Well, anyway, have a good one, whatever you do," Jackie told me, smiling benevolently.

Which made me feel even worse.

Chapter 24

Now, under the best of circumstances, I'm pretty much of a tortoise when it comes to getting myself shaped up for an evening out. Tonight, however, thanks to Emaline's corkscrews—along with one or two much more minor crises—I outdid myself. And in the event you have any doubt, I do not mean this in a positive way.

Even cutting my bubble bath down to a measly ten minutes didn't give me that much leeway. As soon as I got out of the tub, I had to apply my makeup. Which, in my case, is no one-two-three job. I require a fair amount of help from Estée and Princess Marcella and a couple of other ladies you might be familiar with. Plus I've just never learned to wield my eye pencil or mascara wand with any great skill. And I'm no whiz with a lipstick brush, either.

Anyway, once I'd done what I could with my face and gotten into some underthings, I concentrated on my dress. I'd already made up my mind to this light blue silk which, regardless of the fact that I'd originally bought it for a date with Bruce, has remained a favorite of mine. And now I examined it closely for any small stains that might heretofore have escaped my notice. The thing is, you see, not being exactly sylphlike, every once in a while some insensitive dolt may refer to me as "fat." But I'm damned if I'll ever give anyone cause to regard me as "fat and sloppy." At any rate, I was relieved to note that the dress was absolutely spotless. But for some reason—maybe it was the Bruce thing—an instant later I had second thoughts about wearing it tonight.

I quickly made a return trip to the closet, this time choosing a two-piece black pique with an asymmetrical top. Which, of course, required I change to a black bra, slip, and panties. Not such a big hassle, right? Except that this little outfit also demanded off-black panty hose. And it wasn't until I had them on that I discovered my off-blacks were actually navy. And—wouldn't you know it?—ditto all the other dark-colored panty hose in my drawer. So I wound up in my original underthings and the light blue silk after all.

And now I had to tackle the *real* chore: unscrewing the corkscrews.

I brushed that hair of mine until my scalp ached and my arm just about dropped off and the clock told me it was 7:05. I had to call it quits then. And while I wasn't completely satisfied with the results of my efforts, I did manage to make quite a bit of headway. (No pun intended.) But it had taken so much time that I had to put on my earrings and bangle bracelet in the elevator.

The cabdriver was a heavyset, balding man of about sixty, with a thick accent and a square, weather-beaten face. His name—according to the sign on the partially open Plexiglas partition separating us—was Sergei Kurov. He scowled at me as I was giving him the address of the restaurant.

"You can keep your Clinton," he said as we lurched away from the curb.

"My *what*?"

"You know what gentleman he should be President?" He allowed a decent interval for a reply, and when none was forthcoming he provided one himself. "Clayton Powell."

Now, I make it a practice to stay away from political discussions with the same determination I avoid asparagus. But I was taken aback, and the response slipped out. "*Adam* Clayton Powell?" I said, referring to Adam Clayton Powell IV, a man who's held local office here in New York but who has never, to my knowledge, been touted by anyone—even his nearest and dearest—for the position of Commander in Chief.

Sergei nodded vigorously. "He is man of courage. Know

how to be leader." And then slowly, to provide maximum impact: "I was general, too. In Russian army."

Oh, for heaven's sake! He means Colin *Powell!*

"You no believe, huh? You wait. I show you."

"No, no, I believe you," I assured him quickly.

But about a minute later, when he was stopped for a red light, Sergei leaned over and thrust a half-bare arm in front of the opening in the partition. "See? You take look."

A deep scar ran almost the complete length of his forearm. "I get two operations," he informed me proudly after I'd had sufficient time for an inspection. "Three bullets I have. From Afghanistan. One doctor tell me I going to lose arm even."

"Uh, I'm glad to see he was mistaken."

"You believe now, huh?"

"Yes, of course," I said, although it was just as possible Sergei here had gotten those bullets robbing the Russian equivalent of a convenience store.

Horns were honking impatiently at this point, the light having changed to green by now. A woman who had to switch lanes to get around our taxi pulled alongside to apply a few adjectives to Sergei that they don't even use on *NYPD Blue.* Following which she suggested that he would be better suited to piloting a kiddy car.

Sergei promptly retrieved his arm and, practically throwing himself across the front seat to the passenger side, utilized the open window to acknowledge the lady with a gesture involving his middle finger. Then he immediately dismissed her from mind. "Russian doctors," he groused to me as the cab shot forward. "What they know?"

We drove the rest of the way in silence, and Sergei managed to find the restaurant without taking so much as one wrong turn.

But if I thought he'd abandoned politics, I was mistaken.

"So you vote for Clayton Powell next time, huh?" he said, swiveling around to collect the fare.

"If he runs, maybe I will."

Ready to make my exit now, I tugged on the door handle,

but the door wouldn't budge. And then I realized that Sergei had locked me in the cab!

"No 'maybe,'" he declared sternly.

This was ridiculous. But what could I do? "All right, I'll vote for him." Sergei was regarding me skeptically, so I added, "I promise." It was, thank goodness, my open sesame.

Needless to say, though, I got as far away from that curb as fast as my under-utilized legs would carry me.

I tell you, as often as not, taking a taxi in this city turns into a singular experience.

Lee Wong's was a light, airy restaurant decorated in soft peach with green accents. Huge potted plants in shiny silver containers were strategically placed throughout the room, imparting a lush, tropical note to the surroundings. The chairs here, I noted, were large and comfortable looking and the tables spaced far enough apart to make it impossible to play kneesies with a neighbor—an activity I was happy to forego. All in all, the place gave the impression of being relaxed and uncrowded, even though almost every table was occupied.

The maitre d' led me toward the back of the room, where a smiling Al Bonaventure was already seated. He jumped up quickly. "Desiree! We meet at last," he proclaimed with mock drama, holding out a hand so huge it might have made two of mine. In fact, everything about this man—from his height (easily six two) to his shoulders (which were out to *there*) to his even white teeth—seemed oversized. And also slightly intimidating. At least at first.

Sitting down now, I was able to get an up-close look at his eyes, which were positively the warmest shade of brown—the color, in fact, not too dissimilar from the shade of his thick, straight hair. He looked like a teddy bear, I decided. A *great big* teddy bear. I was certain that lots of women must find Al very attractive. And even on this short an acquaintanceship I was a little sorry that my need to nurture kept me from being one of them.

Over drinks he mentioned how nervous he'd been when he

phoned me all those months ago. "You were the first woman I asked out after my wife and I separated. You have no idea how long it took me to summon the courage to pick up that phone. After being married for eighteen years, I was way out of practice." He grinned now. "And I suppose my being a natural coward wasn't much help, either."

"I didn't exactly make things easy for you, did I?"

"I wouldn't put it like that. You tried your best. You were very pleasant, very polite. But I could tell you weren't that thrilled to hear from me."

"Umm, I—"

"Please. Don't explain. For whatever reason, you weren't up for anything like that at the time. When you told me you'd get in touch with me once you'd wrapped up the case you were working on—well, let's just say I would have been very surprised to hear from you."

"You must have been totally floored when I called you Sunday."

He smiled broadly. "Totally." And then: "Would it embarrass you if I asked what prompted you to change your mind about meeting me?"

"I'm not quite certain myself. I'd held on to your phone number—I'm not even sure why—and I happened to come across it that morning. And on an impulse, I just decided to use it."

"I'm glad you did," he responded quietly.

And you know what? So was I.

We had a lovely dinner. The food was really outstanding. And the conversation was easy and relaxed. I found Al to be a friendly, genuinely nice person. Not only that, but I couldn't remember the last time I'd met a man who looked right in my eyes when he talked to me. And how many people do you know who listen—*really* listen—to what you have to say?

I'll tell you something. In spite of the fact that I'm normally such a piss-poor judge of character, this was one instance where I'd have been willing to bet on me.

Al took me home in a cab and insisted on seeing me upstairs. He opened the door and then, handing me back my keys, bent down to buss my cheek.

"I'll call you soon," he said.

Chapter 25

The first thing I thought when I woke up on Saturday was that I couldn't remember when I'd had a better date. But then, it was a challenge to remember the last time I'd had *any* kind of date.

Don't misunderstand me, though; I haven't exactly been devastated by this lack of male companionship. While it can certainly be pleasant to have a man in your life, this is not something I *require*. Unlike some women of my acquaintance—my friend Pat Martucci immediately springs to mind—I'm quite capable of managing solo, thank you. After all, it's not as though I can't open my own doors or take out the garbage myself. Still, I had to admit that I wouldn't really object to hearing from Al Bonaventure again.

It occurred to me as I was washing up a few minutes later that Al reminded me of Stuart Mason, who is my accountant and also a very old friend, and who, once upon a time, was a little more than that. What I'm trying to say is that Stuart and I were physically close for a while. Not that we were ever romantically involved, however; the physical part just gave an added dimension to the friendship, that's all. At any rate, Stuart eventually met and fell for this Gretchen person (and what kind of a name is Gretchen, anyhow?), and although I do miss being with him, I'm happy about that. I mean, since neither of us ever had *a thing* for each other, it would be selfish of me to feel any differently, wouldn't it? Anyhow, while I still see Stuart, these days it's only at tax time.

But about Al's reminding me of Stuart . . .

As I was having breakfast, I kept trying to pinpoint the reason for it. Aside from their both being tall, the two men are hardly alike in appearance. Stuart's blond and not anywhere near as large as Al is. He's also more conventionally good-looking. I quickly concluded that whatever similarity there was had little, if anything, to do with their physical makeup; it was more a matter of character and personality.

For starters, both Stuart and Al are intelligent and well-read. And they have a very keen sense of humor, too. Also, like Al, Stuart is a really good listener. Plus they're both decent human beings—which, in my experience, is even more of a rarity among eligible single men than attentiveness. (As you can tell, I hadn't wavered at all in my conviction that, with Al, my judgment was on the mark for once.)

But even after drawing these parallels, I wasn't satisfied. And then as I was finishing my second slice of French toast, it finally trickled through to me that the *real* likeness between the two lay in my reaction to them.

You see, as much as I had cared for Stuart and treasured his friendship and even enjoyed our more intimate moments together, I'd been aware from the beginning that the relationship would never evolve into anything serious. No matter how much either of us might have wished it. I was certain of this with Al, too. And inexplicably, for an instant the thought brought me close to tears.

Why worry, though? I ruminated as I was clearing the dishes away. *Who knows if he'll even call again? And anyway, maybe it would be just as well if he didn't.*

Which took me right back to Stuart. After all, Stuart wasn't my type, either. And I know I wasn't his. But that didn't stop us from sharing some wonderful times together, did it? And why shouldn't that be enough in itself? You don't have to fall in lo—

The phone put an abrupt end to this angst-producing postmortem on what had been a thoroughly delightful evening.

As soon as I lifted the receiver—and before I could even get out the second syllable of my "Hello"—I heard Ellen's "So?" There was no need to ask what she meant. I'd kept my forthcoming date with Al Bonaventure a secret from her for almost three days, but that was as long as I was able to hold out. "How did it go last night?" she demanded.

"It went very well."

"Do you like him?"

"Yes, he seems to be a really nice person."

"I'm not talking that kind of 'like,' " Ellen responded impatiently. "Do you *like him* like him?"

"Oh, for heaven's sake! I just met the man."

"Is he good-looking?"

"In a way. He's about six two and—"

"Uh-oh."

"What's that for?"

"I don't really have to explain it, do I? Honestly. You and your penchant for skinny little dorks!"

I smiled at the "skinny"—*this* from a girl who's the width of a pencil.

"You know, I'll never understand your taste," Ellen ranted on. "Not if I live a thousand years." And then she sighed. "That maternal fixation of yours is such a detriment to your love life, Aunt Dez. Why don't you just adopt a kid and stop ruining things with the men you meet?"

"Hey, there's no reason to be so preachy. It's not as if I've even been getting the opportunity to ruin anything. What men have I met lately, anyhow?"

"Exactly my point." I didn't have to see the self-satisfied look on Ellen's face to know that it was there. And now she added, "Promise you'll do me a favor, will you?"

"What's that?" I inquired cautiously.

"Just give the guy a chance. Okay?"

"Okay. That is, if I ever hear from him again."

"Oh, you will." My niece—a.k.a. Little Mary Sunshine—apparently had no problem in ascertaining this from the next-to-nothing she knew about the evening. For good measure, she even tagged on a "Wait and see."

Immediately after this conversation with Ellen, I gathered up my courage—what little there was of it—and dialed Jackie's apartment.

Part of me was wishing she wouldn't be there, while an equal part of me was hoping she'd be in so I could make my confession and get it over with.

Five rings later—just as I was about to hang up—there was a breathless "hello?"

"Hi. It's Desiree, Jackie. I was beginning to think you weren't home."

"I wasn't. I just this second got back from the cleaners." And then predictably: "Is everything all right?"

"Of course. I, uh, wanted to speak to you about something, that's all."

She was instantly wary. "They're not selling the firm, are they?"

"What firm?"

"Gilbert and Sullivan."

"Lord, no. Why would you think that?"

"I heard a rumor about a year ago."

A year ago! That is s-o-o Jackie! "Really? You never mentioned it to me."

"I didn't want you to worry. Anyway, what did you want to talk to me about?"

"It's about Al Bonaventure."

"He called!" It was more of a squeal than a mere exclamation.

"Well, uh, no. That is, not lately. I called *him*."

"Terrific! When are you going to see him?"

"Umm . . . last night."

There was no sound on the other end of the line. And then Jackie asked with a lethal softness, "Did you say last night?"

"That's right," I admitted sheepishly.

"You mean the two of you have already been out together?" There was ice in her voice now. "When did you make the call, anyway?"

"Sunday."

"I presume you're talking about a week ago tomorrow."

"Yes. Look, Jackie, I didn't tell you before because I didn't want to make a big deal of it. I figured it would be better to just wait and see how things turned out."

"You think I would have treated it like a big deal? Sometimes, Desiree, I wonder if you even know me," she sniffed. "I'm not like that at all."

With that squeal of hers only moments behind us, I had to laugh—but, of course, I didn't dare. I swallowed the sound that was building up in my throat. "You're taking this wrong; it's certainly not a criticism," I explained. I spoke slowly—my best chance of avoiding any verbal pitfalls. "I'm grateful that you care enough to be excited for me, Jackie. But that's just it. You're so anxious that I find someone—someone nice, I mean—that you'd have been anticipating this date all week if I'd said anything in advance. And you would have been that much more disappointed if things didn't go well."

"And how *did* they go?" Jackie responded after a brief pause, her tone more cordial now. Apparently, I'd succeeded in placating her somewhat. Either that, or it was a case of curiosity triumphing over anger.

"I had a great time."

"You liked him, then?"

"Yes, I did."

"Didn't I tell you you would?" If she sounded impossibly smug now, well, I suppose she was entitled. And at least she didn't ask if I *liked him* liked him.

It was a relief getting that off my chest. And actually, things with Jackie hadn't really gone that badly, I thought. In retrospect, I even considered it possible that if I'd mentioned the date to her earlier, she would have managed to keep her cool somehow.

Nah, not Jackie, I concluded an instant later. *As soon as she heard Al and I had made plans to go out, she'd have started phoning the caterers.*

The call from Nick Michaels came at four-thirty, as I was about to leave for the supermarket.

He apologized for not getting back to me sooner. But he'd just returned from Nassau, he said.

I asked when I could meet with him.

"How's tomorrow night?" Michaels suggested. "My place. About nine-thirty would be good. Is that okay with you?"

"Sure."

"I live in the Village—on Jane Street." He gave me the address.

We were already exchanging good-byes when he put in hurriedly, "Listen, I have this appointment to meet some friends for dinner at seven, and in case I should be a little detained—although I can't imagine why I would be—let yourself in, turn on the air conditioner, and make yourself at home. The apartment's 2-E, and the key's under the mat."

We were at the good-bye stage again when Michaels had another afterthought. "By the way, there's a bar in the living room wall unit and a wine rack in the compartment right below the bar. Mixers are in the fridge. Oh, the wall unit also has a TV and a stereo, and you'll find some magazines on the end table."

Then he added reassuringly, "But don't worry. I'll be back in plenty of time."

Chapter 26

My clue should have been all those explicit instructions as to what could be found where. Of course, anyone else would have had a pretty fair idea of what to expect from the invitation alone—I mean, Michaels's telling me to just walk in and make myself at home. But I was so anxious to meet with this man I hadn't really paid attention to either of these things. Even if I had, though, I don't think I could have anticipated how late it would be before Nick Michaels finally showed.

More than an hour before, I'd taken what was starting to feel like permanent possession of the copilot's blue tweed living room sofa. And since then I'd been fighting to stay awake. Twice I had to rouse myself. And twice more the telephone did it for me.

A Myrna asked my absent host to dinner next week via the answering machine. And a furious Bobbie Jo left the message that she never wanted to hear from him again—that is, unless he could explain what he was doing at Indochine's last night nuzzling that blond bimbo.

Anyhow, each time I came out of my stupor I would focus halfheartedly on the made-for-TV movie I'd turned on earlier. And each time I'd receive further confirmation that it was no less boring than it had been last year, when I'd watched it initially. And this was the best of the television offerings that night, too. (I swear, the more channels they give you, the worse the choices.) I'd had to rule out the stereo immediately, though, since I couldn't figure out how to work it. And the magazines went by the boards as soon as I saw that they consisted of two *Sports Illustrated*s and four *Playboy*s. I'm no sports fan. And as for the *Playboy*s, not being a masochist, I try my damnedest to avoid looking at women who have legs that go up to their armpits—and without so much as a speck of cellulite on them, too. (Although I do like to think that at least some of those ladies contribute to keeping all the retouchers out there off the unemployment line.)

At any rate, the movie had just ended, and I contemplated leaving—as I had fifteen minutes before. And fifteen minutes before that. Once again, however, I rejected the idea because of my eagerness to question Michaels. And besides, by now I'd already put in so much time here that I felt I had to protect my investment. I checked my watch, then gnashed my teeth together: 10:37.

It was maybe a minute after this that Nick Michaels came home.

His presence was announced by three loud raps on the door, immediately followed by an "It's me, Desiree—Nick. Let me in."

I opened the door to a short, thin man with medium-dark hair that spilled onto his forehead with what looked to me like deliberate casualness. "I'm so sorry I'm late," he murmured, a sheepish expression on his small, narrow face. "I hope you'll forgive me, Dez."

In view of the fact he'd kept me waiting so long that my buns had gotten numb, I really resented the familiarity. "I was about to give up on you, Mr. Michaels," I told him.

But if he was aware that the "Mr." was intended to make a statement (although I wasn't quite sure what it was myself), Michaels blithely ignored it. "You have to call me Nick. It is so written," he said playfully as he trailed me over to the sofa. "The restaurant screwed up on our reservation, and it took forever to get a table. And then the service was just so damn slow. . . . But I'd have walked out without even finishing the main course—and prime ribs are a passion of mine—if anyone had mentioned that you have red hair. Redheads being an even greater passion of mine—particularly if they're pretty."

Oh, swell. He was one of *those*. It didn't exactly surprise me—not after Donna Wolf's rundown on him. Which had, of course, been reinforced only a little while ago by Bobbie Jo's accusatory message. Still, seeing Michaels in the flesh was throwing me a bit. The man wasn't nearly attractive enough to play an acceptable Casanova. Not in my opinion, at least.

Anyway, his flirting only succeeded in making me more irritated than ever. I hastily reminded myself that it was possible Michaels might have some key information for me. So plunking myself back down on the seat I'd warmed up for over an hour, I willed a smile to my lips. "Well, I'm glad I didn't separate you from your prime ribs," I told him sweetly.

He was standing in front of me then, and I noted that his white shirt had defied tonight's unbearable humidity, looking as crisp and immaculate as if he'd just put it on. I took some perverse satisfaction, though, from the gravy spots that adorned one leg of his well-fitting, sharply creased chinos.

"Have you had anything to drink?" he asked.

"I didn't really want anything."

"How about now, though? I've got a pretty well stocked bar." He crossed over to the large fruitwood wall unit and opened one of the doors, then stepped aside so I could view the contents. The compartment contained more than two dozen liquor bottles, while displayed on the two shelves directly above the bottles were an ice bucket, bar tools, and four or five sets of glasses in varying sizes and shapes. "We've got bourbon and scotch and gin and rye. Also, Dubonnet, rum, cordials—anything you like." It was said with obvious pride. "Or, if you prefer . . ." Michaels bent to open another section of the unit, this one revealing a built-in wine rack. "Voilà! Here we have red wines, white wines, rosés, champagne. . . ." He turned to face me. "So? What's your pleasure, madam?"

"Could I have a cup of coffee?"

"*Coffee* the lady asks for?" Eyes opening wide in feigned horror, he slapped his cheek. After which he shook his head as if in sadness. "You are a terrible disappointment to me, Desiree

Shapiro." A couple of seconds' pause. "But you were only kidding, right?"

"No, I'd really love some—if it's not too much trouble."

"Well, that's the last time I stock up my bar for you. But okay," Michaels said, grimacing, "if you'll settle for instant, I suppose you can have your damn coffee." And then he grinned. It was a charming, elfin grin that completely transformed what until that moment I'd regarded as an almost homely face. And now it was a lot easier to figure out how Nick Michaels had won his stripes as a ladies' man.

He was gone less than a minute when he poked his head back in. "I'm sorry. A friend was over this morning, and sh— this friend must have used up what was left of the coffee."

I thought of Bobby Jo's telephone call again. *I'll bet that friend was a blond bimbo.*

"How about a Coke?" Michaels suggested.

"That'll be fine."

He was soon back with my Coke, which he set down on the lamp table next to me. Then he settled into one of the tan-and-blue-plaid club chairs facing the sofa.

"You're not having anything to drink yourself?" I inquired, reaching for the soda.

"If you'd seen what I consumed at dinner you wouldn't ask," he informed me, chuckling.

"There's always something soft," I reminded him, tapping my glass.

He manufactured a shudder. "God forbid."

"What is it you do drink?"

"Bourbon. Neat. I only keep all that other stuff on hand for sissies."

I took a couple of healthy swallows of the Coke—I hadn't even realized how thirsty I was. And then I said, "Do you think you could answer some questions for me now?"

"Must I? Can't it wait a few minutes?"

"It's getting late."

He glanced at his watch. "I suppose it is." And now he turned serious. "I liked Cheryl very much, you know. She was a real good kid. You think that someone deliberately pushed her off that platform, don't you?"

"Yes, I do."

"Look, I seriously doubt that I have any information that would be of use to you. But, well, who knows? And assuming you're right about how Cheryl died, nothing would make me happier than helping you find her killer.

"So go ahead, Desiree Shapiro, ask away."

Chapter 27

"What can you tell me about the three flight attendants who worked with Cheryl?"

The copilot smiled. "That's a pretty broad question. What is it you'd like to know?"

"Well, why don't we start with which of them would have been most likely, in your opinion, to engage in a profitable, if illegal little sideline?"

"You're really convinced one of them was involved in transporting drugs, aren't you?"

"I gather Laura didn't tell you, then."

"About what?"

I related the purported contents of the last telephone call Laura Downey had received from the victim.

For a moment Michaels was stunned. "Then Cheryl's husband has been telling the truth all along."

I nodded in response.

"I wonder why Laura didn't mention that call to me."

"I don't think she said anything to anyone about it. Because that phone call means that one of her two closest friends is a drug smuggler and—although Laura refuses to admit to the linkage—a killer. Either that, or this dual honor is one Laura can claim for herself."

"Oh, man," Michaels mumbled, running his hand through his hair. "This is so hard to even imagine."

"Nevertheless, it's true. So please. Any information you can give me on the three of them . . ."

For a brief time Michaels sat there deep in thought. Then he said, "You asked me who I considered the most likely smug-

gler, and the truth is, I haven't got an answer for you. It seems
so out of character for all of them."

"I don't suppose you ever witnessed any sort of suspicious
meeting over in Nassau?" I put to him, although with very little hope of a positive response.

"Never."

"That's what I figured." (Like I said, I hadn't held out much
hope.) "Look, I'm particularly interested in finding out who
might have had a need for additional funds. But I'd also appreciate your filling me in on whatever else you know about these
people."

"I'm not sure what I can tell you. But I'll certainly do my
best."

"That's good enough."

"I guess we might as well dispose of Laura first—bad choice
of words. What I mean is, since we were just talking about her."

"Might as well," I agreed. "Would you happen to be aware
of any money problems there?"

"No. And besides, her mother's married to a very wealthy
man, so I assume that if Laura ever did require some ready
cash, she wouldn't have too much trouble laying her hands on
it."

"But you have no knowledge of anything occurring in her
life that could have made this necessary?"

"Uh-uh." And unexpectedly he laughed, and there was mis-
chief in his eyes. "Unless it was to support the baby."

"What baby?"

He was still laughing. "The one she left up in Toronto."

I sat up a little straighter. "I'd like to hear about that."

"It was only a little joke, Dez. Somebody got some ridiculous idea last year that Laura was pregnant."

"And she wasn't?"

"Definitely not." But one look at my expression and
Michaels knew he wasn't going to get off the hook that easily.
"All right," he said, just the least bit impatient now, "I suppose
the whole thing really started at Bloomingdale's."

"Bloomingdale's?" I parroted.

"Just pay attention, will you?" he chastised jokingly. "One day last fall Alice Thorne—she's the flight attendant Cheryl replaced—happened to bump into Laura in the lingerie department at Bloomingdale's. Laura was over by the cash register, paying for a couple of bras. A couple of really *big* bras. Laura noticed Alice staring at them, and she mentioned something about picking them up for her aunt. I heard that the two of them even kidded around a little about the size."

"And this is what led Alice to believe Laura was pregnant?" I demanded, my eyes widening in disbelief.

"No, of course not. But a couple of weeks afterward Laura broke her leg, and she went up to Toronto to stay with her mother for a while. Well, she had some complications—I understand the bones didn't knit properly—and it was close to three months before she came home. When she did, there was quite a bit more to her than there'd been when she left. In fact, I couldn't get over how she filled out her uniform. You see, until then Laura was really skinny. I used to tease her about it, too—I like my women a little more well-padded." He leered at me now, manipulating his eyebrows up and down à la Groucho Marx. But I realized it was intended to be comical. And it was. And I smiled. Then Michaels added, "I suppose it was stupid of me, though—giving her the business like that."

"You're right," I told him lightly, so as not to sound too judgmental. But a moment later I couldn't stop myself from throwing in, "Not to say unkind."

"Go ahead, make me feel even worse. Anyhow, it was when Laura returned from Canada that Alice began speculating about her having been pregnant.

"I should make it clear," Michaels inserted here, "that Alice wasn't a bad kid, but she was kind of a dingbat—a dingbat with an exceptionally active imagination. She'd always suspected that there was a little something going on between Laura and Chet. And now, for some dopey reason known only to Alice herself, she came up with this notion that maybe the weight gain was the result of a pregnancy. That maybe Laura hadn't broken her leg at all but had taken off for Toronto in order to have Chet's baby in secret. And then she remembered Laura's Bloomingdale's purchase. And she got it into her head that in all likelihood Laura had bought those 36Ds—or whatever—for herself. Well, Alice came to regard those bras as a sort of proof. The more she thought about it, the surer she was that Laura was beginning to look pretty zaftig even before she left for Canada. Oh. I'm assuming you know what the word means."

"Zaftig? Don't be silly. My name is Shapiro, isn't it?" I didn't, however, feel it necessary to inform him that I'd only acquired this name through marriage.

"That's right, I forgot."

"And *had* Laura begun to add any extra pounds before she left?"

Michaels chuckled. "Not that I noticed. And I would have noticed. Trust me, this is the one area where I'm an expert."

I didn't doubt it for an instant.

"And not that anyone else noticed, either," he added.

"Did the others place any stock in Alice's theory?"

"Are you kidding? Everyone else knew there was nothing between Laura and Chet. While Chet thinks Laura's a great person, he's never been the least attracted to her—and vice versa. But none of us could disabuse Alice of her dumb idea. She even used the fact that Laura had discouraged her friends from flying to Canada to visit her as an indication she was with child." He smiled wryly at this. "The truth of the matter, though, is that Laura just didn't want anyone to bother making the trip.

"At any rate, we were all concerned that Alice's nutsiness might get back to Laura. So I finally drew Alice aside one day and told her something the rest of the crew wasn't even aware of, something Chet wanted kept confidential: He'd been living with another woman that entire year.

"I guess you could say I betrayed a trust, but the way I looked at it, it was for a good cause."

"So you convinced Alice she'd been wrong about the baby thing?"

"I wouldn't go that far. But I think I managed to plant a

doubt in her mind, at least. Because from then on, she put a lid on it. Whatever suspicions she still had, she kept to herself."

"So, as far as you know," I concluded now, "Laura didn't have any pressing need for money."

"Right. Not any more than the rest of us. Most likely less, actually. However, if *need* is the criterion, I could probably qualify as your prime suspect."

Recalling what I'd heard about this man's fondness for gambling, I thought this could very possibly be true. "But Laura does have expensive tastes, doesn't she?" I persisted.

"You mean the jewelry?"

"What jewelry?"

"Oh, she collects good jewelry, *expensive* jewelry. She says it's a smart investment. She rarely wears any of it, though. Everything pretty much stays in the vault, while she walks around in the cheaper stuff."

"What about her furniture? Some of those pieces look like they could be antiques."

"Maybe they are. But you can't prove it by me." And then he added firmly, "Look, I've told you all I can think of about Laura."

"All right. Let's move on to Hank. How does he stand financially?"

"Well, I suppose Hank could have used some money a while back when his lover left him for another, wealthier man. Incidentally, Hank's gay. But I suppose you already know that."

"Yes, I do. And I understand he was in a bad way after the breakup."

Michaels nodded. "He was even talking suicide for a time; I was damn worried about him—we all were. The days we weren't flying, I'd call him almost every night just to make sure he was okay. We'd get together here in town every so often, too, and take in a movie or just go out for a bite so he could vent a little. But I wasn't the only one who was trying to look after him. Not by a long shot. Laura and Donna—Cheryl wasn't working at Bahamian yet—were *really* there for him. I wouldn't be surprised if those two ladies saved his life."

It was at this moment that I decided that Nick here—I suddenly found myself referring to him in my head by his given name—was a lot more sensitive a person than I would have suspected. "Do you think Hank's finally reconciled to the loss of his lover?"

"Well, he doesn't really talk about him anymore."

"That's not what I asked you," I reminded him softly.

The answer came reluctantly. "Okay, from some offhand remarks Hank's made fairly recently, it wouldn't surprise me if he still cares for Paul a little. But he's never actually said anything of the kind. Honestly. This is only my own impression. And, believe it or not, Dez, I've been wrong before." And with this, he broke into another of those very engaging grins of his.

"But if Hank did want to get back together with his ex," I plodded on, "an additional income wouldn't hurt, would it?"

"No, I suppose not," Nick was forced to concede. And now he opened his mouth as if to elaborate, then promptly closed it again.

"What were you going to say?"

"Nothing. Nothing relevant, that is."

"Please. Let me decide that."

"All right. But this was over a year ago—when Paul first moved out. Hank talked about getting a second job at that time. He wanted to be able to afford a nicer apartment, a place that this prick Paul—excuse the language, Desiree—would consider more suitable for someone of the station to which he was aspiring."

"Hank wasn't able to find anything? Job-wise, I mean."

"No. But I don't think he really looked, either. Or if he did, he wasn't putting that much effort into it. I never saw him checking the want ads or making any phone calls. He never mentioned going on any interviews, either. And as I said, I spent a fair amount of time with him in those days, so I think I would have been aware of it if Hank was into any serious job-hunting. I imagine he began to appreciate that getting part-time employment wouldn't be any help at all in coaxing that little money-grubber back to Queens. That would require really big bucks."

And now, realizing he'd just inadvertently supplied Hank with a dandy motive for doing a bit of smuggling on the side, Nick hurriedly attempted some damage control. "Listen, a year is a long time to carry a torch. And while it's conceivable Hank isn't over Paul completely, his feelings are nowhere near as intense as they used to be."

"Let's say for a minute that you're right about that," I countered. "The thing is, though, who's to say when the perpetrator's affiliation with El Puerco started? It might go back a year, you know."

"Look, Hank's far too moral a person to traffic in drugs, regardless of how much he may have wanted Paul in his life again. Also, he faced up to what Paul is a long time ago, right at the beginning. What you have to understand is that even at the height of his feelings for Paul, he's always been aware that no matter how much he might be able to give the little shit, Paul would only stick around until he found a new love who could give him more. And, morals aside, Hank's too smart to risk jail time for someone like that."

"You've met this Paul?"

"No, but I've heard enough about him so I can hate the man without having had any direct contact with him."

"Can you give me his last name?"

"It's Garay." Even saying this brought a furrow to Nick's forehead.

"Any idea how I can get in touch with him?"

"He's living with a stockbroker name of Wilson Cummings. Cummings owns a townhouse in the East Sixties somewhere. I don't have his number, though."

"That's okay; I can get it."

"What do you say we move on to Donna now?" Nick suggested here. "I've just about shot my load when it comes to Hank."

"Of course. What can you tell me about Donna's situation?"

"Basically, Donna's a happy-go-lucky kind of person, but

the poor kid has her share of problems—although she tries not to let things get to her. To start with, there's the fact that she's a single parent and the baby's father is a real scuzz. The guy cut out when she became pregnant, and he's never contributed a single cent to the raising of his own son."

"What about Donna's mother? Does she help out financially?"

Nick screwed up his narrow face, the corners of his mouth turned down in distaste. "I would assume that 'Mommie Dearest' lends a hand whenever and wherever needed."

"Have you ever met her?"

"Once. And she's a kick and a half." He said this in a tone heavy with sarcasm.

"In what way?"

"Well, let me tell you what I know of her. Right after Donna gave birth, Hank and I stopped over at her apartment with a gift—Donna was still living in her old place then. Anyway, Mrs. Wolf was there, and at first Hank and I were both very impressed with how gracious the woman was." Here, Nick's voice shifted to a falsetto. "Can I get you fellows a drink? Or maybe you'd rather have some coffee. How about a sandwich? Oh, I just baked a delicious blueberry cake, and I'll be awfully disappointed if you don't at least try a piece."

I couldn't keep from laughing. The man was quite a mimic.

"Before we left there, though, I'd revised my opinion considerably," he went on.

"Why's that?"

"She was *too much*. Mrs. Wolf is a lot more than just pleasant; the woman's positively cloying. She was fawning all over us. And I don't mean that she was being flirtatious, either. It was as if she considered herself an earth mother. At least, this was my take on her. That's not what really bothered me, though."

"That being—?"

"The way she kept after Donna about how to handle the baby. It wasn't merely suggesting or even instructing. It was almost like Donna was the puppet, and she was pulling the

strings. I got the very strong impression that if Lettie Wolf—
she insisted we call her Lettie—could have grabbed that infant
from her daughter and nursed him herself, she wouldn't have
hesitated for a second. I recall thinking, 'Uh-oh, poor Donna's
got herself a real big headache with Mama here.'"

"What about Mr. Wolf—or isn't there one?"

"He died when Donna was very young. He didn't leave a for-
tune by any means, from what I've heard, but it was enough to
allow his wife and daughter to live fairly comfortably."

"Tell me, did Hank share your opinion of Mrs. Wolf?"

"Not entirely. He thought she was a little overbearing, but he
didn't see her as being the piranha that I did. However, I think
that time has proved me right." And with a straight face:
"Which, of course, was to be expected."

"Okay, stop patting yourself on the back, will you? How
were you proved right?"

"Well, this one afternoon in Nassau, Donna appeared to be
kind of upset—and this was really unusual for her. It was rare
that you even saw a frown on her face. Anyway, I persuaded
her to come into the bar with me for a drink, and after a little
time and a fair amount of scotch she owned up to having some
trouble with her mother.

"It seems Donna had a vacation coming, and Mrs. Wolf had
been after her to go away. She kept insisting that Donna could
use a rest, that it would be a chance for her to meet interesting
people—you know, all that stuff. She even offered to help pay
for the trip. But Donna had no desire to jet off somewhere; she
wanted to spend her vacation at home with her son. The mother
kept pushing her, though. And without a letup. It had reached
the point where it was driving Donna crazy.

"And then before I had a chance to get a word out, Donna
said that she knew I was going to tell her that her mother had
her best interests at heart and that she should be grateful to her
for helping so much with Rusty.

"Naturally, I assured Donna that she wouldn't be hearing
anything of the kind. Not from me. I told her I'd seen for myself how proprietary her mother was with the baby. And that's

when Donna admitted that lately she'd had the feeling that her
own mother was trying to get her out of the picture so she could
be the one to bring up the boy."

"Just when was all this?"

"It must have been when Rusty was only a couple of months
old." And now Nick grinned impishly. "I remember thinking
that there wasn't much of a wait before my initial, highly per-
ceptive assessment was confirmed."

"Spoken with your usual humility," I remarked dryly. "But
to proceed: Did Donna mention anything else to you?"

"As a matter of fact, she did. She had to get away from her
mother, she said. As soon as she could swing it financially, she
was planning to move out of state."

"Has she talked to you about this since then?"

"Oh, yeah. The following morning she took it all back. She
asked me to forget what she'd told me. She informed me that
she didn't mean anything she'd confided to me in the bar. She
claimed she hadn't been feeling well the last couple of days and
that this is what must have triggered all of that 'bitching and
moaning'—her words, not mine. According to this latest bulletin, Lettie was now absolutely *the best*. 'I really don't know
how I could possibly manage without her,' Donna said. And
ever since that time I've never heard her utter a single com-
plaint against Mama."

Nick sat back in his chair then, a subtle way of letting me
know this was all I would be getting on Donna.

I took the hint. "Well, I guess that's about it," I said, rising.

Nick stood up, too. "I suppose you're aware that you made
me feel like a complete louse tonight."

"Why?"

"You've managed to induce me to sit here and rat on three
friends of mine."

"Don't look so worried. As far as I can tell, you haven't
given me anything damning about any of them—and much to
my disappointment, too. Besides, you did this to help catch
Cheryl's killer, remember? And wasn't Cheryl also a friend of
yours?"

"Yes, of course. But these are nice people we're talking about here. I can't quite believe—"

I cut him off. "I know it's hard to accept," I said. "But take my word for it, Nick. One of these 'nice people' of yours is a murderer."

Chapter 28

Nick couldn't be dissuaded from waiting with me for a taxi. "I'm not going to let you stand out there by yourself, so just shut up about it." Which was really very sweet of him—the thought, if not the way it was expressed.

"So . . . uh . . . nothing I told you was of any help to you, then?" he asked as we were walking over to the curb.

"That's not how it works, Nick—anyway, not for me. Maybe you did give me some useful information. But until I put it with whatever else I know about Cheryl's death and then study everything together, I can't be sure one way or the other."

"Well, having just become a Grade A fink, I hope it at least turns out to be worth it."

"Hey, you don't hope it any more than I do," I said, as we continued to stand there talking, both sets of eyes focused on the street. "But at any rate, thanks for your time. You were very patient."

"I enjoyed meeting you, Dez," he told me, energetically signaling for the empty taxi we spotted in the distance. And then just as this relic of a cab stopped in front of us, belching gas fumes: "Look, would it be okay if I called you for dinner sometime?"

"I'm sorry, Nick. But I've been seeing someone for quite a while now. It was a pleasure meeting you, too, though. And I mean that."

"Okay," he said cheerfully, holding the door open for me. "But you're making a mistake."

Well, don't lose any sleep over it, I thought perversely, disappointed that he was taking the rejection in such good spirits.

Not that I wanted him to be devastated or anything, but it wouldn't have killed him to act a *little* let down, at least.

The driver had already begun to pull away from the curb when Nick—shouting now in order to be heard above the rumble of the departing taxi—added, "Maybe I'll still give you a ring one of these days." And then yelling even louder so his words would catch up with me: "In case you have a change of heart!"

I provided the cabdriver with my address, after which I sat back and allowed myself to be floored.

Who would have thought that Nick, of all people, would want to go out with me? Now, I'm not putting myself down. But let's face it, I don't have a prayer of ever making the center spread of *Playboy.* And the guy already had more than his share of female companionship. I mean, I'd been in his apartment less than an hour when I learned of two women who were interested in him. No, make that three. (After all, if she weren't attracted to him, I doubt that the blond bimbo would have gone in for all that nuzzling at Indochine.) And who knew how many women had called the apartment before I arrived there tonight—or how many would be phoning him tomorrow?

He must be years younger than I am, too. Well, maybe not years. But I couldn't deny I had *some* mileage on him.

I grinned at his saying he might give me a call one day. That wouldn't surprise me in the least. I could see this man being persistent as hell when he felt like making the effort.

But much as I liked Nick—and I did—I had no intention of dating him. Ironic, isn't it? I finally meet a nice guy who's just my type—physically, at any rate—and what happens? I have to pass.

What I certainly did not choose to have in my life, however, was a lover whose little black book would have to be a loose-leaf so he could keep adding pages. Plus Nick's reputed addiction to gambling couldn't exactly be termed an attribute, either. But the clincher was the obvious fact that—small and skinny though he was—Nick Michaels needed mothering about as much as I need another inch on my hips.

And speaking of ironies, there was, of course, an even bigger one. As you well know, men haven't exactly been burning up my phone wires of late (or earlier, either, for that matter). And then within days of each other two eligible and appealing men show an interest in me. I felt like Cleopatra, for God's sake.

Cleopatra Shapiro . . . You have to admit it has a ring to it.

On Monday morning I hauled the Manhattan telephone directory out of my desk drawer and looked up Hank Herman's former lover's present lover. (I do hope you can follow that.) I'd pretty much anticipated that the man would have an unlisted telephone, though, so I was really pleased to find a number for a Wilson Cummings on East Sixty-fourth Street.

The phone was answered by a very proper sounding gentleman with a British accent—or someone attempting to emulate a British accent. "Mr. Cummings's residence."

"I wonder if I might speak to Mr. Garay, please."

"May I tell him who's calling?"

Now, this was the tricky part—inducing Garay to come to the phone. "Yes, my name is Desiree Shapiro. Mr. Garay and I have never met. But I'm a private investigator, and an old friend of his is involved in a case I'm working on right now. I'm hoping Mr. Garay may be in a position to verify some facts for me."

"And the name of this friend?"

"I'm sorry. But due to the sensitive nature of the case, I prefer to give that information directly to Mr. Garay."

"I'll see if he's in," I was told in a tone that had just turned at least twenty degrees chillier. "And the name again is Ms.—?"

"Shapiro. Desiree Shapiro. And that's *Mrs.*"

And now I waited. And waited some more. I was beginning to wonder if I should just hang up and try to figure out another way to get to Garay when, sure enough, his curiosity induced him to pick up. "What's this about?" demanded an impatient, gravelly sort of voice.

Rude little shit, isn't he? But you'd never have been able to ascertain my opinion from my manner. "Mr. Paul Garay?" I inquired politely.

"Yeah, that's right. Harris tells me you're investigating a friend of mine. Which one is that?"

"Well, Harris didn't get things precisely right. I'm not investigating your friend; I'm investigating a murder. And your friend happened to be close to the victim. I contacted you because I believe you can substantiate some information I've recently received."

"A murder, huh? No kidding!" Damned if he didn't actually sound pleased. "Now, just who are we talking about?"

"Hank Herman."

"I can tell you practically anything you want to know about Hank. We used to live together."

"Yes. So I've heard."

"Who bought it, anyway?" Garay asked eagerly. In fact, he sounded positively ghoulish.

"A woman named Cheryl Simon, a flight attendant who only recently went to work for Bahamian Air. I'm certain you've never met her."

"Oh." He apparently felt that being acquainted with the deceased would have been a bonus. "Well, go ahead."

"You don't understand. I was hoping we could do this in person, so we'd have a real chance to talk."

"Yeah, you're right. That would be much better," Garay agreed.

"When would it be convenient for you to see me?"

He gave this some thought. "Tomorrow night would be good. Wilson—he's the man I'm living with now—always has dinner with his mother on Tuesday nights, and I don't want him to know anything about this. Y'see, he's pretty straight-laced, so he might not approve of my being involved in any kind of murder investigation. But the way I look at it, it's my civic duty to do what I can to help, right?"

"Absolutely," I replied. Luckily, he wasn't able to see the smirk on my face.

Since Garay didn't want to take the chance of meeting with me in his own neighborhood, we arranged to get together at six-thirty at Timothy's coffee bar on Eighty-first Street and Second Avenue. (Which, being that the place happens to be only a couple of blocks from my apartment, was more than okay with me.)

Garay was certainly making a real cloak-and-dagger affair out of this thing, though, wasn't he? And even if it served the practical purpose of keeping our little rendezvous a secret from his lover, I was convinced that Paul Garay was enjoying every minute of this minor league intrigue.

I spent the remainder of the day typing up my notes regarding last night's questioning of Nick Michaels. I warned myself not to try and make sense of them as I went along. But I didn't listen. With the result that the job took hours longer than it should have. While nothing at all sank in.

Al Bonventure called right after supper, just as I was finishing my second cup of coffee, having already polished off the dish of Häagen Dazs that had been keeping it company. He told me how much he'd enjoyed Friday night, and I told him how much *I'd* enjoyed it.

And then he invited me out for dinner the following evening. I explained that I had a business appointment, and he sounded disappointed. Which was nice.

"I can't make it Wednesday—I teach a course on Wednesday nights—but how about Thursday?" And now he put in uncertainly—evidently remembering our initial go-around months back—"Unless you're too tied up with your work right now."

"No, Thursday would be great."

Al asked if there was someplace special I'd like to eat. Which was also nice. I told him I'd leave it to him.

"How do you feel about Italian food?" he wanted to know.

"I love it."

"Good. There's this restaurant in Little Italy that has *the* most sensational Italian food."

"Guaranteed?" I teased.

"Guaranteed. And if you don't agree, I'll even pay for your meal," he teased in return.

After settling on a time—eight-thirty suited us both—we hung up. And I sat there for a moment with a smile on my face, really glad to have heard from him. But then, being me, I couldn't keep the second thoughts from creeping in.

Was it so wise to see Al again this soon? Why let him think I was champing at the bit to go out with him? Especially in view of my feelings toward him. After all, it wouldn't be fair to give the man the wrong impression, would it?

Fortunately, reason now intervened.

I had absolutely nothing to be concerned about. From what I'd gathered, it was probably less than a year since Al had separated from his wife—most likely he wasn't even divorced yet. So the last thing he'd want right now would be a serious relationship.

It takes some kind of chutzpah to imagine he has anything more in mind than just a good dinner and some pleasant conversation, I rebuked myself.

I mean, who did I think I was, anyway—Cleopatra Shapiro?

Chapter 29

I walked into my office on Tuesday morning with a very optimistic outlook. I had a feeling, bordering on the mystical, that somewhere in that manila folder marked CHERYL SIMON was a clue to the woman's killer. And today was the day I was going to uncover it.

Taking out the file, I carefully read through the interview with Nick Michaels—twice. And then, once again, I began to go over all of my notes, right from the beginning. But I was only able to get partway through them when my twelve o'clock gynecologist's appointment necessitated my calling it quits.

To be honest, though, I was glad about the forced interruption. The further I read, the more frustrated I was becoming. If there was a clue hidden on those pages, it remained well hidden.

Leaving work at quarter to twelve, I had more than enough time to get to Dr. Cantor's by noon, her office being only a few blocks from my own. The instant I entered her waiting room, however, I felt a tension headache coming on.

There were six other women already seated here, a pretty fair indication that this was going to be yet another of those interminable visits. But with Dr. Cantor, there really weren't any other kind.

I spent three-quarters of an hour leafing through one dog-eared, many-months-old magazine after another before I heard those very welcome five little words: "Desiree Shapiro? This way, please."

I knew, of course, that I was still far removed from Dr. Cantor's probing finger. But at least I was about to enter phase two of the doctor's system.

Getting to my feet, I followed Tina, Dr. Cantor's office assistant, into a tiny room, where I was ordered to remove everything but my shoes. Tina handed me the requisite blue gown. "Don't forget, the opening goes to the front," she instructed, exactly as she has once a year for the past five years.

As soon as I got into the gown, I availed myself of the straight, high-backed chair—the only seating accommodation here (other than the examining table, which doesn't count)—and tried to make myself at least reasonably comfortable. It was impossible. The seat's dimensions were a lot narrower than my own, plus the damn thing was rock-hard. What's more, for some weird reason the air conditioning in this room was going full blast, and my paper gown was—as you might expect—paper-thin. Plus there wasn't a single magazine—no matter how outdated—to be seen anywhere. I was so anxious for something to occupy me that I actually regretted not having brought the file I'd been so happy to get away from.

After a while, I began to seethe. Didn't these doctors realize that people had other things to do with their lives besides spending them in a damn gynecologist's office? And why couldn't Dr. Cantor at least allow her patients to remain in the waiting room until she was almost ready to examine them? I mean, wasn't that what it was for—waiting? But no, she had Tina stick me in this damn refrigerator for—I checked my watch—close to fifteen minutes now. With nothing to do but shiver. I shifted my afflicted bottom. And nothing to sit on but *this*.

Well, today I'd tell her just what I thought of this system of hers when she showed up. If she ever did, that is.

I'd been closeted in here for twenty minutes when there was a light rap on the door, instantly followed by Dr. Cantor herself. In person.

"Desire," she said, smiling amiably at me. "It's nice to see you again. I hope you've been well?"

"Oh, I've been fine, Doctor. Although maybe a little chilly

these past few minutes." I rubbed my bare arms to illustrate.
"How have *you* been?"

· And this, wuss that I am, was as close as I came to giving her
a piece of my mind.

The examination lasted about ten minutes, followed by a
routine consultation that took all of five. By the time I got out
of the place, though, it was after one-thirty. And now I was desperately in need of sustenance.

There was no way I could even consider bringing something
back to the office; I was in danger of passing out at any moment, right here on the sidewalk. So I stopped off at the first
luncheonette I came to. Where I was quickly revived by a ham
and cheese, plus a little cole slaw and a few French fries on the
side.

When I finally sat down at my desk again almost three-
quarters of an hour later, I gave myself a pep talk before re-
opening Cheryl Simon's file.

After all, I'd marched in here at ten o'clock this morning
feeling really positive about finally unearthing a clue to this
case, and now—before even getting to the end of my notes—I
was ready to throw in the towel. Which was dumb. I still had
quite a few pages to go, didn't I?

But late in the afternoon I did get to the end of my notes. And
all I can say is, so much for positive feelings.

I hadn't bothered to ask Paul Garay for a description of himself, since Timothy's is pretty small; besides, a fairly clear picture of the man was already etched in my mind. (Oddly enough,
it was the personification of a slimy little weasel.) Fortunately,
however, I did mention my red hair. Otherwise, we might still
be hanging around there waiting for each other.

I mean, I've had enough mouths lower to half-mast to realize that I'm not exactly what people expect to see when they
hear "private eye"—even if they already know the P.I. is a
woman. (Thanks to the movies and TV, they apparently antici-
pate something between Téa Leoni and Lucy Lawless.) And

Garay didn't quite match up to my mental image of him, either. He was tall, light-haired, athletic-looking, with a square jaw, bright blue eyes, and a straight, near-perfect nose. I'll tell you, if Paul Garay wasn't actually handsome, he was close enough to it to fool me.

He was already seated at one of the small tables, a near-empty Styrofoam cup at his elbow, when I walked into the coffee bar. "Desiree?" he inquired tentatively getting to his feet. He didn't try very hard to conceal his surprise when I smiled in acknowledgment.

"Nice to meet you," I told him. We shook hands. His, I noted, was cool and dry. Like Nick Michaels, he seemed impervious to hot, sticky summer evenings, looking neat and unmussed in navy jeans topped by a cream-colored T-shirt that was snug enough to reveal a set of very nicely developed pectoral muscles.

I offered to get him another cup of coffee, and he graciously accepted.

"Would you like anything with it?"

"Something sweet might be nice," he told me.

A couple of minutes later I returned to the table with two large, steaming mugs and two brownies. This time Garay didn't bother to stand.

He took a bite of his brownie and without even waiting to swallow, said in this hushed tone, "Tell me something about the murder, Desiree." There was no mistaking the gleam in his eyes.

I hastily got down the piece of brownie I was chewing on. I'd comply with the request—while providing as few particulars as possible.

I restricted my answer to informing Garay that the victim—a member of Hank's flight crew and someone with whom he'd formed a close friendship—had been run over by a subway train a few weeks earlier. Anticipating Garay's next question at this point, I cut him off at the pass. "I'm not at liberty to say why the police suspect that Cheryl Simon was tossed off that platform by someone she knew, but the fact is, they do."

"Listen, you don't think *Hank* killed her, do you?" There was horror in his voice, but again, his eyes were a dead giveaway to his excitement.

"Oh, no. I'm just gathering as much information as I can on Cheryl's coworkers—that's pretty routine. But Hank isn't really a suspect," I lied.

"Good. Because he's a wonderful, gentle person. I sincerely loved him, you know. I still do, if you want the truth. But when I left him I was going on thirty years old my next birthday, and there just didn't seem to be any future with Hank."

"I'm not certain if you're even aware of this, but after you walked out, Hank talked about taking a second job in order to win you back."

"I know. He called soon after we split up and told me he was going to look for something. I said he shouldn't bother."

"Oh? Why's that?"

"What would it pay? Diddly. Just like his job at the airline. And diddly doesn't get you a Mercedes, or Armani suits, or dinners at Le Cirque, or trips to Paris every six months. Believe me, Desiree, our breakup was just as traumatic for me as it was for Hank. I literally had to *force* myself to be practical and look down the road a few years."

The hypocrisy of this man! I could barely contain my contempt for him. "Are you yourself employed, Mr. Garay?" I inquired, managing somehow to keep my tone neutral.

"In a manner of speaking, I am. And call me Paul."

"All right—Paul. What is it you do?"

"I'm a writer."

I tried to sound impressed. "Really. What kind of things do you write?"

"Historical fiction. I'm working on a novel about the Civil War now."

"I'd *love* to read one of your books," I said, feigning enthusiasm. "Has anything been published?"

"Not yet. But three publishers are very interested·in my first book, which takes place during the time of the American Revolution. I expect to hear something—something positive—any day now."

"Well, I certainly wish you the *very* best of luck," I gushed with total insincerity. "But to get back to Hank . . . When did you last talk to him?"

"A month ago."

"Would you say he still cares for you?"

"He adores me."

"If you haven't heard from him in a month, how can you be certain of that?"

"I didn't say I hadn't heard from him," Garay shot back. "You asked about the last time I *talked* to him. We haven't spoken because I've been in Paris; I just got back Sunday night. But Hank wrote me notes while I was away. Lots of them." And from his disdainful expression he might just as well have added, "So there."

"Weren't you afraid that Mr. Wilson might intercept one of these notes?" I was thinking of how Garay had even taken the precaution of getting together with me here, outside his immediate neighborhood, so his latest lover would be less likely to learn of our meeting.

Garay grinned slyly. "You don't think I'm stupid enough to let Hank mail anything directly to me, do you?"

"I should have figured that out myself."

"And it's not Mr. Wilson, by the way; it's Mr. Cummings. His name's Wilson Cummings."

"Sorry," I mumbled. "Something puzzles me, though. Since you and Hank have obviously been in touch, I'd have expected him to write you about his friend's death."

"Hank doesn't like to upset me. He knows how sensitive I am."

This guy had a special talent for triggering my gag mechanism. So it took a moment before I was up to continuing.

"Let's talk about Hank's notes for a minute. Would you mind telling me what they were about? In general, that is."

"About how much he loves me."

"He never said anything at all about part-time employment in any of them?"

"No. But he did bring up the subject when he called this one time. It was the only instance where he mentioned it—other than right after I moved out, that is. He said he was planning to take on a second job, and he assured me it was the kind that would pay very well. He wouldn't be any more specific than that, though."

"When was this?"

"Oh, quite a while ago."

"Would you say it was . . . umm . . . six months ago?"

"Could have been," Garay answered indifferently.

"Could it have been earlier?"

"Maybe. Or maybe it was later."

I gave up on attempting to establish a time frame. "Did it sound to you like he already had additional employment lined up, or do you think he was still trying to land something?"

"I had the impression he was trying to land something. I'm pretty sure I was right, too, because he never said another word about it. I brought it up myself once or twice, but he was very evasive. So I figured he wasn't able to get anything. I'm one hundred percent certain that if he was actually on the job, he would have wanted to keep me posted about what was going on. Especially if it was the sort of work that had the potential to be really profitable, like stocks or real estate—that type of thing." At this instant, I could envision the invisible dollar signs that must now be dancing enticingly in front of the chiseled face across from me. And suddenly not quite so confident in his opinion, Garay asked almost timidly, "Don't you think so?"

"Oh, yes," I agreed. *Unless he's keeping mum until he's amassed a bundle big enough to win back a bloodsucker like you.*

"Listen, Desiree, I don't understand why you're so interested in some part-time job that probably doesn't even exist. But I've told you all I know. And I've been very forthright with you about everything else, too. Answered all of your questions, no matter how personally painful. So can't you be a little flexible and let me in on why the police suspect Hank's coworker was murdered by someone she knew? I swear, whatever you say would be just between us. I'd never tell another soul." And then he immediately threw in, "It would be a big help to me, honestly. I intend to write a murder mystery next."

Yeah, sure you do. "I'm sorry, but I can't divulge anything more," I responded, succeeding, I believe, in injecting a good measure of regret into my voice. "I wish I could oblige you, though. It would be s-o-o gratifying to be able to assist a budding novelist in his career."

Leaving a somewhat disgruntled Paul Garay to battle for a taxi in front of Timothy's, I walked over to Uncle Otto's, a little bar-cum-restaurant that has absolutely the best Southern fried chicken and candied yams you've ever tasted.

It was pretty crowded when I arrived, with a fair number of people queued up near the entrance waiting impatiently to be seated. I wondered how long it would take before I could be accommodated. Well, I'd better make sure I got put on the list, I thought. And I went over to the lectern to give my name to Chuck, the establishment's owner. (Don't ask me whatever became of Uncle Otto; I have no idea, and neither does Chuck.)

I was greeted with a warm smile. "Good evening, Desiree. How are you tonight?" And before I could answer: "Now, let's see," Chuck said, running his finger down the right-hand page of the ledger in front of him. "Ahh. Here it is," he announced loudly, giving me a conspiratorial wink. "I have your table for you. This way, please."

I followed obediently as he showed me to what appeared to be the one available table in the room. In an instant he had removed the "reserved" sign that explained its availability. I guess I looked a little astonished or maybe even a bit guilty, because he reassured me. "It's okay, Desiree. you're a good customer and a nice person. Felice"—this is Mrs. Chuck—"and I like you." And then he shrugged. "So these people have to wait a little while. So what. It'll kill them?"

Five minutes later I was sipping a glass of Chablis and reviewing my just-concluded meeting.

The only things I seemed to have accomplished was to confirm that Hank Herman was still pining for his former lover. If I believed Garay, that is. And I did—where Hank was concerned, at any rate. Plus I'd learned of Hank's second, more recent mention of part-time employment to Garay. Had he ever found additional work—a job that both Garay and Nick Michaels were apparently unaware of? It was something I should definitely pursue with Hank. Although if he was now involved with El Puerco, I couldn't quite picture his sharing this with me. What's more, even if he'd gotten something legitimate, that didn't negate his trafficking in drugs as well. I mean, Hank could be relying on this legitimate new job to explain a change in his financial status in the event it was discovered that he suddenly had a swollen bank account.

Oh, hell, I realized dejectedly, there was no point in even bothering to speak to him about this.

It was really disheartening. I didn't seem to be making any progress at all here. And for the first time since taking on this case, I felt as though I'd reached the end of my rope. I had talked to anyone I could think of, read through that miserable file again and again, gone over everything in my head ad infinitum—and nothing. Absolutely zero.

Naturally, it was possible that the reason I hadn't uncovered a single clue in that folder was that there just wasn't any to be found there. God! I hated myself whenever I thought like this. But I had to face it: Maybe Cheryl Simon's killer had actually committed the perfect crime!

No. Stop being so negative. Tomorrow I'd type up my notes on this meeting with Paul Garay. Could be he had provided some key information, after all. Information I hadn't assimilated yet. I mean, as you know, before I can appreciate the significance of a fact, I almost always have to see it in black and white—and even then as part of a total picture.

And this led to my recalling a remark Cheryl Simon had made the night she told her husband about the incidents in Nassau, a remark I'd been more or less skipping over of late. She'd mumbled to herself that it all fit together now. Or words to that effect.

Well, from here it was only a short step to asking myself once again what else the victim could have seen or heard or suspected prior to witnessing that crucial meeting in the lounge between her friend and El Puerco.

I determined that I would certainly have to review the case with this question in mind. Of course, just then I would have grabbed on to anything that offered a different direction for me to pursue—no matter how slight that difference might be. The thing is, by committing myself to another tack, I was able to feel as if I were breathing new life into my deteriorating prospects for solving Cheryl Simon's murder.

And now I was sufficiently cheered so that when Felice brought over a big white plate practically overflowing with Southern fried chicken, candied yams, string beans with mushrooms, and orange-cranberry relish, I was able to attack this feast with all of the gusto it merited.

Chapter 30

On Wednesday I had to cope with the great-great-grandmother of all headaches.

I must have checked my watch every five minutes to see when it would be okay to take another couple of Extra Strength Tylenols—and after that, another couple, and later, still another. A fat lot of good they did me, too. I mean, maybe the pills dulled the pain a bit (and then again, maybe not), but I certainly couldn't serve as the poster girl for a miracle cure.

At any rate, after calling Bruce to give him a progress report (which would be better termed a nonprogress report), I began transcribing my notes on the meeting with Paul Garay. When I was through, I turned to the beginning of the file, abandoning my usual procedure of first studying the most recent addition to the folder. Today I would go over everything in chronological order. I don't know why, really. Except that it was probably in the back of my mind that changing my routine would change my luck.

Forget it.

My antennae were really out then, too, searching for the slightest hint of any additional incident or incidents—or whatever it was that Cheryl had been referring to just before her death. But revising my work habits didn't do beans for the results. And I wound up not learning one iota more than I had the countless previous times I'd tackled this same maddening job.

Of course, hampered by my headache and all, I can't say I was particularly sharp that day. I'd do better when my temples weren't pounding like this, I decided. And I almost made myself believe it, too.

*   *   *

I was a lot better on Thursday. Health-wise, anyway. But I still thought it might be a good idea to take a break from the case. Maybe removing myself from it for a day or two would give me a fresh perspective. Besides, I was beginning to feel like a masochist whenever I reached for that file.

Now, you might assume that since I wasn't presently involved in any other investigation, shelving the Cheryl Simon murder could present a problem as to how to productively spend my time at the office. But never fear. It enabled me to engage in fairly lengthy telephone conversations with Ellen (who was home with a sore throat that had rendered her hoarse, but far from silent), Pat Martucci (whose boss eventually suggested—very strongly—that she hang up the phone), and my neighbor and friend Harriet Gould (who might still be talking if her doorbell hadn't rung). After this I manicured my nails, checked out the latest fashions in *Mode* magazine, and—when I was ready for something really challenging—sharpened a handful of pencils.

I took a late lunch, during which I stopped off for a quick hamburger and then headed for Macy's to buy a blender at twenty percent off, my own twenty-five-year-old model having emitted its death rattle the week before. I also picked up a couple of pairs of desperately needed off-black panty hose while I was at the store.

On returning to the office, I dropped in on Elliot Gilbert for a brief visit, and immediately following this had a somewhat more extended get-together with Jackie in the ladies' room. (And yes, I told her I would be seeing Al later, since I had no doubt that if I committed a second transgression with regard to Al Bonaventure, I was chopped liver.)

Back at my desk again, I made one more phone call—this time to Christie in Minneapolis—sharpened a few stray pencils, and then left for home.

Have you ever gotten ready to go out when—without expending any more effort than you normally do—virtually everything turns out perfect? Well, this was me tonight. In fact, I was so mesmerized by the reflection of that stunning woman in the mirror that I just stood there and gaped at her for I don't know how long.

This may sound conceited, but believe me, it wasn't like that at all. What I was experiencing was delight. Mixed with a very large dose of astonishment.

I mean, the makeup was flawless. You couldn't tell where the base ended and the actual me began. My cheeks were aglow with a subtle, masterfully applied coral blush. My eyelashes were curled practically up to my eyebrows. And I had on this dynamite new shade of coral lipstick that, wonder of wonders, wasn't bleeding into any of those zillion little cracks around my lip line.

Plus that glorious hennaed hair of mine had never looked more glorious.

As for the rest of me, it was clothed in a two-piece black pique (the same one I'd had to forego last week after discovering that all my off-black panty hose were navy). And it turned out that the dress was a lot more flattering than I'd ever realized. The accessories were exactly right, too: black-and-gold drop earrings, along with this beautiful gold bamboo necklace that had been a gift from my late husband Ed.

Still held captive by the woman in the mirror, I began to turn slowly. And twisting my head so far around now that I was actually in pain, I was treated to a side and semi-rear view.

Well, I'm not going to claim I was svelte—you wouldn't believe me if I did. But the way I see it, who needs svelte when there's voluptuous?

And damned if I didn't qualify as voluptuous this evening!

I got to Vincente's five minutes early—at twenty-five past eight. Al was already at the table, waiting for me.

A big smile spread across his face as I approached. He got up quickly, then bent down—*way* down—to kiss my cheek.

"How pretty you look," he said appreciatively when we were

both seated. (Not in the same league as "stunning," but what the hell.)

"Thank you," I simpered. "You look very nice, too." And he did. He was wearing an oatmeal tweed jacket, a bone-colored sport shirt, and tan pants. Very nicely coordinated, he was. But wardrobe aside, the man was definitely appealing—in a teddy bearish sort of way, of course.

"I guess I should have warned you that Vincente's isn't too fancy," he murmured apologetically as he caught me checking out the rather small, very crowded room. One of the restaurant's three dining areas, it was presently occupied by a really eclectic clientele consisting of young families, sedate middle-aged and elderly couples, and hip Generation X-ers.

"It's homey," I said, glancing around some more. The wood floor was bare and unpolished. The stucco walls were a soft beige and decorated with colorful prints of the Italian countryside. And the sturdy oak tables were covered with starched white cloths and set with simple white china, a quartet of fresh blossoms in little white vases adorning every tabletop. Naturally, I was also appreciative of the fact that the seats of the wooden chairs were generously padded in vinyl and wide enough to accommodate an ample derriere—and with inches to spare. "I like it here," I pronounced.

Al seemed pleased at this. "I do, too. And just wait till you taste the food."

I reminded him of the arrangement he'd proposed in jest the other night. "Remember, Al, if it's not the best I've ever eaten—you pay."

"I have complete confidence that you'll end up with the bill," he responded, deadpan.

Well, the dinner turned out to be quite wonderful—my second great meal this week. And while I can't say for sure that it was the best ever, it was certainly a worthy contender.

Al ordered a bottle of Chianti, and although I'm no wine connoisseur, as far as I was concerned, it was a fine choice. (At least it didn't have a twist-off cap.) We shared the appetizer—mussels in a red wine and tomato sauce—and also the house salad, which was humongous. Following this, we were each served a really excellent entrée, with me choosing the veal parmigiana and Al the osso buco. These were accompanied by side dishes of spaghetti marinara and grilled portobella mushrooms, as well as a basket of Vincente's special garlic bread.

Everything was so delicious—and so abundant—that by dessert time I discovered that I didn't have a millimeter of space left for anything more than a cup of espresso. Al, however, had found some room for the rum cake. Which he absolutely insisted I sample.

Mmm. Primo.

He urged me to have a second helping. After which he prevailed upon me to dig in again. Fortunately for Al, the portion was sizable enough so that when I finally withdrew my fork for good, there was still something left on the plate.

Now, all the while that I'd been scarfing down this irresistible food, I'd been doing pretty damn fair in the company department, too.

Al was every bit as attentive as he'd been on our previous date. Also just as stimulating. And smart. And funny.

We discussed movies and current events and Ella Fitzgerald and I can't even recall what else. And while our opinions clashed once or twice, it was even a kick to disagree with this man.

"I had a terrific time," Al informed me at my door.

"The same here." And now I behaved in a manner that was totally *un*-me. In fact, I actually startled myself. Reaching for his hand, I gave it a little squeeze. After which I moistened my lips and then looked up at him with what was intended to be a seductive expression. I stopped short of batting my eyes, however. Or, anyway, that's my recollection.

Al did the gentlemanly thing and responded with a lingering kiss, practically scraping his knees on the ground in order to oblige me. (It was a very pleasant kiss, by the way, in case you're wondering.)

When we broke apart he hesitated a moment, probably because he was unsure of what else was expected of him. (He had a right to be confused, too, because I wasn't certain myself.) Apparently, however, he opted for caution, because he followed the kiss by saying that he hoped to see me again soon. And I told him I'd be looking forward to it.

Closing the door to my apartment a few seconds later, I decided that I was happy Al hadn't asked to come in and that the evening had concluded exactly as it did.

Chapter 31

I didn't berate myself until I was taking off my makeup. But by then I was fuming. I had almost allowed my libido to call the shots tonight. I mean, if it weren't for Al's showing some restraint, there was no telling how things might have ended up. And what was I trying to start here, anyway?

Looking for self-justification, I attempted once again to draw a parallel between this relationship and the one I'd had with Stuart Mason. But I didn't let myself get away with it this time. In the first place, I hadn't gone ahead full steam like this with Stuart. In that instance the initiative had been entirely mutual. Even more important, though, Stuart and I had tacitly agreed from the beginning that a warm friendship—albeit with a little physical bonus—was all we were seeking from one another. But I certainly couldn't be sure that this was also what Al Bonaventure had in mind.

And then it came to me.

It was conceivable that I was misjudging myself. Was I, at this far-from-tender age, actually growing up, perchance? Could I finally be ready to set aside this silly search for *my type* in favor of pursuing a possible romance with a nice, menschy teddy bear?

Okay, so I'd been a little overzealous tonight. But still, maybe I was—hallelujah!—showing some sense at last.

The next morning, however, I woke up filled with doubts, thoroughly unnerved by the memory of a very vivid dream. . . .

I was in an enormous laboratory, and I was dressed in a long white coat, which is why I realized at once that I must be a scientist. (I also had on a shower cap—a pink, ruffly one, no less—for a reason I have never been able to fathom. So let's just forget about that part, okay?) Anyway, in a corner of the room were these two gurneys, positioned side by side, and strapped to each of them was a shadowy, unidentifiable figure.

I was a good distance from the figures, standing over this enormous vat. I kept pouring the measured contents of test tube after test tube into the vat, stopping after each addition to stir frantically and then drain a small sample of the mixture into a fresh test tube. Following which I'd hold the newly produced solution up to the light and examine it very carefully.

I'm not really certain, but I think I had just arrived at the precise molecular combination I'd been striving for when suddenly the door behind me burst open.

"Stop!" a voice shouted. "You can't do this!"

I wheeled around to find Jackie waving her fist and glaring at me.

She rushed over to the gurneys and undid the bindings of the occupants. I could make out both people very clearly as they sat up, dazed and rubbing their wrists.

One was Al Bonaventure, and the other was Nick Michaels.

Now, I have no idea how I know this, but when I awakened it was obvious to me that I'd been attempting to create a formula that would allow me to transplant Al's character into Nick's body.

Well, I thought disgustedly, *so much for your finally attaining some degree of maturity.*

Jackie attacked me the moment I arrived at the office.

"How did it go? Tell me!" she commanded, her cheeks flushed. (I swear she was breathing hard, too.)

For an instant I thought of saying "lousy," just to see how she would react. But that was because, still put off by the dream, I was feeling less than sunshine-y this morning. I didn't have the heart to do that to Jackie, though. Or the nerve, either, for that matter. "We had a lovely time."

"So?" she demanded.

"What are you asking me?"

"Anything *in-ter-est-ing* going on?" The emphasis, along with the avid expression on her face, left little doubt that she was hoping to hear big things from me.

"Yeah. We're eloping at four today," I answered sarcastically. I couldn't help it; I felt like I was being set upon by a pit bull. And then instantly regretting the response: "Seriously, Jackie, I enjoy the man's company, but it's much too early to even think about whether something serious could develop between Al and me."

"Well, if you let him go, you're missing out on one terrific guy!" she shouted at my rapidly departing back.

In the safety of my cubbyhole, I decided that the wisest thing for me to do for the next six or seven hours would be to re-sharpen my pencils, add another coat of polish to my nails, and then call up whatever friends I hadn't yakked with yesterday. In other words, this was another day I intended to avoid trying to make sense of Cheryl Simon's file. The reason being that I had grave doubts about my ability to concentrate at present. And the thing is, each time I failed to come up with anything, I tended to get a little more discouraged. Which, I suppose, was understandable, especially at this juncture.

To make matters worse, in spite of my renewed sense of purpose on Tuesday night, just now I found myself returning to the possibility that that entire stack of typewritten pages might not contain a single clue. It was also conceivable—and this was even more unsettling—that there *was* something significant to be found there and that I might never spot it.

And if, God forbid, I wasn't ever able to learn anything from my notes, what then? There didn't seem to be a soul left to interview. And if there were any additional questions that should be put to the people I'd already spoken to, I didn't know what they were.

Obviously, this called for another little pep talk.

The truth was, I reminded myself, that since deciding to focus on Cheryl's cryptic statement, I'd read through my notes exactly once. And I'd had an abominable headache then. I would take a good, long look at everything tomorrow when, hopefully, I'd be in a better frame of mind.

Momentarily satisfied, I removed the nail polish bottle from the top left-hand drawer of my desk and began unscrewing the top. But out of the blue I found myself wondering how Tim Fielding's investigation was progressing. Was he still determined to hang this thing on Bruce? Bruce hadn't mentioned hearing from him lately, but that didn't mean Fielding had abandoned him as a suspect. Not if I knew my old friend Tim. Oh God! What if he should somehow be able to build a plausible case against my client?

And so I put the nail polish back in its drawer and, gritting my teeth, got out the folder. Maybe my mood this morning wasn't conducive to any brilliant deducing. But I couldn't see my disposition improving if—while I was waiting for the perfect conditions under which to apply myself to the case—Bruce should be arrested for killing his wife.

I worked slowly, stopping every so often to think about what I'd just read. To my great surprise, I was able to shut out everything but Cheryl Simon's murder—and the urgency I felt to solve it.

I didn't even break for lunch, continuing to pore over the file as I gulped down a BLT and a Coke at around one-thirty. (Which is why pages seventeen through twenty-one still feature somewhat prominent mayonnaise splotches.) I stayed committed to my task until the bitter end, too, finally winding things up at close to five o'clock. When I was forced to admit that I'd made no headway at all.

Well, where do I go from here?

For a while I just stared into space. And then I recalled the advice Hercule Poirot has been giving me since I was practically in toddler sizes. It's a course of action I've turned to in other desperate situations over the years—although, unfortunately, not often with a great deal of success. At any rate, Poirot

maintains that the more you induce people to talk, the greater
the likelihood something of consequence will come out.

Okay, what did I have to lose? I decided to take the advice of
the great detective and initiate another conversation with
Cheryl's friends. At this point, it did seem like the wisest thing
to do. The *only* thing to do, really.

I'd start with the three suspects. Being that it was Friday,
though, I expected that they were all in Nassau right now. I'd
get in touch with them over the weekend and set up the ap-
pointments. Anyhow, that would give me time to dream up
some pretext for asking for another meeting.

I was almost cheerful about the whole idea; it was a relief to
once again fix on an alternate route I could pursue. *And who
knows?* I mused. *Maybe—just maybe—somewhere along the
line I'll acquire that one little piece of information that will
help me unmask the killer.*

There was a message on my machine when I walked into the
apartment.

"Hi," Al said in that nice, friendly way of his. "I couldn't call
you earlier; it's been one of those days—three emergencies. I
wanted you to know how much I enjoyed last night, though."

"Me, too," I told the machine.

"I'm leaving for Nantucket any minute—my sister has a
place there, and it's my nephew's birthday tomorrow. But I was
wondering if you were available for dinner on Tuesday. I'll call
you when I get back to town to find out if you can make it and
to firm up the arrangements. How do you feel about seafood, by
the way? And, uh, listen, when I speak to you—Sunday
evening, if you're home—maybe we could set something up
for the following weekend, too. If you're free next Saturday or
Sunday, hold the day for me, will you?" The last couple of sen-
tences came out in a rush. "I have to go now, but I'll talk to you
soon. Take care."

Standing there next to the answering machine, I vowed to put
that dumb dream behind me and just let things with Al take
their course. And this also went for the physical aspect of our

relationship. I still wasn't very proud of sending out the kind of signals I did when he took me home. And the fact that it had been a while since my libido had had cause for celebration was really no excuse. Besides, I think I once heard that abstinence is a very good character-builder—although, in my case, I couldn't see where it had been any great shakes so far.

Chapter 32

It may sound funny. But I've begun to get the idea that maybe the early morning air nourishes the brain or something. Because it's most often in the wee hours that I'm finally able to see what's been staring me in the face for weeks.

Just like now.

Since coming home from work I had managed to completely avoid thinking about the investigation. I hadn't even attempted to come up with a reason for requesting a further meeting with the suspects. It was really no big deal, though; I'd take care of that tomorrow.

Anyhow, I went to bed at around one o'clock. And that's when that remark of Cheryl's began to go around and around in my head.

It all fits now, she'd mumbled.

Well, once again I proceeded to challenge myself with the victim's puzzling statement. *What could she have been referring to? What is it that fits now?* And it occurred to me then that these might not be Cheryl's exact words—or at least, the words that Bruce had repeated to me. Being curious—and unable to sleep anyway—I got out of bed to check it out.

I staggered into the kitchen and put up the coffee. After which I removed the dog-eared manila folder from my attaché case and set it on the table. As soon as the coffee was ready I poured myself a cup and sat down with the file.

Thumbing through my notes, I located the passage I was looking for almost immediately. Bruce's actual quote of Cheryl was *But everything fits. Everything fits now.* What's more, he'd assured me that this was "just what she said."

The net takeaway was the same as *It all fits,* though, wasn't it? That's why I hadn't been too scrupulous about committing the precise words to memory. In fact, I hadn't even made the distinction those countless times I'd read—and reread and reread—the crucial phrase.

But looking down at the page in front of me now, I slowly became aware that there was actually a slight difference between the two statements.

Strictly translated, *Everything fits* means *They all fit.* Not *it—they.* And all at once it occurred to me that another interpretation—a literal interpretation—could be applied to Cheryl's words.

And this is how, at long last, I was able to identify the killer.

Chapter 33

When I finally went back to bed it was around three a.m. Apparently I dropped off as soon as I made contact with the pillow, in spite of being wildly exhilarated by my discovery. Also, in spite of having consumed a cup of coffee so nasty, so eye-openingly bitter that a less resilient soul would have been sleep-deprived for days.

I didn't come to until well past ten o'clock, at which time I was instantly wide awake. And then a moment later I started humming. And I never do that. But I suppose it was some kind of release after all the self-doubts I'd been struggling with lately. I have no idea as to the name of my little song—assuming that it was an actual song—but I continued to hum even while I was brushing my teeth. Which, of course, wasn't easy. But there was no denying that the sound I managed to eke out vaguely resembled a tune.

At any rate, I was totally delighted with myself—my perception, my determination, my drive. And I was certain I'd reached the right conclusion, too. Because as the victim herself had observed, *Everything fits now.*

Just as I finished consuming my third slice of French toast, however, a very unwelcome concern began to drizzle on my parade. Exactly what, I wondered, did I intend to use for proof?

But not willing to relinquish this all-too-infrequent feeling of triumph, I assured myself, *Don't worry, you'll think of something; you always do.*

*   *   *

After breakfast I did some long overdue housecleaning, grumbling out loud as I bent to scrub the toilet bowl. This was hardly an appropriate job for a top-notch investigator.

Nevertheless, I continued with my menial chores until around two o'clock, when I finally threw in the towel—also, the dust cloths and mops and brushes. Following this, I got into some supermarket-friendly clothes. But as I was about to head out the door, I hesitated. And in a few seconds I walked back into the living room. This definitely seemed like an appropriate time to put in a call to my client. I mean, it would probably be nice to inform him that I had just solved his wife's murder. My hand was poised to reach for the telephone on my desk when I hesitated again. Why not hold off a couple of days longer? By then, there was a chance that everything would be all wrapped up. After all, it shouldn't be too difficult—should it?—to figure out a strategy that would enable me to deliver the perp to the police.

Rarely has such optimism been so unwarranted.

It was late that afternoon when the phone rang. I was standing at the kitchen sink, washing off a newly purchased peach that was intended for immediate consumption.

"Desiree? It's Hank. Hank Herman. I . . . uh . . . I have to talk to you about something," the timid voice informed me as I finished drying my hands.

"About what, Hank?" I responded cautiously.

"I spoke to Paul the other day. I understand you met with him and that . . . umm . . . that you think I was the one who murdered Cheryl."

Why, that miserable skunk! As you know, I hadn't told Paul anything of the sort. In fact, I'd bent over backward—lied, actually—to make him believe that Hank wasn't even a suspect. Paul couldn't be that thick-headed, for heaven's sake. But the alternative made no sense either. What purpose could fabricating something like this possibly serve?

"I have reason to believe he's finally beginning to appreciate that money is no replacement for love," Hank went on. "Cummings—the man he's with now—has been treating Paul miserably lately, and I'm certain he was seriously considering coming back to me. But after the conversation you two had, he won't even hear of discussing the future. Not while there's this cloud hanging over me."

Ahh, so that's it! Didn't Hank realize yet that Paul had no intention of ever getting tied up again with a man he considered to be a pauper? There was absolutely no question in my mind then that Paul had merely found himself an excuse for not entering into a commitment—and used me to do it, too. What's more, he was devious enough to still hold out false hope to his besotted ex in order to keep him on the string. I came close to blurting this out to Hank, but I quickly censored myself. It was really none of my business (although I have to concede that this doesn't always preclude my sticking my nose into somebody else's). And anyway, this was hardly the time to go into Hank's love life. So in the end I had to be satisfied with a terse statement of fact. "I didn't say a single word that would give Paul cause to think I had you pegged as Cheryl's killer."

"Oh, he didn't say it was something you actually *said*. But he got that impression. And Paul's amazingly intuitive."

"Not in this case, he isn't."

A pause. And then Hank asked tentatively, "Does this mean you've found out who really *did* kill Cheryl?"

It was a few seconds before I responded. "Uh, I'm afraid not," I mumbled. But I doubt there was a whole lot of conviction in my tone.

This was pretty much confirmed an instant later by Hank's retort. "You're not leveling with me, are you?"

"Of course I am."

My assurance was about as convincing as my denial had been. But I couldn't seem to help it. Arriving at the truth hadn't exactly been a picnic, you know. And I really resented having to lie about my success.

It was a conceit that would very nearly cost me my life.

Chapter 34

Right after Hank's phone call I ate my peach. And then I made some coffee and had a seat at the kitchen table, where I seem to do my best thinking lately.

It took maybe an hour or so before I'd admit that it was all well and good for me to pretend to myself that I could devise some absolutely brilliant means of trapping the murderer. Just as long as I didn't hold on to this absurd fantasy for very long.

The fact is, the only course of action that had even occurred to me to this point was to get together with the perp and reveal what I'd discovered. Hopefully, this would result in a conversation—one that would produce the evidence needed to make an arrest.

I went through a tentative scenario in my mind.

As soon as we sat down with each other, I would announce that I'd figured things out at last, which should certainly lead to a request for clarification. So I'd explain just how I'd arrived at the solution to Cheryl's death. *But you have nothing to worry about,* I'd say. *Unfortunately, I can't touch you, since I haven't got a shred of proof. I'd appreciate it, though, if you'd satisfy my curiosity.* Then, depending on the response, I'd maybe reiterate, deep regret in my voice, that there was nothing to fear from me. Once this was established, I could move on to my probing.

I might start off with *How did you ever get involved with El Puerco in the first place?* And then follow that with *What did you say to Cheryl when she told you what she'd seen in Nassau?* And somewhere along the line I'd be sure to put in *Where was Cheryl supposed to be headed when she inquired about the trains to Canal Street?*

There were really a million questions I could ask, and it wasn't that far-fetched—was it?—that I'd get some answers, too. I mean, it was entirely possible the killer would be eager to unload. After all, murdering your close friend can't be too easy to live with.

Okay, so maybe I was grasping at straws. But I *had* seen hundreds of people confess under similar circumstances—on television, at least. (I, myself, however, have not yet encountered a single soul who was that accommodating.) Anyway, at the same time that I'd be providing assurance that this was just between us, there'd be a tape recorder whirring away in my handbag.

Now, I recognized that my game plan wasn't particularly original. And admittedly, it certainly hadn't worked for me in the past. But I didn't see what else I could do. The odds on my actually coming up with a more inspired scheme in the foreseeable future went from absolute zero all the way up to highly improbable. Which in my heart, I suppose, I'd realized all along.

So the way it looked, I could either proceed with the tape recorder thing and pray for the best—or just give up and let Cheryl's treacherous pal get away with murder.

It took three tries before I was able to connect with a real-life person.

"There's something that I'd like to discuss with you," I told the perpetrator. "And I was wondering if I could come over for a few minutes."

The response was amicable enough. "Of course. I'm going out soon, though, so I hope you weren't thinking of tonight. I could make it tomorrow, but it would have to be in the evening. Say, around nine? Can whatever it is hold until then?"

Well, we were talking more than twenty-four hours away here. And I was impatient to get on with this. Nevertheless, I answered that Sunday at nine would be dandy.

What choice did I have?

* * *

In the morning I phoned Ellen to give her the news. (I considered myself to have shown great restraint in waiting all this time, too.)

"I know who killed Cheryl," I informed her.

"You're kidding!" she screeched—to the detriment of my eardrum. And before I could say anything else: "Are you sure?"

"Yes."

"How did you figure it out?"

And so I gave her an abbreviated tour of my thought processes.

"Well, for goodness' sake," she murmured with something like awe in her voice. And then she added hurriedly, "Not that I ever had any doubt that you'd solve this."

Which was probably true. I mean, if there's anyone in the entire world who has unflinching, unreasoning faith in me, it's Ellen.

"Have you spoken to the police yet?" she wanted to know.

"Uh-uh. I have to try to gather a little something in the way of evidence first."

"Oh. Any idea how you're going to do it?"

Now, for some reason I was reluctant to divulge my agenda in advance. Even to Ellen. Maybe it had to do with my misgivings. So I said, "Not so far. I'll have to give it more thought."

"I'm positive you'll come up with something." *If only that optimism of hers were contagious.* "Can I tell Mike about this?" she asked then.

Well, knowing my niece, it wouldn't matter much whether I said yes or no. It was extremely unlikely that even if she were sworn to secrecy she'd be able to resist bringing Mike up to date. Not for very long, anyway. So I gave her the go-ahead. "If you want to." At least it would keep her honest.

Soon after speaking to Ellen, I began firming up a list of questions for tonight. And when I was fairly well satisfied with what I'd decided on, I devoted some thought to my general approach. I shouldn't be too friendly, of course—that would definitely arouse suspicion. But on the other hand, I also had to avoid being overly accusatory—which could provoke the perp into shutting down on me altogether. It was really critical to strike the right balance.

I took another look at my list at around one o'clock and made a few revisions. Then later that afternoon I checked it over again and made quite a few more. Both times I practiced asking the questions aloud, too, in order to get my manner down pat. And with each rehearsal I could feel my anxiety level building.

I'm sure that what I'm going to say next will sound incredibly naive to you. (Or maybe *stupid* would be more like it.) But anyway, believe it or not, my nervousness stemmed solely from a concern that I might not be able to worm a confession out of the killer.

You have to understand something, though. The way I figured it, I wouldn't be presenting myself as any kind of threat in this meeting. So it didn't even dawn on me that I had reason to be afraid for my life.

Chapter 35

On the way to Forest Hills that evening my palms were so moist they were practically sliding off the steering wheel. Plus my hair was sticking to my neck, my forehead was decorated with little beads of sweat, and my bone-color cotton suit jacket was plastered right up against my back. None of which had anything to do with the temperature. In fact, the Chevy's air conditioning was operating at peak efficiency tonight, actually throwing out genuinely cold air.

I found a parking space half a block from the red-brick apartment house and on the same side of the street. Walking back to the building, my heart threatening to burst out of my chest, I said a silent prayer: *Please, God. Let me get that confession.*

I repeated this same prayer in the elevator. And not one to worry about overkill (not the best word to use, I suppose, considering the circumstances), I most likely would have given it a third try at the door—if it hadn't swung open just then. . . .

Chapter 36

"Hi." The smile was broad and ingratiating. "C'mon in."

I gulped once, then smiled back halfheartedly. "How are you, Laura?"

Following her into the living room, I was astonished that I had managed to sound so normal. I guess I hadn't been a member of my high school drama club for nothing.

"I'm fine, Desiree. You?"

"Pretty good."

She gestured toward the sofa, and I plunked myself down obediently.

"I baked the most delicious honey cake this morning. And you're going to have to try it. Our talk can wait a few minutes until we've had our little repast, can't it?"

Now, I was so anxious to get to what I'd come here for that I'd have loved to pass on the honey cake. Particularly since it's never been a favorite of mine, anyway. But I had the definite feeling that this would not sit too well with my hostess. So I said, "No problem."

"Iced coffee or hot?"

"Whatever you're having would be fine."

"Then it's hot. Oh, just a second." Crossing the room to a small table in the far corner, she picked up three magazines. "Here," she said, handing them to me. "You should be able to find something interesting enough to keep you busy while I put up the coffee and set the table." And with this, she went into the kitchen.

An *Architectural Digest* was on top of the pile, so I opened it. Probably because it was there. I didn't turn the page, though.

Actually, I didn't even look down. I just kept cautioning myself, *Whatever you do, Desiree Shapiro, don't screw this up!*

A short time later, Laura called out to me to join her in the kitchen. I went in to find the table beautifully set with an off-white linen cloth, gleaming flatware, and delicate blue-and-cream china—porcelain, no doubt. In the center of the table was a round crystal plate containing a formerly rectangular-shaped cake that was now a square—a sizable portion of it having obviously been hacked off.

Laura was standing with her arm draped across the back of one of the chairs, a rather large piece of the cake at the setting in front of her. "Sit down," she said. I took a seat at the opposite end of the small table, where an even more generous slice of cake awaited me. I mean, it was BIG. I think I may have turned a little green.

As I mentioned before, I'm not exactly crazy about honey cake. And it used to be more or less foisted on me, too. Or at least that's how I felt. You see, before moving to Florida, Margot, Ellen's mother, would have all the relatives over for Passover every year. Mostly to please Ellen's father, I think. And guess what she invariably served for our holiday dessert—and with seconds positively mandatory, besides. Plus to make matters worse, my sister-in-law is as comfortable in a kitchen as I am in a fitness center. And it shows.

Anyway, just as I was about to plunge my fork into the cake, Laura stopped me. "Hold it," she instructed, passing me a small sauce boat. "You've got to try it with the raspberry sauce."

Well, raspberries being something I absolutely adore, I had no difficulty accommodating her. I drenched the cake with the sauce.

I had my first taste as Laura watched expectantly. "It's really delicious," I pronounced. Which was definitely an exaggeration. But I didn't think the woman would be too pleased with "not bad." And besides, even if this wasn't your usual accompaniment to honey cake, the sauce did an admirable job of masking its flavor. Almost as admirable a job as Laura's exceptionally strong and uniquely terrible coffee did of overpowering the raspberries. (And believe me, I know from strong, terrible coffee.)

I finished the cake and, somehow, every last drop of the bitter vetch in my cup. I looked over at Laura's plate then, and it, too, was empty. Thank God! It had been a nerve-racking ten or fifteen minutes. I was so intent on starting my spiel that I'd barely been able to engage in the requisite chitchat. But since Laura had made it clear that she intended for me to save the weightier subject matter until we were through eating, I'd had to go along with her. I was really walking on eggs here.

"Some more coffee, Desiree?" she asked then.

"Oh, no, thank you."

"You'll have another piece of cake, though, won't you?" And without waiting for a response, she picked up the cake knife next to the crystal plate.

"I couldn't," I protested. "This was a real treat, honestly, but I haven't got room for another bite."

"I'm sure you can manage one more teensy little slice," she cajoled, proceeding to cut into the square.

At that moment the doorbell rang.

Oh, shit! High school drama club or not, it was impossible to conceal my dismay.

Laura appeared to share it, however. "I have no idea who that could be," she told me, frowning. And then in a conspiratorial whisper: "But why don't I just ignore it?"

"I was hoping you'd say that." I could only manage to partially stifle the sigh of relief.

She motioned for my plate now. *Well, what the hell. Make her happy. And what was another five minutes, anyway?* I passed the plate across the table. *It beats having to deal with some damn intruder, doesn't it?*

The doorbell rang again, more insistently this time. "Whoever it is should go away in a moment," Laura murmured encouragingly, handing back the plate, which now carried a not so teensy little slice.

At this point we heard some muffled shouting. Laura got up

and walked into the living room to listen; I was right behind her.

"—you're in there," the man continued loudly.

"Oh. It's a friend of mine," Laura apprised me softly, apparently recognizing the voice. Then as the friend began to pound on the door: "I suppose I'd better have him come in."

And with seeming reluctance, that's what she did.

Seeing Bobby Lomax standing there, my initial reaction was resentment. He couldn't have made a more untimely visit. But seconds later I became alarmed.

Maybe his appearance tonight had been planned. *Had he lent his sweetie here a helping hand in silencing poor Cheryl?* I asked myself. If so, I was probably dead. And I mean literally. A shudder made its way down my spine.

Instructing myself not to jump to conclusions, I took stock of Lomax. He was dressed in skintight jeans again—this time, blue ones. And he had on a rumpled black T-shirt that didn't appear any too clean to me. *Probably the same one he wore when I met him. I wouldn't be surprised if he hasn't washed it since then, either,* I thought nastily, attempting to block out my fear. *And doesn't this guy ever shave?*

Lomax acknowledged me with a nod, then focused on Laura. "What's going on?" he demanded. "You had me worried."

"Why, for God's sake? And what made you so sure I was even here?"

"Mrs. O'Donnell let me into the building—she was on her way out to walk the dog. She told me you were home, that she saw some woman entering your apartment only a few minutes ago. And if you want to know why I was worried, a friend of yours *was* murdered not that long ago, remember?"

"I remember," Laura responded tersely. She turned to me. "Mrs. O'Donnell's my neighbor across the hall, and I think she must spend half the day at her peephole."

"So? What's going on?" Lomax repeated.

"Nothing for you to get all steamed up about, I assure you. Desiree wants to talk to me, and it's something she'd like to do in private. I had no idea it was you ringing, you realize." And now she put to him, her tone almost accusatory, "I thought you weren't coming over tonight. If I recall correctly, you were going to meet your cousin in Manhattan, and the two of you were planning to do a little clothes shopping and then have some dinner and take in a movie."

I was thoroughly confused. Laura was certainly giving the impression that she was annoyed at Lomax's stopping in. But she'd already proven herself to be quite the little thespian, hadn't she? And as for Lomax, he seemed genuinely agitated. Who could be sure, though? Maybe, like me, he'd once joined a drama club.

"You did say you needed some new things for school, didn't you?" Laura was asking.

I was reminded then that the guy was a teacher, which, looking at him, wasn't too easy to accept. *He's the hygiene instructor, no doubt,* I informed myself facetiously. And there was a smirk inside me—right before the apprehension kicked in again.

"We did the shopping part, but halfway through dinner Phil got sick, so we called it a night," Lomax told her. After which, tilting his head to one side, he asked, "Do I smell coffee?"

"There's none left," Laura answered.

"Okay. I'll make my own. It's safer that way anyhow." And he grinned at her. Now, all this time the three of us had been standing a few feet from the door. But just then Lomax began to head for the kitchen.

Laura grabbed his sleeve. "Don't be silly. I was only giving you the business. I'll go make a fresh pot. You sit down here and keep Desiree company."

"*I'll* fix the coffee," Lomax said firmly. "And don't worry. I'll close myself up in the kitchen, so you two can have your confidential talk." Gently extricating himself from her grasp, he walked briskly from the room, Laura hurrying after him.

Still on tenterhooks, I remained where I was—close to the exit. I heard Lomax observe, "Cake, huh? Looks homemade, too."

"Don't touch that!" Laura exclaimed. But almost immediately she added reasonably, "You probably didn't even get to finish your meal before, so why don't you have a sandwich instead? Come on, leave that alone. I can give you salmon, or I have a little—"

Lomax broke in, and his voice was frightening in its calm. "What is this about, Laura?"

"Nothing, I swear. I just want you to eat something sensible, that's all."

"That's all, huh?" he retorted sharply. At least, I believe those were his words, since they were uttered so softly I couldn't be sure. Or it's possible I wasn't really listening anymore. Because almost at this same moment, one horrifying fact became clear to me:

Laura had put something in that cake!

For a couple of seconds I was in shock. My brain had shut down completely. I couldn't think, much less move; it was as if I were rooted to the floor. And then this stubborn, self-preserving core that I'm convinced lies dormant in all of us suddenly activated itself, commanding my legs to function, willing me to get out of there—THIS INSTANT!

As I fled from the apartment, my heart pounding in triple time, Bobby Lomax yelled after me, "Desiree! Stop! You can't go now!"

Chapter 37

The elevators were directly across from Laura's apartment. And by the light inside one of the cars, I realized with great relief that it was right on this floor.

I stabbed at the button. The door was maddeningly slow to respond. I stood there bouncing from one foot to the other, thought after thought racing through my mind.

I'd been *poisoned*! Maybe, this very minute, I was even *dying*! I had to get to a hospital—and fast. Where *was* the nearest hospital, anyway? *Don't worry, you'll find out,* I assured myself, trying to put down the panic. I wondered about Lomax then. Had he really been unaware that Laura had tried to kill me? Possibly. But it was also possible that this was part of the act. And besides, let's say he wasn't in on this from the start. That didn't mean he wouldn't be willing to help his lover finish me off.

The elevator creaked open—just as I imagined I heard something behind me. I cast a fearful glance over my shoulder as I got in. But there was nothing to see. Still, I was half expecting that at any second Lomax would burst from the apartment and drag me out of here at knifepoint. Frantically I punched the button marked L, then immediately pressed it again, keeping my finger on it this time. I was quivering from the crown of my hennaed head right down to the toes of my taupe leather pumps.

At last the car began its interminable descent from the third floor. It occurred to me now that those two upstanding citizens might have decided to spare themselves any further trouble and planned to simply allow the poison to do its work. *What did that damn bitch put in that crappy cake of hers?* I chided myself at once. *Never mind that; the real question is, how much longer do I have?* God! At the rate this elevator was moving, I could be dead before it ever reached the street level!

When the car jerked to a stop and it registered on me that I was still alive, I was actually a bit surprised. I was also determined to keep things that way—for as long as I could, anyhow. So before leaving the comparative safety of this little four-by-five-foot cubicle, I peered out and surveyed the lobby.

Empty. *Thank you, God!*

I dashed—yes, *dashed*—from the elevator and out of the building, moving with a speed I never dreamed I could attain. And no doubt will never duplicate.

I should mention that although it takes a little while to explain what transpired next, the incident itself most likely lasted about three minutes—if that.

I'd covered about half the distance to my Chevy when somebody yelled, "Desiree!"

I didn't have to turn around to realize that it was Bobby Lomax's voice and that he was only a few yards in back of me.

"Wait up, will you!" he shouted.

I kept running. Just ahead was a street lamp, and going by it now was an elderly man walking briskly in the opposite direction. As we passed one another, I called out to him. But at this point I had so little breath left in me that my "Phone the police" was weak. And chances are, he didn't even hear me.

"Stop! Let me help you!" Lomax yelled. He seemed to be closer now.

As hard as I pushed myself, though, I couldn't go any faster. But evidently Lomax could. And moments later he had hold of my arm. His hands were a lot more powerful than I'd have imagined.

A couple of cars came down the street at just about this time. But either they didn't see what was going on—although the area was fairly well lit—or they didn't realize its significance. Or could be they preferred not to get involved.

"You don't have to be afraid of me, Desiree," Lomax said then. "I'm a cop."

Right. And I'm a missionary, I thought, struggling to break away. But it was useless. The man's fingers were like a vise, digging deep into my flesh. "I only want to drive you to a hospital," he told me in a tone dripping with sincerity.

Yeah, sure. And your girlfriend only wanted to fix me a nice, healthy snack. And now I attempted a scream. But as a result of the breath shortage I was only able to eke out a small, pitiful whimper. (See? As I've always suspected, exercise really *isn't* that good for you.) There was no opportunity for a second go at it, either, because Lomax promptly clamped his hand over my mouth. And then he hastily checked out the immediate vicinity to determine if anyone might be witnessing our scuffle. Apparently no one was. "Try that again," he hissed in my ear, "and I'll knock you cold. I won't even hesitate, so I advise you not to test me. Do you understand?" I nodded. He removed his hand from my mouth. "It's important that we get you taken care of as quickly as possible. Where is your car?"

I didn't answer. Partially out of defiance and partially because this took more energy than I cared to part with.

Exasperated by my silence, Lomax spat out the next words. "Listen, there's no time to fool around. You need medical attention fast, and I'm parked three blocks away." I wouldn't have thought it possible, but his grip on my arm became still tighter, and I cried out in pain. "Now, where the hell is your friggin' car?"

"Over there," I gasped, pointing. "It's that Chevy over there."

"Good. Okay, move."

He propelled me over to the car. I didn't go with him willingly, but I was too spent by then to offer much resistance.

"All right. Give me the keys," he ordered.

"They're in my handbag." (Can you believe I hadn't had the foresight to take out my car keys while I was in the elevator?)

"Get them."

Lomax continued to clutch my arm as I fished around in that portable junk shop I call a handbag. Two women strolled by together while I was still occupied with my search, but before I was even aware that they were there—they weren't anymore. Anyhow, when I finally extracted the keys—which had somehow worked their way to the bottom of the bag—I turned to Lomax as if to place them in his outstretched palm.

But instead, I summoned up my last bit of strength and aimed my knee at his groin. Unfortunately, however, the knee was a couple of inches off target, and while the attack caused him to wince, its effect was short-lived and not nearly as debilitating as I had hoped for.

"You stupid woman," he muttered, wrenching the keys from my grasp. And opening the car door, he shoved me onto the seat. Then he locked the door and ran around to the driver's side.

I remember very little of what happened after this. All I know is that Lomax was using only one hand to steer so as to retain his grip on my left arm with the other. And I recall that we had barely pulled away from the curb when I twisted around and, with my right hand, made a desperate grab for the wheel.

There was a crash.

And then there was nothing at all.

Chapter 38

I opened my eyes to find Lomax looming over me. Well, at least whatever happened with the car hadn't been fatal. And it was obvious the poison hadn't done me in yet, either. I mean, I could be certain that I wasn't in heaven, because there was no way this creep would have ended up there, too.

"How're you doing?" he said.

"Where are you holding me?" I croaked. My throat was sore and my head hurt. Also my stomach felt as if an elephant had been dancing on it. Or maybe *in* it.

Lomax chuckled. "I'm not holding you anywhere. The doctors are. In spite of your best efforts to cancel us both, I managed to get you to the hospital." I glanced around to verify this. I really was in a hospital, in a small, semiprivate room—the other bed in here being presently unoccupied. I noticed now that daylight was peeping in between the partially opened window curtains. "They wanted to keep you overnight for observation, but you'll probably be released sometime this morning."

It was coming back to me. "I had all these tubes going down me. In my nose, in my mouth—everywhere," I mumbled, grimacing.

"Not quite everywhere," Lomax corrected. And his eyes seemed to be grinning at me. "The doctors said they gave you a lavage with a saline solution to wash out the poison—for that there was a tube in your nose. And then later they inserted a tube in your mouth that had activated charcoal in it to absorb any remaining poison and prevent it from entering the bloodstream. The important thing, though, is that you're going to be just fine."

"Last night's still a bit hazy," I admitted.

"I can understand your being slightly confused." Lomax dragged a chair next to the bed and took a seat. "We had an accident—an automobile accident—on the way over here. Does that ring a bell?"

"Kind of."

"You hit your head on the dashboard and blacked out for a while." He half rose, then leaned over and reached for my hand, placing it on my forehead. "See? You've got a nice little lump there. Anyhow, you didn't come to until the doctors had already started working on you."

"The accident—" I put to him fearfully, recalling now that I'd been the cause of it, "was . . . was anyone hurt?"

"No. We slammed into a parked car, that's all. But I had to flag down another car to get you here. Listen, lady, you certainly make it tough for a guy to play hero."

I was both relieved and embarrassed. "I'm sorry, *really* sorry that I gave you such a hard time." And then it occurred to me that I hadn't even said thank you to this man for saving my life. "I'm very grateful to you for bringing me to a hospital," I told him. "I imagine that if not for you, I'd be playing a harp right now."

Lomax wasn't going to let this pass. And who could blame him after what I'd put him through? "I wouldn't be too sure of that. Maybe you'd have wound up down below shoveling coal."

"Uh, about my car. It wasn't totaled or anything, was it?" I mean, I suppose you could even call the Chevy a heap. But it was *my* heap.

"I doubt it. But I'll have it checked out. I really don't think the damage was too bad, though. So don't worry."

"Thanks. Thanks a lot."

"Listen, you seem beat," Lomax said then. "Why don't you try and get some more sleep. I have to take off now anyway."

"What time is it?"

"Just after six." He smiled. "A.M., that is."

"You've been here all this while?"

"No, I just popped in a few minutes ago to have a look at

you—my apartment's not that far from this place. I was about to cut out when you woke up."

"What hospital is this, by the way?"

"Saint Anne's. In Queens."

Well, at any rate, he was right. About my being tired, that is. I was completely exhausted. In fact, my eyelids were starting to droop. But I forced them open. There was something I had to know.

"Can you stay just a couple of minutes longer?" I didn't give him a chance to say no. "I wanted to ask if you and Laura . . . that is, you had no idea she planned to murder me?"

"Would you be here if I did? And never mind *that.* I was even ready to sample her poisoned honey cake myself." I'm not positive, but I think Lomax turned a little paler at the thought. And then he said, "Look, Desiree, I'm a cop. Well, a cop of sorts. I tried to tell you this before, but you're not that easy to convince."

"What do you mean 'of sorts'?"

"Not now. I'll explain everything when we talk again. I promise."

"Tonight?" I pressed.

"All right, tonight. I'll even stop by your house, okay? I have some questions for you, too."

"Okay. But just one more thing before you leave. Did the doctors find out what kind of poison Laura used?"

"I was able to provide *them* with that information. Why do you think it took me so long to go after you? I had to apply a little pressure to Laura's throat before she'd agree to tell me what she'd cooked up for you. It appears, though, that she made the honey in that cake herself, from something called California buckeye."

"California buckeye?"

"Yeah. Also known as horse chestnut."

"You've heard of it before, then."

"Never. But while the doctors were treating you, I put in a phone call to someone who *is* familiar with it—a toxicologist I know. He tells me that's pretty lethal stuff. How did the cake taste, anyway?"

"I can't really say. Laura served it with raspberry sauce, and that's mostly what I tasted."

"Anyhow, this California buckeye—which incidentally, from what I understand, is fairly easy to come by—takes a day or two before it affects you. That's no doubt why she chose it. She most likely figured that by the time it started to work, nobody would connect the poisoning to her. It's conceivable that even you might not have thought to blame your symptoms on Laura's little dessert."

Well, at this point my eyes had reached the stage where they were like slits. And my stomach still wasn't feeling too swell, either. But I wasn't about to let the man walk out. Not yet.

"What about Laura? Why wasn't she poisoned, too?"

"Let me put it like this. Did you actually see her cutting any of that cake for herself?"

"Yes. Of course." And then I reviewed that scene in the kitchen. Both portions were already on the plates when I entered the room. "Wait a second. No, I didn't."

Lomax nodded with satisfaction. "There was evidently a second cake around somewhere, a nontoxic one. Had to be. But anyway, I almost forgot. Before I get out of here, there's something you might want to see."

"What?"

He stood up then. And removing a handkerchief from his jeans pocket, he unfolded it to reveal a very crumbled piece of honey cake. "This was the slice Laura was yelling at me not to eat," he informed me, extending his arm so I could get a better view.

I realized instantly that I was looking at my second helping— the one I didn't get to consume because Lomax, bless him, had begun raising a ruckus at the door by then.

As he put the cake back in his pocket, Lomax's lips curled in something resembling a smile. "*Now* let her try saying there was nothing the matter with that cake."

Chapter 39

They released me from the hospital at around eleven that morning, and I took a taxi into Manhattan.

Once I was back in my apartment, the first thing I did was to retrieve the messages on my answering machine.

I'd had two calls on Sunday night. One was from Al, who was checking to find out if I could make it for dinner on Tuesday. And the other was from Bruce, who apologized for breaking his promise about getting in touch with me—only he "just *had* to know how the investigation was coming along." Well, I was charitable enough not to blame him, since I really should have contacted him with the big news on Saturday.

This morning's messages were from Jackie and Ellen, both of whom were demanding to know where I was and why I hadn't contacted the office.

Having established—to my own satisfaction, at any rate—that there was nothing here requiring immediate attention, I unplugged the phones, peeled off my clothes, and crawled into bed. And it wasn't because I was so tired, either. Or even because I was feeling ill—actually, by now I felt somewhat better. The truth is, at present I was more shaken than sick as a result of last night's events. And the remedy I prescribed for myself was to bury my anxiety in sleep.

In the course of the next few hours I must have opened my eyes half a dozen times and then stubbornly closed them and drifted off again. During my waking moments, though, I did give a thought or two to the calls I should be returning.

I had some genuine—if transitory—guilt pangs about Ellen; she'd sounded worried. However, even before I remembered about unplugging the phones, I convinced myself that I lacked the energy to reach over to the night table and lift up the receiver. Not that I honestly believed it; I was well aware of being overly self-indulgent. But I considered that I had a right to be, never having been poisoned before. And besides, I absolutely *knew* that Sunday's screeches would be like pallid rehearsals for the high C's Ellen would let loose when I told her about the California buckeye. And I definitely wasn't ready for that.

Jackie would have to wait, too. I mean, you have no idea of the snit that woman gets into if I dare show up late at the office without prior notification. ("Late" being by her own definition, which varies considerably from one episode to the next, depending on her mood.) I figured that by this time I was most likely in imminent danger of being fired. (Jackie has never quite recognized the fact that *she* works for *me*.) Either that, or she was attempting to induce Governor Pataki to call out the National Guard for a Desiree hunt. But one thing you could bet on: Dial that number, and I'd be in for an interrogation the likes of which would make another lavage seem almost benign.

I should definitely get in touch with Bruce, though. Thanks to Laura's creativity in the kitchen, charges could now be brought against her for attempted murder, at the very least. What's more, this second violent action of hers should certainly let Bruce off the hook for his wife's death. But the thing is, he'd want to know how I had finally come around to IDing the killer. And I'm sorry, but at the moment I was hardly up to dealing with all that.

Then there was Al—and the dinner. Well, I couldn't possibly face a real meal yet, and I was bound to still be off my feed tomorrow. I suddenly recalled Al's mention of seafood in the message he'd left for me on Friday—which only reinforced my conclusion. I mean, I had this image of a whole bunch of shrimp swimming around on my plate in a yellow garlic-butter sauce. *Ugh.* I hated those slimy little creatures; I hated *food*. There was no question I'd have to let Al know I wouldn't be able to see him on Tuesday. And it wasn't very considerate to let this slide until the last minute, either. Nevertheless, it might be advisable to spare myself from going through a tedious explanation in my present fragile condition. (Was I milking this thing for all it was worth, or what?) Actually, it wouldn't hurt if I postponed that call until tonight, I decided. Or even until tomorrow, for that matter.

Being poisoned, I suppose, can color your thinking.

It was past three o'clock when I dragged myself out of bed. I had a cup of tea and a couple of slices of dry toast. And after that I prepared some lime Jell-O, which was to be the highlight of tonight's supper.

Now, under normal circumstances I'm passionately anti-Jell-O. I can't name another edible that's as boring. The only reason there was even a package in the house was because I'd picked it up one time right after having a couple of wisdom teeth pulled. But then when I got home that afternoon I'd quickly rethought the menu to avoid eating the stuff. Today, however, I was actually happy it was still in the back of the cupboard. (*Jell-O!* Can you imagine being practically delirious over having *Jell-O* on hand?)

Anyhow, while I was diddling around in the kitchen, Ellen crept into my mind again.

She was undoubtedly beside herself by now. I wouldn't be surprised if she'd tried to phone me during these last few hours—and more than once, too. (In all honesty, that's one of the reasons I'd unplugged the telephones.) So after taking a couple of minutes to work up to it, I finally dialed her at Macy's.

What was it I'd said about high C before? Well, forget it. Ellen's "Aunt Dez!" was all the way up around E. Following which she peppered me with questions. "Where are you? Where have you been? Are you okay? Do you realize I've been trying to reach you this entire day? Have you any idea how upset I am?"

"Now, don't get excited, Ellen," I inserted when she took a breath. "I'm home. I was in Queens overnight, though—at

Saint Anne's Hospital." And then I instantly threw in, "But I'm okay now. Really."

Evidently, however, Ellen didn't find this terribly reassuring. "Hospital!" she shrieked. "When Jackie called me this morning, I got this cold chill all over. I just *knew* something awful had happened to you."

Jackie, it seems, had contacted her with the bulletin that I was a no-show at work and that she hadn't been able to get me on the phone. Ellen, of course, had immediately made it clear that she wasn't harboring any secret information about my hideout. At which point, Ellen told me, Jackie decided to get hold of my Rolodex and start calling everybody and his brother to try and locate me.

Swell!

"Wh-why were you in a hospital?" Ellen was asking anxiously.

"Laura Downey fed me poisoned honey cake last night."

Another shriek. "Oh, my God!" And then somewhat closer to her normal voice range: "A *what* did you say she fed you? Never mind. The main thing is that you're all right. You did say you were all right, didn't you?"

"Yes. It turns out that Laura's boyfriend—I think I may have mentioned him to you—is a cop of some kind. He brought me right to the hospital, and they were able to wash the poison out. But let me tell you, this was not a pleasant process. I had these tubes down me, and—" I broke off. "Yecch. I don't even want to think about it. But, anyhow, I guess I was pretty lucky."

"I'm coming over."

"No, no. Don't do that. I'll be going to bed very early; I'm still a little tired."

"I could leave this minute and bring you some supper. I'll just stop off at the deli for a container of soup and some nice crackers and, let's see, maybe—"

"Honestly, Ellen, I do appreciate this, but I've already prepared something for later." (I couldn't bring myself to say what it was.) "And besides, they told me at the hospital to be sure to get plenty of sleep."

Now, I'd already had more than enough, as you know, plus they hadn't made any such recommendation. But the last thing I needed here today was my lovable worrywart of a niece fussing over me until I went totally—and maybe permanently—out of my mind.

"Uh, well, all right," Ellen reluctantly agreed. "You'll call if you need me, though, won't you?"

"Absolutely—but don't hang up yet. I have a couple of favors to ask of you." And I laid two of the chores I'd been dodging in her lap. "Would you phone Jackie and let her know what's happened? And then ask her to get in touch with Al Bonaventure and tell him I can't see him tomorrow but that I'll talk to him soon." I was resigned to contacting Bruce myself— and this afternoon, too. In all conscience, I realized that there was just so much I could foist off on Ellen.

"No problem," she responded with her usual good nature. And then she added, "Gee, it's a shame, though."

"What specifically are you referring to?" I mean, I had no idea. Was it my being poisoned? Landing in the hospital? The tubes?

"That you won't be going out with Al tomorrow."

There are times I wonder about Ellen's priorities.

I knew that having restored my telephone service, I'd be hearing from Jackie in a matter of minutes. But at least Ellen would have taken care of the explanations—for the most part, anyway.

Smiling to myself, I checked my watch: 4:20.

At 4:29 the call came in.

"Ellen told me everything," Jackie said, her tone grim. "My God, Dez, I feel so terrible about this. Being mad at you for not coming to work today, I'm talking about. Of course," she added hurriedly, "after a while, I became a lot more worried than angry. Anyway, Ellen says you're all right, and that's what counts."

"Yes, I was fortunate."

"What kind of a person would do a thing like that?"

"A not overly nice one."

"Very funny. Look, I understand that you have to get your rest, so I won't stay long."

Icy tentacles of dread clutched at my heart. "What do you mean?"

"I just want to come by with some dinner for you. I'll pick up something that's very easy to digest."

"That's really thoughtful of you, Jackie, and I thank you. But I can get around. In fact, I fixed my supper for tonight about an hour ago. I'm only hoping I can eat it; I don't have much of an appetite."

"Are you sure you can't use some help?"

"You're a good friend, Jackie. But I'm managing fine."

The words came out slowly. "All right, then, if I can't give you a hand."

"Everything's under control. I swear."

"Well, if you decide you want some company this evening, just holler. I'll be in from about six o'clock on. Oh, and Dez?"

"What?"

"I tried Al before—only he was with a patient. But he'll be getting back to me, and I'll let him know about tomorrow night and the poisoning and everything."

"I appreciate that."

"I have something else to tell you, too. I spoke to him this morning—that was to see if he might have some idea about where you were." *Oh, crap!* "He didn't, naturally." *Naturally!* "And he was very concerned that something might have happened to you."

Now, I won't deny that I liked the "very concerned" part. But immediately afterward Jackie left me openmouthed.

"The man cares, Dez. It's too bad you couldn't hear how he sounded. You know, I'm aware that this was a *terrible* experience for you. But, umm, I can't help thinking it might have been almost worth it. In a way, anyhow."

Did I say I wonder about *Ellen's* priorities?

*   *   *

Having recently finished with Jackie and noting that I wasn't banging my head against the wall, I figured I could tackle Bruce now, too. Well, not only *could,* but *should.*

I reached him at his office, catching him just as he was leaving to meet a friend for drinks.

"I gather you got my message," he said.

"Yes, but I was going to get in touch with you anyway. I have a lot to talk to you about. Look, why don't you call me later—I'm at home."

"Not on your life. My friend can wait."

"This will probably take a while."

"I don't care. Go ahead. And please, don't leave anything out."

"All right. To start with, I know who killed Cheryl."

There were a few seconds of stunned silence, followed by a whispered "Thank God."

I filled him in then on how I'd arrived at my conclusion, after which I proceeded to Laura and her cake, finally winding up with my rescue by a cop "of sorts."

"This is wonderful, Dez!" Bruce exclaimed. "I guess it means that at long last I'm off the hook with your buddy Fielding, doesn't it?"

"I'd say so." At this mention of Tim Fielding, I found myself grinning. Being perennially childish, I was really looking forward to rubbing Laura's guilt in his face. I'd phone him tomorrow, by which time I could hope to have accumulated a little more strength for gloating.

"See? I was right all along. I was positive that I could count on you," Bruce said happily.

Our conversation ended without any indication that the man was disturbed in the slightest about my close-to-fatal encounter with the killer. I mean, there'd been no acknowledgment of it whatever.

Worse yet, though, he hadn't said a single word about my revelations in relation to Cheryl.

It dawned on me then that my client had never been as interested in learning who killed his wife as he was in exonerating himself.

And so I was reminded once again—and it's no great reflection on me that every so often I required reminding—that underneath all of his charm, Bruce Simon was just plain scum.

Chapter 40

Bobby Lomax was on my doorsill at five-thirty.

"It's great to be home, I'll bet," he remarked as he was seating himself in the living room. "But I thought that by now you'd probably be out jogging."

"Jogging? I'd sooner have another helping of Laura's honey cake."

He laughed. "You're looking pretty good, you know that?"

"Liar." The last time I'd checked the mirror—and things certainly hadn't improved since then—I was a sight. My oversprayed, stiff-as-a-board hair was shooting off in all directions, having triumphed handily over a somewhat mediocre effort to make it presentable. (I really should have gotten out my wig— a conclusion I'd arrived at just as the downstairs buzzer rang.) Also, I had a brand-new, humongous zit right alongside my nose. And what's more, with my "good" bathrobe presently one of the many occupants of an overstuffed clothes hamper, I was attired in a nifty little number that should have been tossed out ages ago. It was a faded yellow chenille adorned here and there with colorful red splotches—the colorful part being the price it paid for that time it rolled around in the washing machine with a crimson shirt. And as if that weren't enough, there was a noticeable tear under one arm, so I'd have to remember to avoid any broad gestures.

I should mention, however, that Lomax was hardly a thing of beauty himself. For openers, there was the straggly ponytail and that eye- (and crumb-) catching Fu Manchu mustache of his. And when you factor in the sallow skin, the crumpled black

T-shirt, and a pair of torn black jeans that fit him like the skin on a baloney—well, he was one sleazy-looking character.

"Can I get you something to drink?" I couldn't quite bring myself to make an offer of food.

"Thanks, but I'm fine."

"Listen, I have a lot of questions for you," I informed him as I settled myself on the sofa.

"I kind of figured you would."

I kicked off with my major concern. "What's going on with Laura?"

"Don't worry. She's in custody."

Praise the Lord! "Have you gotten her to confess to the murder?"

"Uh, listen, Desiree, I'm not a member of the police department. I'm with the DEA."

"The DEA?" Now, I'm absolutely convinced that ordinarily I wouldn't have found it necessary to ask, but for some reason—I like to think it was because of my recent trauma—just then I was blank.

"Drug Enforcement Administration. I've been working undercover to find out who Laura was passing the cocaine to here in the States."

"Oh, for heaven's sake," I murmured. And after I'd absorbed this: "Well, have you?"

"Found out anything? You might say so. We're reasonably sure we've made her New York connection. The problem is, though, that the two of them have been pretty damn clever about things, and we've never been able to get a fix on when she was actually handing over the junk. Which is why I happened to be around her place last night."

"And thank God for that," I responded fervently. "But you were saying?" I prompted a moment later.

"Well, the point is, as vigilant as I try to be, in the past I could see—in retrospect, naturally—where there might have been a tiny window when she could have unloaded the stuff. But I would have sworn she hadn't had a single chance to do that since returning from Nassau on Saturday. So I figured that

either I'm not as smart as I think I am"—he grinned here—
"which is highly unlikely, or she wasn't carrying this weekend.
Or—and this is what I was counting on—the thing hadn't gone
down yet. At any rate, that's why I told her I'd be in Manhattan all day Sunday. I was hoping she'd take it as an opportunity
to have the meet, and also, with me out of the way, she just
might be a little less circumspect about it."

"You were staking out the house?"

"Right. That—in case you're wondering—is why my car
was parked a couple of blocks away. I wanted to make certain
Laura didn't spot it."

To be honest, I hadn't given any thought at all to Lomax's
transportation. Nevertheless, I nodded politely.

"To go on, though," he said, "since leaving Laura's apartment early that morning, I'd been watching the building, waiting to see if anything would transpire. But she didn't so much
as stick her nose out of the door that entire day."

"Probably too busy baking my cake," I observed dryly.

"I wouldn't be surprised. Anyway, the guy I was laying for
didn't put in an appearance, either. And neither did anyone else
who was even the least bit suspicious. So I was still hanging in
when you showed up. Initially I had no idea whether it was
Laura or Hank you were there to see. And the thought it might
be Laura had me a little edgy. Then when Hank went out about
ten minutes later—which definitely narrowed it down—I got
really nervous. I finally came to the conclusion that I'd better
check on things."

"You suspected that Laura had murdered her friend—was
that what made you decide to investigate?"

"You bet. I'd heard about your theory on the killer's motive
from being privy to some conversations Laura'd had with
Donna and Hank. And obviously, knowing what I did, your
version of things made perfect sense to me. I considered it
highly unlikely that anyone *but* Laura was responsible for that
woman's death."

Now, I have to admit that my thought processes are not exactly lightning-quick. Still, it shouldn't have taken *this* long for

the implications of a certain piece of information to register. "Wait a minute," I said, suddenly alarmed. "Being that you— the DEA, I'm referring to—were the ones who collared Laura, does this mean you people are trying to convince her to cooperate with your agency?"

Lomax looked uncomfortable. "I can't discuss anything like that with you."

"All right. But just answer one question for me. If she *should* give you what she knows on the drug thing, am I to assume that she won't be charged with murder?"

This apparently called for a fingernail check. And then when Lomax finally raised his eyes, he seemed to focus on a spot somewhere behind my left ear. "Uh, as I said, I can't go into that. All I'll tell you is that in cases where the perp assists us with our investigation, something may be worked out where she—or he—is allowed to cop to a lesser charge." And now in response to what he was seeing on my face: "But even if that does happen here, this wouldn't necessarily preclude Laura's still going away for quite some time."

"Yeah, like what? Six months, maybe?" I grumbled, disgusted.

"I would hope it's a lot longer than that. Anyway, I don't know that Laura's even agreed to help us so far."

I glared at him. "And you wouldn't tell me if you did."

Lomax smiled weakly. "I realize you're not happy about this, Desiree. But there doesn't seem to be any option. You have to appreciate that for years we've been trying to get something concrete against El Puerco and his pals. This is a very nasty bunch—an *extremely* nasty bunch—we're talking about. The deaths they're responsible for—and I'm only referring to the ones they're directly responsible for, those they've actually had a hand in—well, the body count must be in the dozens. At any rate, I'm trying to explain that it's possible—and I'm only saying 'possible,' " he injected hastily, "that Laura may hold the key to torpedoing the whole stinking operation. And that includes bagging El Puerco himself. So if nailing those mothers takes making a deal with her—"

"Making a deal with someone who's *also* a killer," I reminded him. "And almost a two-time killer, if you recall."

"I know," Lomax admitted. "And I can't say I'm too thrilled about that myself."

Chapter 41

For maybe a minute no words were exchanged between us. Then Lomax suggested softly, "Why don't we wait and see how it all works out?"

"I guess we'll have to, won't we?" I responded grudgingly.

And now he said in a lighter tone, "It's your turn in the barrel, though. And I've got a bunch of questions for you, too. For starters, what put you on to Laura, anyhow?"

This seemed to loosen the knot in my chest. (I have to admit that even under these circumstances, I couldn't forego the opportunity to show off a little.) "Well," I began, immediately warming to my task, "I presume you're aware that the victim witnessed a couple of suspicious incidents in Nassau. I mean, you did mention agreeing with my theory that this is what led to her death."

"Yep. Although since I wasn't personally involved in the murder investigation, I probably don't have all the facts."

"I'll fill you in as I go along. And anything I don't cover, just ask. But to give you your answer, it was actually a remark that Cheryl herself made a couple of days before her death that pointed to Laura. She said—in her husband's presence—'Everything fits now.' And he repeated this to me.

"The thing is, though, from the first I had taken Cheryl's comment as an indication that she'd seen or heard something more, something she hadn't put any stock in until that night in the Nassau cocktail lounge." I looked at Lomax meaningfully here.

He picked up his cue. "But you've come to believe that this wasn't what she had in mind?"

"Exactly. And it was when I figured out that there was another way to interpret these same words that I was able to identify the murderer."

I derived some small satisfaction from the puzzled expression creasing Lomax's forehead.

"Cheryl could also have been referring to somebody's *clothes* fitting now," I went on. "Which would certainly suggest that they hadn't before. And who in Cheryl's circle had, in the not-too-distant past, suddenly developed a nice round shape? No one but dear, sweet Laura. In fact, their copilot told me—and in so many words, too—that prior to this Laura didn't even fill out her uniform. Well, where did that roundness come from?" I demanded excitedly. "From padding, that's where. Naturally, the—"

"Hold it a minute. Why were you so convinced you'd arrived at the meaning the victim had actually intended?"

"Because it finally dawned on me that if Cheryl had been referring to an additional *incident,* she would have spoken to her husband about it. After all, she was trying to give him a complete picture of what had alerted her to the possibility that her friend was involved in drug trafficking."

Lomax didn't entirely agree with me. "You're probably right—but not necessarily. Also, it could be that she did tell the husband about a third sighting or whatever—most likely something that was of no great consequence—and he forgot about it before he met with you."

"We-ell, maybe. Although I really doubt it. Anyhow, there's more. I—"

"Back up again—to that padding. Let's assume you're correct and that Cheryl *was* referring to the way Laura fit into her clothes these days. How could you be sure this wasn't just about her putting on some extra pounds?" It was obvious that Lomax was playing devil's advocate here—and I had the feeling he was enjoying it, too.

"If Cheryl were merely alluding to Laura's having gained weight, that wouldn't tie in with the drug thing—not as far as I can see, at any rate. And this is what was on Cheryl's mind that night; she was almost sick with worry that her friend might be smuggling drugs.

"You want *real* evidence, though? Another flight attendant caught the perp buying these oversize bras in Bloomingdale's not long before she had that *supposed* horseback riding accident in which she *supposedly* broke her leg. And I have it on very good authority—the best, actually—that Laura was as thin as ever when she left for Toronto. In other words, she was straight as a stick."

"Listen, Desiree," Lomax put in hesitantly, "I just thought of something. I hate to say this—and I'm not absolutely certain—but, well, it seems to me there could be a flaw in your reasoning."

"A flaw?" I repeated, feeling as if my stomach had just dropped straight to my toes. (And Lord knows, my insides had already been through enough since yesterday.)

"While Laura's obviously your killer, it's possible your fingering her was a coincidence. What bothers me is how Cheryl could have been aware of any change in Laura's figure. At the time of the Toronto trip, Cheryl hadn't even started working at Royal Bahamian—unless I've got my facts wrong, that is."

Greatly relieved now and my stomach back in position, I smiled. "You're not wrong, but—"

Lomax didn't appear to be listening. "Of course," he murmured thoughtfully, "the others might have mentioned the difference in Laura's appearance, but that's not the same as seeing it for yourself." And here he looked at me apologetically. "What I'm trying to come to terms with is whether just hearing about something like that would have made enough of an impact on the victim for her to recall it in connection with the smuggling. And frankly, my initial reaction is that it wouldn't."

"I agree one hundred percent. But didn't you know that the two women were acquainted while they were both living in Chicago? In fact, they were with the same airline for a time. And then when Cheryl comes to New York—*voilà!*—this former coworker is squeezing a whole new body into her uniform."

"Geez," Lomax mumbled, practically hanging his head. "I feel like an idiot. Chicago completely slipped my mind." There was a three- or four-second interval before he asked sheepishly, "Where were we, anyway?"

"With Laura's bras, I think."

"Okay. So your view is that Laura got those bras in order to—?"

"In order to stuff them full of drugs, as you very well know."

Lomax grinned. "How did she explain her purchases to this other woman—or didn't she?"

"Oh, she did. She claimed she was shopping for her grandmother or her aunt or somebody." Naturally, in light of everything else I'd discovered, I no longer gave that contention of Laura's the slightest bit of credence. And I rolled my eyes to indicate this—just in case there was any doubt.

"And another thing," I pressed on, "if my theory's correct, Laura would have had to substitute the drugs for the padding, and, of course, it would be advisable to do it as quickly as possible. Well, when Cheryl was telling Bruce—her husband—that she'd come upon her mysterious friend and El Puerco sitting side by side in that cocktail lounge, she mentioned the friend's switching shoulder bags with El Puerco and then taking his bag into the john with her. And obviously Laura went into the bathroom during that other meeting with El Puerco, too—in the luncheonette, I mean—because she informed Cheryl that the toilet was stuffed up. Actually, it's more than likely that Laura herself was responsible for clogging it by attempting to flush down the cotton or whatever it was she used for padding."

"You make a couple of good points."

"I think, too, that those rest room visits—particularly in light of the exchange of bags—are what suggested to Cheryl that Laura's curves might not have come naturally."

"Could be. But listen, you said her 'supposed' accident before. You don't believe Laura really broke her leg?"

"Not for a minute. Once I'd reinterpreted Cheryl's words, I realized that by manufacturing the accident, Laura had provided herself with the perfect excuse for leaving town long enough for a decent weight gain to be conceivable. Something she obviously considered vital to her forthcoming business association with El Puerco et al."

Lomax absently scratched his chin. "But didn't any of the people she worked with go to see her during all that time?"

"No. Laura insisted that they not come up there."

And now he mused, "I wonder what would have happened if when one of them called her—and I presume that being her friends, they did call—someone else had answered the phone. What I'm getting at is, what if this party was asked how Laura's leg was?"

"That occurred to me, too. The way I see it, Laura either had a private line or else she dreamed up a plausible little tale for dealing with this sort of contingency. I'll give you an example. She could have told her mother that she had to get away from New York for a while, maybe claiming she was very stressed out or that she was trying to get over some man—I don't know. And then she'd have said that in order to take off from the job like that, it had been necessary to pretend that she'd had an accident. Well, under those circumstances, I can see the mother instructing the rest of the household to go along with the broken leg story, can't you?"

"I guess so," Lomax conceded.

"And while we're on the subject of Laura's legs—or at least one of them—they helped convince me I was on the right track." I thought that statement was kind of provocative, so for a brief time I didn't say anything further, anticipating that Lomax would be only too eager to question me on this. But he sat there mutely, apparently making up his mind to wait me out.

I gave in. (It was a silly game, anyhow.) "You noticed that her legs were too thin for the rest of her, didn't you?" Lomax's lips parted, a good indication he was about to reply. I prevented his uttering so much as a syllable, though. "And before you tell me that this happens," I said hurriedly, "I agree that it does. But not that often. Besides, I'm not through yet; I have more for you."

This time I allowed him the space for a response. "Go on."

"Are you aware that Cheryl spoke to Laura the day before the murder?" I asked.

"No, this is the first I've heard of it."

"That's what I figured. Well, the phone company records show that Cheryl telephoned Laura that afternoon. I have no doubt this was to arrange to see her the following day. Laura's version, however, is that Cheryl asked for her advice on confronting someone she suspected of smuggling drugs. Cheryl refused to give her the name, but from the conversation, Laura was able to deduce that the victim was talking about either Donna or Hank. At any rate, Cheryl wanted to know whether or not she should call whoever it was to make certain they'd be home before she went trekking out to Forest Hills. And Laura told her it might be a better strategy to go for a surprise visit. All of the aforementioned crap as per Laura, of course."

"This is news to me."

"The thing is, if I'd taken the trouble to really examine it, I would have realized right away that Laura's story didn't hold up. Or anyway, I like to think that I would have. After all, Cheryl had already demonstrated how committed she was to playing this entire matter very close to the vest until she was satisfied she had the facts. Just consider the pains she took to protect the perp's identity when she was relating the Bahamas incidents to her husband. So I find it hard to imagine—in retrospect, naturally—" and I made a face here, "that she'd bring another party into this and risk having that person speculate about the guilt or innocence of their close mutual friends. And it's particularly unlikely she'd have done it for a reason that's actually pretty damn slight."

Lomax nodded. "I tend to agree with you there."

"There's no denying that Laura's fast on her feet, though. I almost have to admire the woman for producing an instant lie that's even *that* credible."

"Oh, she's a sharp customer, all right."

"At any rate," I said, "when you add all these things up . . ." I concluded my presentation with a self-satisfied smile.

"You know, you haven't done a bad job of piecing everything together. For a P.I., that is," Lomax teased.

"Thanks a bundle."

And now there was a prolonged silence. I took it as a sign that Lomax had run out of questions. There was something I was anxious to ask *him* about, however, and I decided I'd better do it immediately, since I was most likely only a few minutes removed from my Jell-O. (Which, incidentally, was beginning to lose its earlier appeal for me.) Anyhow, I was trying to come up with a genteel way of phrasing things when he sat forward in his chair.

"What you've been telling me does seem to—excuse the expression—fit," he said. "But there are a couple of points I'd like to talk about."

"Sure."

"For example, do you have any theories about how Laura wound up on that train to West Fourth Street with Cheryl? I assume they *were* traveling together."

"I'm pretty positive of that. And one possibility is that Cheryl persuaded Laura to accompany her into the city—to see an attorney, for instance. But although I still wouldn't rule this out, after I thought things over for a while I began to feel that it was more probable the initiative came from Laura. This way seems just a little too convenient, a little too *easy* for the perp, if you know what I mean."

"I'll level with you. For some reason, I hadn't even considered that Laura might have made the trip at Cheryl's suggestion. But you're right. It does seem too convenient."

"Okay, try this. Laura may have tailed Cheryl to the Forest Hills station and then sat in another car of the train. In which case Cheryl wouldn't even have been aware that she had company."

"I can go along with that one."

"The third option is that Laura convinced Cheryl of the need to return to Manhattan with her."

"And how did she manage that?"

"Well, I can give you one scenario, at least, that I consider quite plausible."

"Somehow I knew you could." Lomax's face was close to being a blank, but I was certain there was a grin hovering very close to the surface.

"It might be," I speculated, "that once Cheryl aired her suspicions, Laura proposed that the two of them go to see Captain Byrnes—he's the pilot."

"And this visit would ostensibly serve what purpose?"

"Maybe Laura was insisting that Byrnes could prove she had nothing to do with any smuggling. Or conversely, maybe she admitted to her involvement and told Cheryl she wanted Byrnes's counsel; I understand he's considered the most sensible member of the crew. And she might have said to Cheryl that she'd like her to be there for moral support. By the way, I settled on Byrnes because we know that on arriving at the West Fourth Street station, Cheryl asked someone where to get the train to Canal Street—which is very close to Byrnes's apartment. But, of course, Laura could also have stated her intention of consulting with a lawyer in that neighborhood. Or anybody else, for that matter."

"Coming back to Byrnes—he wasn't expecting them, I gather."

"No, he wasn't."

"But if that was where they were supposed to be headed, wouldn't Cheryl have wanted to check out whether the man would even be in?"

"Look, follow me on this—and I don't doubt that there are other possibilities, too. Laura tells Cheryl not to bother phoning Byrnes, that she's sure he's going to be home this afternoon because she just spoke to him. Then when the two women get to Manhattan Cheryl says she'd better give him a ring anyway, just to let him know they're on their way over to talk to him. At this point Laura says never mind, that she'll take care of it, but that in the meantime it would be a good idea if Cheryl got the information on the Canal Street trains—something Laura most likely had no need for at all."

"So why dispatch Cheryl on a phony errand?"

I'm afraid I sent Lomax a pitying glance. "Laura certainly wouldn't have wanted her intended victim with her, since, obviously, she had no intention of making that call."

"That wasn't too swift of me, was it?" he acknowledged meekly. "But here's another question for you. Don't you think Laura would have been concerned that someone might remember seeing her traveling into Manhattan with Cheryl?"

"She had to be. I'll bet she'd been hoping to dispose of Cheryl back in Forest Hills, only she didn't get the opportunity. The thing is, though, the woman was really up against it. She was aware that it was crucial she act before Cheryl blew the whistle on her. She may have taken some steps to minimize the risk, however. Like when they were on the subway, for instance, maybe she buried her nose in a book or held a newspaper in front of her face or made believe she was asleep. That way it might have appeared to the other passengers that Cheryl was on the train alone."

"Well, I suppose this little playlet you've laid out isn't too far-fetched," Lomax conceded after mulling things over for a few seconds. "I'll have to give it some more thought later on. But right now I want to know if you're ready for the big question."

"Fire away."

"What *really* arouses my curiosity is why in God's name you went to Laura's apartment last night."

I explained about my not having any hard evidence and my tape recording scheme and everything.

"You were hopeful that this would work, were you?" The voice was skeptical.

"You never know," I responded a shade defensively. "But let's just say I prayed that it would."

"Well, in the event you haven't already figured it out, you were extremely foolish to put yourself in jeopardy by going up there alone like that. On the other hand, though, I can't understand why, after all these weeks, Laura suddenly made up her mind to get rid of you."

"I believe I can be fairly safe in taking most of the credit for that myself," I confessed. "You see, I allowed my egotism to deep-six my common sense—what there is of it—which led to my making a stupid, almost fatal mistake." And I proceeded to relate how ecstatic I'd been at finally getting somewhere with the case. "I was so disgustingly pleased with myself, in fact, that when Hank called me on Saturday and—in the course of our conversation—asked if I knew yet who had murdered Cheryl, I couldn't bring myself to say no with any conviction."

"You decided you'd rather die, right?"

"Anyhow," I continued, ignoring the sarcasm, "I imagine Hank guessed that I was lying and—" I stopped short; I'd just had a thought. "You know, it's even conceivable that Laura instigated that call from Hank. What I mean is, he was under the impression I had him pegged as the murderer. And it wouldn't surprise me if he voiced his anxiety to Laura and she encouraged him to confront me as a way of learning herself how things stood with the investigation. At any rate, after Hank and I spoke, he must have relayed to his good friend Laura that I'd all but admitted finally identifying Cheryl's killer. You see, in spite of my denial, I think he still feared that I figured him for the perp. Laura, of course, would have been concerned that I'd actually discovered the truth. And then when I phoned her later that same day to set up a meeting, she took it as confirmation that I was on to her."

Lomax's quick, almost curt nod, along with a surreptitious glance at his watch, made me suspect once again that he was almost ready to call it quits. And I wasn't about to let him out of here yet. I still hadn't asked that question of mine—and I intended asking it no matter what. Not that you could consider it relevant to the murder; I admit that. Still, I swear I would have kicked myself all the way to New Jersey if I didn't spit it out.

"Uh, I wonder if I could put *you* on the spot now."

"Sure," he responded agreeably. "Go to it."

I could feel my face growing warm the instant I began to speak. "You must have seen Laura without . . . I mean, when you were alone together, she wouldn't . . . that is, the padding—"

Mercifully, Lomax jumped in. "I think I have a pretty good idea of what you're getting at," he said, "so let me make this easier for you. Laura told me she was extremely self-conscious about being so skinny. And I believe that this much is true. She was also constantly taking a ribbing about her figure, she said. And that's at least partially true, I would guess. Anyway, according to her, she tried to put on some weight while she was up in Canada recovering from her accident, but it just didn't happen. Well, when she was on the plane heading home, she came up with this notion of playing a little joke on her buddies. She decided that that afternoon, for kicks, she'd pick up some large-size underwear—a bra and girdle and whatever—and pad everything. Then she'd show up at work the following morning—her first day back on the job—with all these curves she'd supposedly added while she was away. Initially, she intended that the very next time she put in an appearance it would be as her usual self. But when everyone kept telling her how great she looked, she felt it wouldn't hurt to keep up the charade a while longer, maybe for the rest of the week. The reactions to the voluptuous new Laura were so favorable, though, that she just never got around to being the real Laura again."

What a crock! "And she expected you to *buy* this?"

"It isn't really that outrageous. At any rate, it's not the strangest thing I've ever heard. And after all, she had to think of something when we . . . umm . . . when we got better acquainted. And that was apparently the best she could do." Lomax paused then, his eyes focused on my face. "I'm sorry I'm embarrassing you, Desiree, but this *is* what you wanted to know, isn't it?"

"Yes. And you're not embarrassing me," I protested, aware that I was blushing furiously and cursing myself for being such a stupid prig. But it was even more irritating that this telltale flush of mine had let Lomax in on that fact.

Now, at this moment a follow-up question was right on my

lips, but I didn't have the nerve—or the complexion—to put it to Lomax.

What I was itching to say to him was, "How could you have slept with someone just to make your case?"

All right, I'll grant you he hadn't actually acknowledged that he'd been intimate with Laura—not in so many words, anyhow. However, while I'm reasonably certain this sort of thing—sleeping with a perpetrator, I'm talking about—isn't sanctioned by the DEA, I have very little doubt that it goes on. And even less doubt that it had been going on here. Which didn't sit at all well with me. Especially, I suppose, since I was discovering that I sincerely liked Bobby Lomax. And fair or not, I believe most of us expect more from the people we're fond of.

At any rate, I knew I had to let it pass. At the same time, I made up my mind to expend a real effort not to be too disappointed in Lomax—regardless of his choice of bed partners. After all, so what if his work ethics were, well, maybe a tad questionable. The thing is, if I wasn't willing to cut this man a little slack—this guy who'd just saved my life—then what kind of a person would I be? Also—and on occasion I have to remind myself of this—the truth is, I'm not quite perfect, either.

I moved on and settled for clarifying another point. "Why a teacher?"

Lomax looked perplexed for a second. "Oh, you mean why did I say I was a teacher? I actually was one for a semester—right after I got out of college—so I was comfortable with that role. More important, though, it was critical not to alert Laura's suspicions. And teaching sounds like a harmless enough profession. Plus it would account for my having all that free time during the summer, which naturally I hoped to spend with her."

"And when the two of you met—you weren't afraid that your . . . uh . . . the way you dress would turn her off?" I still can't believe I had the chutzpah to zap him with that one. And I regretted it as soon as it was out of my mouth—my *cavernous* mouth. Although having just poked around in his sex life, I suppose this was comparatively innocuous. And at least I'd substituted "dress" for what I was really thinking.

But apparently Lomax wasn't fooled. Or offended, either. "On the contrary," he informed me, purposefully fingering the Fu Manchu mustache, "the agency did a little research, and for some silly reason—and only God knows what it is—Laura seems to prefer men of my general appearance."

It was very soon after this that it hit me. "Hey, didn't you tell me that Laura claimed she'd decided to play that trick on her friends *after* she failed to gain the weight up in Toronto?"

"That's right."

"But she bought those Bloomingdale's bras *before* she went to Canada."

You could see that Lomax was impressed. "You did say that earlier, didn't you? Damned if we don't have to chalk another one up for your side!" A moment later, however, he amended this. "Unless, of course, that time they really were for grandma."

"Yeah, sure," I retorted. I shot him what I hoped was a truly malevolent glare. Then I saw the grin he was trying to suppress, and we both laughed. After which Lomax got to his feet.

"I'd better take off," he announced, glancing at his watch. "It's later than I thought."

"Dinner date?" (Well, I've never denied being nosy.)

"I suppose you could call it that. I'm dining at McDonald's tonight with a gentleman known on the street as Izzy Double Cross. A nickname he's earned in spades, believe me." Here, he smiled broadly. "Hey, this is my work outfit. You don't think I wear these clothes in real life, do you?"

For some inexplicable reason, I was pleased to hear this.

As we were standing at the door, Lomax promised to stay in touch and keep me advised about Laura. And I said that I hoped everything worked out with his drug case. Considering that in some ways we were at cross purposes, however, it was understandable that my good wishes were extended with very mixed feelings.

Chapter 42

I was to have a very long wait before Laura Downey's fate was finally determined.

And in the interim there was a lot going on in my life, both personally and professionally. But in spite of that, Laura—and what was in store for her—were still right up there in my thoughts.

As the months went by, I spoke to Lomax now and again, but for the most part, he would only give me a vague idea of what was transpiring—agency policy and all that. The only things I knew for sure were that the woman had agreed to cooperate with the DEA, that El Puerco was being extradited from the Bahamas and would be brought to trial in the U.S., and that any concrete negotiations with Laura had to be postponed until the trial was over.

Then, on a rainy Tuesday afternoon more than thirteen months after the attempt on my life, I received the definitive phone call.

"I've got news for you, Desiree," Bobby Lomax said. "It's about Laura. I don't think you'll be too unhappy, either."

But I could tell from his tone that I was about to be furious.

"Let me have it. How much time will she serve?" I held my breath.

He didn't answer the question directly, opting to first acquaint me with how instrumental Laura had been in nailing El Puerco. In addition to supplying the Agency with crucial information and even wearing a wire at one point, she had also given evidence against the drug biggie in court. Which is why her own sentencing had to be delayed; the government wanted to be certain that she delivered on her promise to testify.

"And how many years did she get?" I demanded impatiently.

Lomax was slow to respond. He was obviously not very comfortable with the answer he had for me. "Well, she pleaded guilty to assault first—assault in the first degree, that is—and on the recommendation of the assistant DA, she . . . umm . . . she got seven years." His voice dropped precipitously with these last two words.

I was incredulous. "You mean a *total* of seven years? For *everything*?"

"It couldn't be helped. To be honest, I don't see how we'd have been able to lay a glove on El Puerco without her. And in case you missed it in the newspapers, he was found guilty. It looks like he'll be spending the rest of his natural life behind bars without the possibility of parole."

My mind, however, was not on El Puerco. "I can't believe—"

But Lomax appeared as anxious to postpone returning to the subject of Laura as I was to pursue it. "We were really lucky with this whole business, too," he broke in. "What happened was that the guy who was originally passing the stuff to Laura started coming on to her, and she refused to meet with him anymore. So then El Puerco himself took over."

"Look," I came close to shouting, "just tell me. How much time will she actually have to serve in prison?"

"Well, uh, she could be released in four and change," Lomax admitted.

I felt sick. A little over four years for pushing an innocent human being—and one of her closest friends, at that—under the wheels of a train? And what about all of her drug activity? And don't forget *me*. I mean, that woman had done her damnedest to have me fitted for a shroud.

But listen, I read the papers; I watch *Geraldo*. And while in the present instance I was affected in a personal way, this kind of thing was really nothing new.

I tried to adopt a philosophical attitude. After all, she wasn't being let off scot-free, which has also been known to happen.

"Well, at any rate, she'll see the inside of a jail," I told Lomax. "And I suppose these days that's something to be grateful for."

So that was it. The unthinkable ending to a frustrating case.

I wish I could put it behind me. But every so often I find myself recalling those words of Cheryl's—the words that had led me to her killer at last: "Everything fits. Everything fits now," she'd said. And I invariably become incensed all over again that Laura Downey's sentence didn't fit the magnitude of her acts.

I suppose, though, that if you really want to and you're persistent enough, you can find some tiny measure of consolation in almost anything. And I *have* managed to come up with one semiheartening little fact:

At least Laura won't be baking any more honey cakes. Not for a while, anyhow.

I'm afraid I'll have to settle for that.

"Who referred you to me?" I asked this through parched lips, my mouth having gone bone dry the instant I became aware of the identity of my visitor: a notorious New Jersey mobster.

"One of my"—Vito da Silva hesitated for a moment, and I had the impression he was searching for an acceptable term—"business associates contacted an acquaintance of his—an attorney named Elliot Gilbert—for a recommendation."

Now, Elliot is one of the partners in the firm that rents me my office space and probably the straightest person you'd ever meet. So I had absolutely no doubt that he was unaware as to who actually wanted this recommendation.

"Gilbert told my associate you are the best. Also, he said that you have the time to do what I require. Which is to devote yourself exclusively to finding the person who shot my good friend—my *protégé*. Shot up his face so badly, I've been told, that he no longer resembled a human being."

Well, if I didn't want this cold-eyed mobster as a client, I'd better convince him right now that Elliot was off-target regarding my availability.

"Uh, I'm very sorry about your loss, Mr. da Silva. But as for my being free to handle this for you, I just accepted a big case for an insurance company, and I—"

"Get someone else to take care of the insurance company."

Funny. The soft, even voice that I'd initially regarded as rather pleasant now sounded positively menacing to me—and all the more so for its lack of inflection. "I'm a one-person agency," I managed to croak.

"Have you ever heard of subcontracting? Farm the thing out," da Silva ordered, his tone still not much above a whisper. "Listen, someone murdered somebody I cared about. And I'm determined that I—that *you*—will see to it this person answers for what he did."

"Mr. da Silva, I hope you understand, but I made a commitment and—"

"I'm sure you can work something out," he responded with a perfunctory wave of his hand. "In the meantime, I suppose I should tell you a little bit about Frankie Vincent—the victim. The boy was a chiropractor. But not your average chiropractor. I swear to you, Frankie could perform miracles.

"I always had terrible problems with my back, you see. I must have been to every top man in the country. And I'm not only speaking about chiropractors, either. I saw orthopedists and osteopaths. I went for acupuncture three separate times. I even tried this holistic quack. Then someone told me about Frankie; he said the boy had done wonders for him."

"And he helped you, too."

"No. Frankie Vincent saved me. This was perhaps three years ago. And I've been a different person ever since. At any rate, I was very grateful to him, and I sent him a couple of patients. He called to thank me, and we got to talking, and after that we began having dinner together occasionally. Then, pretty soon, we were doing it on a more frequent basis. Over the years I really got to know Frankie, and I became extremely fond of him. Do you follow me?"

"Of course." I mean, what was there to follow?

"You won't mind if I smoke, Desiree," da Silva was kind enough to inform me now—just prior to removing a silver cigarette case and lighter from his inside breast pocket.

Well, I did mind. In my minuscule office with its single small window sealed up tight, this was not at all a healthful practice. But I was too intimidated by the man to voice an objection.

He lit up and took a long drag on the cigarette, exhaling slowly, and filling every last inch of space in these impossibly cramped quarters with thick, eye-stinging smoke. For a moment, I could barely make out his face—although he was sitting not much more than two feet away from me. And breathing from here on in was no picnic, either.

A few seconds later da Silva resumed his narrative. "At any rate, one night Frankie and I were at dinner, and in the course of conversation he casually mentioned that the greatest satisfaction he could have in life would be to serve his country. For the first time, I became aware of his interest in holding public office. But he was concerned that unlike most politicians he had no legal background. I said never mind about that. If this is what he wanted, I would make it happen. Had he lived, Frankie would have been a senator one day—I'm talking about a *United States* senator. Maybe even president. Trust me, I could have delivered."

"I'm sure you could," I responded. But it was just to be agreeable. Okay, he might have his connections. But Vito da Silva a *president*-maker? Come on!

"He was already on his way, too," da Silva continued. "I saw to it he was given a shot at the New Jersey State Assembly last year. There was never any hope of his winning that one—the Republican incumbent was pretty much of a shoo-in. But winning wasn't the purpose of Frankie's running; it was an opportunity for him to get his feet wet, to get himself known. All he needed to do was to make a respectable showing. Well, the fact is, he did a lot better than anyone expected he would—with the exception of myself. And after that election the party regarded Frankie as a vote-getter, a definite up and comer." And here da Silva leaned back and took another long pull on his cigarette.

Which caused me to start hacking away.

He sat there quietly until the cough subsided. Once he could be reasonably certain my struggle for oxygen wouldn't be disrupting his monologue, he went on. "I suppose you want to hear how Frankie was murdered."

That's what you think sprang to my lips. But, naturally, it never passed them. Instead I answered, "Yes, I do." Mealymouthed coward that I am, I was postponing the moment of truth—the time when I'd have to make it unmistakably and irrevocably clear to this man that I was not going to be accepting any assignment from him.

"Frankie was murdered across the street from his office the night before last, when he was leaving for home," da Silva told me. "At first, the word was that the shooting occurred during a robbery attempt. A woman who was out walking her dog witnessed the entire thing, including the killer bending over Frankie and starting to relieve him of his valuables. I don't know that he actually took anything, however, because she screamed bloody murder and frightened him off."

"You said that *at first* it was believed Frankie died during a robbery attempt." I couldn't help it. My curiosity had been aroused.

"That's right. Now it appears that it was supposed to seem as if robbery was the motive. But it wasn't. You see, the woman gave the police a description of the car—the one the killer drove off in. And yesterday someone who works in that neighborhood came forward with the information that this same car had been parked opposite the building for hours."

"I don't quite—"

"And there was a man in it."

It took a couple of seconds before this registered. "So whoever did this must have been lying in wait for Frankie. " And then I couldn't stop myself from asking, "Any idea who might have wanted your friend dead?"

"No. That is, not really. Frankie and Sheila—his wife—well, the fact is, they did not have a very happy marriage. But Sheila was in Europe two days ago. Of course, there's always the possibility that she hired someone to dispose of her unwanted husband. It's also a possibility, however, that she had nothing at all to do with Frankie's death. I'm leaving it to you to find out the truth."

And now there was no more postponing it. "Uh, Mr. da Silva," I protested, "I wish I *could* help you, but—"

"You can. And you will. I've already had a talk with the mayor of Riverton, which is where Frankie was from—Riverton, New Jersey. The mayor has seen to it that you will be provided with whatever you need at the station house—it's best if you work out of there—and he's assured me that the police will cooperate fully with you. Naturally, my name is to be kept out of this."

I was trying to work up the nerve for another attempt at setting da Silva straight when he put in, "As for your fee, I believe you will find your compensation more than adequate." And he quoted a figure that took away what little breath I had left. I'd never even made *half* that much on any investigation I'd been involved in before. "Is that satisfactory?"

He didn't wait for a response. Which was fortunate. Because my mouth was still hanging open when he wrote out a nice, fat check as a retainer.

Well, that clinched it.

It's more than likely that I'm the most cowardly member of my profession. And maybe even the greediest (although this is something I seriously doubt).

But on the plus side, for a very brief time, I was also the most expensive.